The Curse of the Aztec Dummy

By the same author:

IS THE MOON THE CENTER OF THE UNIVERSE?
HISTORY OF RUSSIA & THE SOVIET UNION in Humorous Verse
MAKE MARZIPAN, NOT WAR: Crazy Rhymes for Crazy Times
CHEESE PIRATES: Humorous Rhymes for Adult Children
CAFÉ BOMBSHELL: The International Brain Surgery Conspiracy
PETS OF THE GREAT DICTATORS & Other Works

See excerpts at www.newacademia.com

The Curse of the Aztec Dummy
A Nebraskan Chronicle

Sabrina P. Ramet

Washington, DC

Library of Congress Control Number: 2017943155
ISBN 978-0-9986433-1-1 paperback (alk. paper)

 An imprint of new Academia Publishing
4401-A Connecticut Ave. NW, #236, Washington DC 20008

 info@newacademia.com
www.newacademia.com

For my cat, Sasha

Contents

Uptown, Nebraska

Some people say that Uptown used to be a sprawling Aztec city, with canals, hanging gardens, pyramids, and paved roads. Uptown has paved roads, but it doesn't have canals or pyramids today or, for that matter, hanging gardens, and no one has ever come up with evidence that there was an Aztec city anywhere near where Uptown is situated today. In fact, Uptown is a very normal place, located just off Highway 80, roughly 30 miles west of North Platte. Although its population is relatively small – just 12,819 inhabitants at the last census, some people say, but that was before Mabel Fillmore gave birth to twin girls and before the census records were lost – it has its own international airport, with an 8-seat Cessna making weekly flights to Denver. The Federal Aviation Administration griped about this at one time, alleging that Colorado is not a foreign country, but the Uptownians are proud of their "international" airport and don't want to give it up. Besides, America is a free country and you can call things what you like.

Since Uptown is small, most people have two roles. For example, the town mortician is also the town florist – which makes sense. The dentist doubles as a therapist and frequently psychoanalyzes his patients free of charge while their mouths are stretched open with metal clamps and a plastic sheet. The only supermarket, if you can call it that, is attached to the gasoline station, although there is also a 7-11 in town, run by a young immigrant from Kansas named Martin Glover. There is no crime in Uptown, and most people don't play with matches. So Geena Dorbin, the police chief,

AKA the fire chief, runs a barber shop in downtown Uptown. It has the familiar barber pole and looks like a barber shop, but the sign reads "Police Station and Barber Shop". There is also a non-denominational church in town with a nondenominational pastor. When it comes to spiritual matters, he can do almost anything you want. Pastor Jim Grace regularly hears confessions from Catholics, knows what he describes as "all five Presbyterian hymns" (no complaints about the small number so far), and once officiated at a bar mitzvah. Rumor has it that Pastor Grace had been a Hindu monk before he came to Uptown. Old Man Marlowe has been mayor for at least 40 years, though no one remembers electing him or having any elections at all. But he doesn't get paid for his mayoring, since he makes a decent living from his saloon, The Fancy Turtle Saloon: this is the town's most successful venture, with people coming over regularly from the towns of Filibuster and Stonewall, both about 20 miles away, since the county in which those towns are located doesn't allow alcohol. For the children, there is the Buffalo Bill Cody Elementary School, which includes grades 1-6. The school library, with its strong collection of children's literature, also serves as the town library. A favorite watering hole is Daisy Doo's Candy Shoppe, where you can also get milk shakes and root beer floats. Across the street from Daisy Doo's is the Museum of Animal Curiosities, where visitors can see a two-headed rabbit, a goat with three tails, a parrot that has learned to sing the Marine Corps Hymn, a "winged mouse" (actually just a dead Big Brown Bat, one of the most common bats native to Nebraska), and what is advertised as the world's largest collection of dead flies (preserved in formaldehyde). There is also a small bookshop on Main Street, but people say that this is just an FBI front and so they won't enter. And yet the shop stays in business. So it probably *is* an FBI front!

About 12 miles west of Uptown, close to the international border with Colorado, is the University of Western Uptown. No one seems to know why it is called "Western", since there is no town by that name, let alone an "Eastern" Uptown. Maybe the name was chosen in order to produce the mellifluous acronym UWU. The university calls itself a "concept university", by which it means that it has only a few departments, which correspond to its concept of education. These are the departments of English literature, astronomy (UWU's smallest department), physics, archeology, zoology, political science, music therapy, spiritualism (where students take part in séances), entomology (the study of insects), art mechanics (a real field of study), automobile safety (the university's major contribution to reducing the death toll on local highways), foreign languages (where Spanish, German, Hopi, Algonquin, and Arapaho are taught), history, and a joint department of philosophy and religious studies. Since UWU is located precisely on the traditional tribal land of the Arapaho, there have been some protests that Arapaho is not a "foreign" language, but the university administration has always replied that, if the language was going to be taught, that was the only department where it could fit. With just 13 academic departments, the university has fewer than 240 regular faculty members and just over 2,300 students, some of them from out of state. All of the departments offer baccalaureate and master's degrees, and two of the departments – spiritualism and automobile safety – also offer Ph.D.'s. After hours, many of its professors frequent the Country-Western Palace, which is where Jeremy Shazoo, the dean of the faculty, met his sweetheart, Debbie Sue Stefanovich, who became the assistant dean. Jeremy wanted her to take his name, which would have made her Debbie Sue Shazoo. But she stood up for women's rights and kept her name just as it had always been. As for the students, they tend to congregate at the local Bingo parlor or play games of chicken on the railroad tracks which run through the town. The students also enjoy a good hootenanny and many of them can play the kazoo. Since the students all live on campus, inevitably some of them like to meet in the Student Union building, where one of their favorite pastimes is to imagine history playing out in different ways. For example, what if the Wright brothers had invented a machine to move from one dimension to another, instead of the airplane? Or again, what if Timothy Leary, who had championed psychedelic drugs in the 1960s and founded the League for Spiritual Discovery, had won the election for Governor of California in 1970 – would that have changed the history of California? Could he have been elected President of the United States in 1980, instead of Reagan? Or again, what if there was no okra in Nebraska? – *that* was something to send chills up one's spine. Of course, the students had homework as well, which, for those enrolled in classes given by the department of spiritualism included practicing séances with their fellow students. They had many conversations with the dead and among those with whom they made contact was an Aztec warrior who never tired of warning them about a cursed dummy. At first, the students insisted that he must mean an Aztec *mummy*, but he was insistent that he meant what he said and the students did not think that it was smart to argue with a ghost. Students majoring in automobile safety were also known to practice their driving skills by cruising in North Platte. They were well loved by the North Plattians because the UWU students had all been trained to be courteous, self-effacing, and indulgent of others' driving preferences. But on the drive between Uptown and North Platte, UWU's automobile safety majors often practice the pit maneuver against each other, sending each other's cars into the ditch.

Such was life in Uptown and UWU – happy, tranquil, and undisturbed until, one day, a stranger moved in. Since he had come from California, Isaac Beanhead Tecumseh Floorboard was immediately treated as a foreigner, since everyone who is not a native Nebraskan is, by definition, a foreigner. Floorboard was a native of Disneyland, well Anaheim, and had served two terms as a congressman from California in the U.S. House of Representatives followed by a two-year stint as president of a university in New Mexico. Now he had been hired in as president of UWU, and there was a lot of excitement both at the university and in the town, where there were some exorbitant expectations. Some folks said that he would bring the next World's Fair to Uptown, others thought that he was going to entice Sears to open an outlet in town. Still others dreamt of NASA moving its headquarters to Uptown. There was even a rumor that he was going to entice the Disney Corporation to open a small version of Disneyland next to Uptown. It's not clear how these stories started, but once they got going some people wanted to believe them.

Foreign or not, Floorboard's arrival was the talk of the town. It was, for Uptown and UWU, the big event of the year – the most exciting news since Professor Joe Friday published an article in *The American Political Science Review*, when – as you can imagine – folks both at the university and in the town could talk of nothing else for weeks on end. Townsfolk decorated the town with banners and streamers, and put up huge posters everywhere. No one seemed quite sure what should be on the posters, but they knew that they could not go wrong with giant posters of American presidents. But amid posters of George Washington, Andrew Jackson, Millard Fillmore (a local favorite), and Abraham Lincoln, there were also posters of Jefferson Davis, Aaron Burr, William Tecumseh Sherman, and George Armstrong Custer, none of whom had been president, although Custer had wanted to be president. The town hall was painted bright yellow for the occasion, and the sheriff's office was painted red, white, and blue, with the result that it now matched the barber's pole.

When the great day arrived, the incoming president was driven through town in an emerald green convertible limousine, while confetti and other colorful objects such as small plastic animals were thrown around in his honor. People lined the streets to witness this great event. The roof of the convertible had been lowered and the university provost, Zoe Ryan, sat in the vehicle together with Floorboard and Floorboard's wife, Eustadiola von Kletten, daughter of a latter-day Austrian waltz king and a Prussian mother, who had taught von Kletten how to handle the world around her. Preceding the limousine was the university marching band, which played Meyerbeer's "Coronation March". Following the presidential convertible were six further convertibles, in which the members of the political science department sat, and at the end of the parade, the members of the university's curling team marched in their bright uniforms, followed by the pupils from the elementary school and their teachers. It was a great day for Uptown. The parade halted at the edge of town in the town park. From there, the limousines drove over to the university. The members of the band climbed into their van and followed the limousines, and most townsfolk got their cars and drove over to UWU in a state of wild excitement and sustained ecstasy. Once everyone had reached UWU, the band reassembled in the bandstand and played a round of "Rule Britannia" – apparently by mistake, and there was some controversy about that later – and then the provost ascended the bandstand and addressed the university's faculty members, staff, students, and those townsfolks who had driven over to the university to hear and remember the speeches.

"My fellow Uptownians," the provost began. "Today is a great day." Everyone knew that already, but it was worth emphasizing. "Today we welcome our new university president, Isaac Beanhead Tecumseh Floorboard of California. As you all know, we lost our dear president, Sylvester McElroy, two months ago. He had been the president of our university for the past sixty-two years and those decades were years of success, joy, and self-congratulation at UWU. Now we welcome a new president and hope that he will be with us for at least sixty-two years of success, joy, and self-congratulation. Floorboard is an enthusiastic fisherman" – roars of approval from all assembled – "and plays a wicked saxophone" – more roars of approval – "and has a Ph.D. from the University of California at Berkeley" – no sound from the audience at the mention of his Ph.D. "He served as president of the University of Truth or Consequences in New Mexico before coming here and has written and published five books, including the near-bestseller, *The Governator in Action.* We are also delighted to welcome his wife, Professor von Kletten, who will join the political science department here. You will all be excited to know that she has written two influential books about the Aztecs" – at the mention of the Aztecs, there were sounds of unbridled excitement throughout the crowd. "And now I shall let President Floorboard say a few words of greeting."

"Provost Ryan, Dean Davis, colleagues, students, and townfolk – my fellow Americans – I am thrilled to be here in Nebraska and coming on board as president of UWU. This university is widely admired throughout our great country and, back when I was at the University of Truth or Consequences, scarcely a day passed without someone making some favorable remark about UWU. From what I have learned, the budget is strong, the university cafeteria has one of the best chefs in this part of the country, and most of the faculty get along famously. But I have already learned of some problems that need to be addressed, perhaps especially in the departments of spiritualism and physics, where there have been constant arguments between these two departments about whether both of them are actually needed at the university. Today, standing here before all of you, I pledge to take UWU, a first-class university sitting on a high promontory of academia, to even greater heights of glory, until we feel that we are literally flying in orbit, with our ivory towers pointing to Mars. If we all work together, there is nothing we cannot achieve – except maybe to rescind the law of gravity, but we wouldn't want to do that anyway."

And with that, the crowd roared its approval, the band resumed playing "Seventy-six trombones", with the members of the curling team singing along, and the president and his wife, together with the provost, walked up the steps to the university's presidential palace and disappeared behind the giant oak doors.

Uptown Civilization and Its Discontents

Pretty much everyone had come to the inauguration of the president, but one person who stayed away was the town malcontent, Big Bill Tarton, who spent the day sitting in front of the Fancy Turtle Saloon, gulping down swigs of whiskey. Mayor Marlowe had shut down the saloon that day, in order to attend the inauguration and thus, Big Bill, who would normally have been sitting inside the saloon, spending his social security check on booze, and grumbling to fellow drinkers about the state of the nation and the state of his digestive system, chose the bench in front of the saloon as his second-best option. As he sat there, he started singing that American favorite, "Home on the range", when the mayor returned from the historic event and opened the saloon door to his most reliable customer.

As Big Bill entered the saloon and slumped into his favorite chair, he slurred his words as he asked, "So whaddid the new president have to say? Will there be big changes?"

Old Man Marlowe was in a playful mood and so he answered, "He is going to build a giant passenger spaceship and will take as many of us to Mars as like to go."

"I'm ready," responded Big Bill in a drunken stupor. "Where do I sign?"

Just then Joe Friday – that's Professor Joe Friday, head of the political science department – came into the saloon with a small retinue of fellow professors. Friday was well liked, mainly because he talked just like his namesake from the television series "Dragnet" but also because he had published enough to qualify as a respectable scholar but not so much that other professors would get jealous of him. He and his "three musketeers" took a table at the opposite end of the saloon from where Big Bill was sitting and beneath a large portrait of William McKinley, our country's 25th president (unless you count Grover Cleveland only once, in which case McKinley was our 24th president). "What can I bring you guys?" Old Man Marlowe asked the quartet. "Your best whiskey," came the reply. In fact, in Uptown almost everyone over the age of 18 drank whiskey – or milk – and there wasn't much demand for vodka or brandy.

Friday's closest friend and ally – and one of his "three musketeers" – was Eddie Bobkov ("call me Bob"), the department's China specialist. His other musketeers were Liam Cleary, who taught the class on Irish politics, and Winston Disraeli, who taught the classes on British politics and American politics. Friday, Cleary, and Disraeli were solid scholars, well respected in their respective fields. However, Bobkov was a bit controversial since, although he taught the class on China, he steadfastly denied that China existed. Some years earlier, he received an invite from the "Chinese government" to visit "Beijing". So, one day, he boarded Air China, which flew westward from Omaha, circling the globe until it landed in Texas, just outside a giant "People's Republic of China" theme park. Of course, he enjoyed his visit to this theme park, since all of the park's employees were friendly and polite and treated him as an honored guest. But among the various things that convinced him that China was just a theme park was the "Cable Car Ride of the Great Proletarian Cultural Revolution", where visitors could look out from their cable cars onto reenactments by park employees dressed in Mao suits of those tumultuous times. After he returned to Nebraska by a more direct route, he was contacted by the US State Department and invited to serve as ambassador to China. But Bobkov had no interest in being ambassador to a theme park in Texas or anywhere else, and politely declined, though not without protesting to the State Department that a mere theme park had an ambassador sitting in the UN. The Chinese "government" found out about this protest and registered its own protest, claiming that, while in their country, Bobkov had ignored the government officials and spent most of his time visiting souvenir shops. Bobkov, in turn, wrote an influential book about politics in the theme park. As for his notions about the Chinese language – well, don't ask.

The conversation began with frets about the university. "Bob, what do you make of our physics department? I am worried about it," said Friday.

"Well, to be sure, I did not encounter anything having anything to do with physics when I visited 'China'," Bobkov replied. "But as far as I know, our own physicists seem to be overly concerned about an allegedly impending threat of black holes, as if we might be about to be sucked into one."

"Have you heard the latest about the physicists?" asked Cleary.

"No, what is it?"

"They want to build a particle accelerator – that's what!" replied Cleary. "There are already more than 30,000 such devices around the world. Isn't that enough? But, no!"

"Perhaps we need one in Nebraska," chimed in Disraeli.

"There is already one particle accelerator at the University of Nebraska at Lincoln," replied Cleary. "But our physicists say that this would be the first particle accelerator in western Nebraska. Apparently it's a question of prestige."

"Sure," said Friday sarcastically, "a particle accelerator really puts a town on the map."

Just then, Professor Wolf Romulus, who claimed to be a direct descendant of the founder of ancient Rome and therefore entitled to rule a revived Roman empire, strode into the saloon, accompanied by his closest associates: Professors Bart and Bret Holloway who, "because they are brothers" – as people liked to say – were usually called "the Maverick brothers", together with a hologram of Professor Giuseppe Pestalozzi, author of *Technology in your Kitchen*. Pestalozzi, despite his given name, was a third-generation immigrant and had never been outside Nebraska. He was a shy man, and hated to be seen in public. So, when he lectured, it was his hologram which appeared in the classroom, with a two-way audio-feed so that his lecture could be heard and so that, from his secret hideaway, he would be able to hear the questions students might ask. Of course, when he – or rather, his hologram – ventured off the campus, there were some imperfections in the system. For example, although he usually asked one of the Maverick brothers to carry along a portable audio system, so that he could take part in any conversations, sometimes the brothers would forget it, or turn off the receiver, with the result that Pestalozzi could talk to people, but not hear their replies. It was, everyone conceded, a flawed system.

Romulus' ambition was to overthrow Joe Friday as head of the department and to take his place on "the imperial throne" – as he liked to say. Romulus, founder and editor of the *Journal of Almost Real Research*, loved the way his silk shirt felt on his chest and, even more, the feel of his orange bandana. He loved walking around the department in his Laredo cowboy boots and liked to sing cowboy songs, such as "The Old Chisholm Trail" and "Cattle Call". He would sit in his office strumming on his guitar and singing. At first, some people in his department objected that these were not Nebraskan songs, so he added a couple of songs that mention Nebraska to his play list – Bob Seger's "Get out of Denver" and Hank Snow's "I've been everywhere". This calmed people down a ton, and since then he'd been able to sing in his office as much as he liked, even with his door wide open. The Maverick brothers and even Pestalozzi thought of themselves as cowboys, even as the real thing, and Pestalozzi even played a Hohner Special 20 harmonica, a favorite instrument among cowboys. The Maverick brothers could play the honky-tonk piano and they could whistle, although just about everybody in Nebraska could whistle, especially in the good old days.

As they strode into the Fancy Turtle Saloon, Romulus and his fellow cowboys certainly looked the part – Justin cowboy hats, silk shirts with puffy sleeves, bandanas, leather vests, chaps, and – as already mentioned – Laredo cowboy boots. They also were wearing holsters and seemed to have some firearms (actually loaded water pistols) in them. As usual, Bart Hollway's clothes were too big for him; judging from the way he was walking, even his boots were too big for him. As they came in, Friday and his departmental colleagues reached under the table into a large canvas bag and retrieved a set of Christian Dior sunglasses, white Fedora panama hats, and four water pistols, which they slammed down on the tabletop. The two groups started staring in a malignant way at each other. Even the Pestalozzi hologram took part in this little exchange.

After perhaps five minutes of silent stares, the Romulus gang stood up and drew their water pistols. Friday and his associates also stood up, water pistols in hand. Old Man Marlowe jumped up nervously and pointed to a sign hanging above the bar: "Attention gunslingers! No water pistol fights on the premises!"

At this moment, the saloon doors swung open and Eustadiola von Kletten, the department's new Aztec specialist and also the department's new deputy head, strutted in, clad in black leather from her black leather bandana to her black leather pants to her black leather Black Harness boots, not to mention also a black cotton shirt that was a little tight against her nipples, a black leather vest, and an authentic Bullhide Thunderstruck black leather cowboy hat. Topping this off, she was wearing a deputy's badge, just like the ones you'd see on "Gunsmoke". Her eyes were blazing, as she shot glances at all the cowboys in the saloon (including her friend, Friday). "Sit down," she barked, "and pour yourself some whiskey. Put your guns away!"

"But this town ain't big enough for both them and us," whined Romulus, even as he obeyed her order. "We just want them to git along."

With that, the entire saloon, including even the almost totally drunk Big Bill burst into a round of "Git along little dogies", except that, where the lyrics were supposed to be "Wyoming will be your new home," they all sang, "Nebraska will be your new home." With that, some semblance of order and even conviviality was restored, and the folks chatted within their respective groups. Von Kletten wandered over to Friday's table and took a seat.

Later, after the saloon closed for the night, Romulus, the Maverick brothers, and Pestalozzi's hologram strolled over to Romulus' yard and sat down in the swings. "Friday's gotta go," said Romulus, establishing the theme for discussion.

Apparently there was a problem with Pestalozzi's reception and his reply was a complete non sequitur, something about Ferdinand Magellan's circumnavigation of the earth – why would he think that might be relevant?

Bart Holloway ("smooth as a handle on a gun") picked up the thread. "What we need is a plan, a way to pitch this to the department, maybe a scandal."

"What kind of scandal, do you have in mind?" asked Bret Holloway ("luck is his companion").

"Something with sex – that always gets people uptight," responded brother Bart ("gambling is his game").

"Yeah," snarled Romulus. "Sex is best. Perhaps we can get a young co-ed to entrap Friday...No, he's above all that. We'd just have to invent something, and start circulating rumors."

"What about the drinking fountain?" asked brother Bret ("riverboat, ring your bell"). "The departmental drinking fountain was out of order for three weeks, and that was on Friday's watch. Perhaps we can get him fired because of that."

"Come on," Romulus replied. "Who's going to get all wound up about a drinking fountain? Besides, our coffee machine has been in good working order the whole time Friday's been head of the department, and he even brought in a cappuccino machine."

"What about the people hired since he became chair?"

"Yeah, like the four of us? He even lets Pestalozzi teach his classes as a hologram."

"OK, what about the duck pond?"

"There is no duck pond!" Romulus shouted, sounding angry at this apparent impertinence.

"That's just my point," said brother Bart. "There's no duck pond. How is it that we political scientists don't rate our own duck pond just outside our building..."

"You're completely nuts!"

"Hey, 'completely nuts' works," replied brother Bart.

"No, it doesn't!"

"Yes, it does!"

"As Josef Goebbels once said, 'if you tell a really big lie and keep repeating it, people eventually gonna believe it.'"

"Why isn't anyone responding to my insight into Magellan's voyage?" Pestalozzi's hologram suddenly interpelled.

"Someone turn on his audio!" barked Romulus and, once that was done, he addressed the hologram and said, "We are not talking about your goddam Magellan, who's been dead for a while. We're talking about how to take power in the department!"

"Oh, OK…" the hologram replied.

"And I don't want to be quoting Goebbels, not even on whether cabbage soup is healthy for you."

"Getting back to the duck pond…"

"Duck pond, duck pond!" götterdämmered Bart darkly, as if it was a matter of deep concern, at the same time resisting the temptation to think about the nineteenth-century German composer, Richard Wagner.

"Hold on," said Romulus, who tended to be more realistic than the Maverick brothers. "If we really want to pursue this duck pond idea, we should probably find out how many universities have duck ponds and how many of these are situated near political science departments. Or we just take another look at the issue of the water fountain."

"Ja," said Pestalozzi, inexplicably lapsing into German before continuing in English. "Friday should have assigned priority to the drinking fountain and put pressure on the maintenance people to get this done quickly."

"It was out of order for only three weeks, and that was in summer, when a lot of people were on vacation," Bart objected.

"It was out of order for fully three weeks, and that was in summer, when it was hot around here," Romulus corrected Bart.

"And he should have consulted the faculty if there was a delay with the maintenance people," said Bret, trying to be helpful.

"But Friday is well-loved and people consider him fair-minded," the hologram pointed out.

"So what! Being fair-minded must mean treating people fairly, and that means getting them water."

"He's an honest broker, everyone knows that" – again, the hologram.

"So what! Water is such a basic human need that it is unconscionable to ignore the crisis for three weeks!"

"I thought that he was calling the maintenance office every day about this," objected Pestalozzi's hologram.

"Who cares?! The point is that he wasn't able to get the problem fixed quickly. And everyone drinks water," Romulus added.

"It's the most essential ingredient in the human body. Sixty per cent of the human body consists of water. If we don't get water, we'll shrink to 40 per cent of our mass." That was, of course, Brother Bart offering these illuminations.

"It's absolutely shameful that the head of the department could neglect this basic need."

"Absolutely shameful," all four muttered simultaneously.

"This is the fountaingate scandal," Romulus announced. "Time to take this to the press." And with that, he started to march out, accompanied by his mavericks, to the office of *The Uptown Herald and Fact Examiner*, until he suddenly remembered that it was past 3 a.m. "I guess it's gotten a bit late," he now conceded. "We'll go in the morning." And with that, the four horseless horsemen retreated to their respective abodes and got some shuteye.

The Cabal

The "campaign for water" began the next day, with the members of Romulus' cabal distributing flyers on campus. The flyers bore the heading, "We demand water!" in bright red block letters. As the flyer made clear, what Romulus and his boys had in mind was to put Friday in virtual stocks over the delay. But they added further flourishes, promising to prettify the campus, to install shag carpets in all the offices at the department, to provide footstools for all the offices in the political science department, to place tropical plants in the departmental office, and – above all – to make "being pleasant" the number one criterion for promotion and increases in salary at the department. It would not be hard to guess who would be assessing how pleasant the professors were. And there they were, Dr. Romulus and the Maverick brothers, passing out flyers around the department as well as in front of the department. Pestalozzi's hologram also took part, but his flyers were also hologramized and were accessible only to students within his hologram. Since there were no hologramized students, Pestalozzi's flyers ended up on the floor of wherever this Nebraskan man of mystery was hiding out.

At first, this campaign made no headway. Then Romulus came up with the bright idea of paying students at the physics department fifty dollars each to come over to the ground in front of the political science department, crossing the entire campus to do so, to march around shouting slogans such as "Friday must go!" "We've had enough water deprivation!" and "Romulus for chairman!"

About forty physics students took part, although some of them shouted other slogans, all popular in ancient Rome, such as "The people rule!", and "The welfare of the people is the highest law", and "Seek only the good of the people." The protesters also held up the dime, on the back of which one finds the fasces, an ancient Roman symbol of power and authority. All of this was an augur of things to come. Some political science students arrived, apparently all supporters of Joe Friday or perhaps just patriotic Americans who were opposed to atavism, and got into scuffles with the physics students. But things were spiraling out of control. It was at that point that Romulus came onto the green and presented the first of in series of striking speeches.

"Fellow Uwuans, fellow Uptownians, fellow Nebraskans, fellow Americans, and visitors from Colorado," he began. "We have heard of outbreaks of Nebraskonitis in neighboring states, with non-Nebraskans becoming so jealous of our way of life, of what we have right here in Nebraska, that they convince themselves that they are native-born Nebraskans. They put on a fake Nebraskan accent, put on our Nebraskan flex-fix cornhusker hats, eat cheeseburger pizzas, and talk about how much they love our state bird – that's the Western Meadlowlark, for those of you from Colorado! They even throw around Nebraskan expressions such as 'Counciltucky' and 'Market rats', without even knowing what these expressions mean. This is too much." Here Romulus drew a breath and was obviously looking for inspiration from the heavens. "But what keeps Nebraskans, what keeps Uptownians, what keeps Uwuans going -- is water. Not water from a cooler, not fizzy water from New York or some other big city slickers, and of course not water from the swamp, but water from a drinking fountain." Cheers interrupted him at this point. "Chairman Friday has let us down. We cannot survive for three weeks without having water splashing against our face, getting our cheeks and chins wet. We are not Californians. We are not Coloradans. We are Nebraskans, and we need drinking fountains! Drinking fountains now! Drinking fountains forever!"

At this, the crowd burst into a round of Tex Ritter's song, "Whiskey, rye whiskey", changing the words to "Water, wet water, water we cry. If we don't get wet water, we think we will die." Or maybe they didn't. Be that as it may, that is how it was reported in the local newspaper, published on that occasion under the banner, the *Uptown Herald and Times Re-examiner*. What is certain is that the crowd started marching around the political science building shouting "Drinking fountains forever!" and "Friday must go!" and "Seek only the good of the people". This went on for something like 45 minutes, until Joe Friday came out on the balcony of the political science building and spoke.

"Friends, colleagues, students, and thirsty people," he began. "I can see that you are troubled, though I wonder what the reasons are. How many people have actually moved to Nebraska in the past five years, pretending to be Nebraskans? According to figures I have seen, we are talking about roughly 43 immigrants from other states in all – 36 of them immigrating to Omaha, six of them moving to Lincoln, and one of them – an outstanding young man – coming here to Uptown to teach at UWU in our Department of Music Therapy. Nebraska is, of course, a great land, definitely the best place to live in America or in the world. Where else can you get Nebraskan Runzas or the Nebraskan Reuben sandwich or seven-decker burgers or our very own blend of ground beef, peanut butter, velveeta, and corn meal, all baked inside cornmeal bread, topped off with a load of ketchup? Just thinking about these great meals makes me glad to be a Nebraskan! And of course we have our cottonwood tree and our Nebraskan anthem, 'Beautiful Nebraska, peaceful prairieland, laced with many rivers and the hills of sand. Dark green valleys cradled in the earth, rain and sunshine bring abundant birth." As Friday sang these words from the Nebraskan state anthem, people swayed from side to side, smiling vacuously. He continued, "Water is, of course, a basic right. Our founding fathers, in their wisdom and glory, may have forgotten to include a right to water in our Great and Glorious Bill of Rights, but we know that we have a right to water, and that is why, from the first day when our departmental drinking fountain went out of order, I immediately contacted the maintenance squad and, at the same time, I had a water cooler installed on each of our department's three floors. I have also taken pains to make sure that these water coolers have never gone dry. I phoned the maintenance people at least once a day to prod them to fix our drinking fountains. I even called the Florence Water Works and the Minne Lusa Pumping Station in Omaha, to see if they could come on 'round and fix our goddam drinking fountain. I did get an offer, at one point, from some Yankees out in Colorado, but I figured that we don't want to get mixed up in international exchanges, at least not without the prior approval of the governor. But, tell you what, I am prepared to hold a faculty meeting so that we can discuss this crisis, if that is what it is."

"All hail Friday!" his supporters cheered. "Don't trust Friday!" his detractors shouted. But a week later, there was a faculty meeting and the topic of discussion was whether Chairman Friday should be forced to resign. Now, Friday was the area's most eligible and durable bachelor and everywhere he went, there were attractive young women holding signs saying "Marry me!" and blowing kisses. One of these attractive misses even knit him a pair of mittens and tossed them after him as he got into his car. As for his credentials, he had earned his Ph.D. at the best university in the entire USA – the University of Nebraska at Lincoln – and had published in various journals, including the *Nebraskan Journal of Political Science.* His book, *Strangers in an unstrange land,* which focused on strange immigrants coming to Nebraska, nearly made the bestseller list and, in any event, made enough money that he was able to build himself a three-story castle on the edge of town.

The political science department – the second largest at UWU, right after the physics department – consisted of 13 regular professors, associate professors, and assistant professors. Four of them were firm supporters of Friday; aside from his "three musketeers" – Eddie "Bob" Bobkov, Liam Cleary, and Winston Disraeli – Eustadiola von Kletten was also firmly in his camp. Romulus' inner core of supporters were "the Maverick brothers" (Bart and Bret Holloway) and the Pestalozzi hologram, but the department's drunk, Gabriel "Gabe" Carver, was also known to be fond of Romulus, although even fonder of drinking. Carver taught an honors seminar on the history of alcohol ("Alcohol through the ages") and was the author of a book on the history of English pubs. The remaining professors in the department were uncommitted "swing voters"; these were Stanton Brookhurst, Katella Beach, and Haldor Mac-Grory. Brookhurst, a specialist in the politics of new technology, was famous for being unable to make up his mind and for changing his mind repeatedly; in a close vote, this could be problematic. Regardless of the issue, Beach also took the position that things could always be better than they were. Katella Beach was a specialist in the politics of Egypt and had redesigned her office to look like an ancient Egyptian pharoah's tomb, complete with copies of ancient tomb paintings. And Haldor, well, his name means "the rock of Thor" and it seems that his heritage was a mixture of Norwegian and Irish although, like most of those working in the department, he was born in Nebraska and was fiercely anti-Coloradan. The only Coloradan in the department was Gabe Carver, but he did his best to keep this a secret – even from his wife of 23 years.

This decisive faculty meeting was scheduled to take place during the very week when preparations were underway to celebrate the 55th anniversary of the founding of the city of Uptown. Needless to say, locals were proud of their long heritage and very excited about the celebrations. Old Man Marlowe, acting as mayor, got to work organizing an old-fashioned rodeo, complete with bucking broncos, an ostrich race, and a don't-feed-the-llama contest. Sheriff Geena Dorbin was hard at work recruiting people for a parade through town, and was promising people that she would persuade the dancers at the local tap-dancing school to tap-dance on a float. Even University President Floorboard got involved, and sponsored a book-reading at the local "bookstore", featuring local authors. The town band would, of course, play at the event, and local folks who were not already involved in one of these other events, were taking various initiatives, usually involving family members and a few friends. The mood in the town was, in general, one of elation.

It was, of course, entirely different at the department of political science, where tensions ran high. Friday and his supporters came to the meeting in business suits; Romulus and the Maverick brothers arrived in full cowboy gear, even wearing their cowboy hats into the faculty room. The Maverick brothers were chewing tobacco until Friday, as chairman, made them stop. Then Friday opened the meeting with a brief recitation of his accomplishments during the three years he had served as chair. These accomplishments included luring the world-renowned political scientist, Seymour Oglethorpe, to UWU to present a lecture, establishing a monthly lecture-picnic which was held outdoors when the weather was good, and indoors when the weather was foul, and, of course, installing water coolers in the building. At the end of his recitation, he opened the floor to questions and comments. The first question came from Romulus.

"So, when are you going to resign?" Romulus demanded to know. This was so brash that it immediately provoked murmuring throughout the room.

"I'll be happy to resign if I lose a vote of no confidence. Otherwise, I will stay on. It depends on all of you present today."

"Well," said Bret Maverick, uh Holloway, "there's the matter of the drinking fountain – "

" – which is once again in good working order," Friday replied.

"It was out of order for three full weeks!" Bret almost shrieked. Well, actually, he did shriek.

"And what about a whiskey fountain?" asked Judge "the Judge" Carver, who wasn't a judge at all, raising his head momentarily from the desk. "They got those in Colorado."

The entire room went still. Someone had mentioned Colorado in some context other than shopping. Someone had cited Colorado as having something better than what people had in Nebraska. Was the Judge perhaps a *Coloradan?* Had he spent any serious time in Colorado, beyond just weekend shopping in Denver? Did he actually like Colorado? For a few moments, people forgot why they were there – all except, of course, Romulus.

"Let's get back on track," said Romulus. "We have a problem and we need to fix it."

"That's right," chimed in Gabe Carver. "We need whiskey fountains in the department – "

"The problem is Friday," Romulus clarified, adding, "someone help the Judge get back to sleep." And immediately, the Pestalozzi hologram produced a pillow hologram, though it was not much help, under the circumstances.

"I for one am not sure what the problem is," said Stanton Brookhurst. "Our man Friday has been functioning very effectively, as far as I can see, and throwing out the departmental chair for the sake of a drinking fountain seems a bit crazy to me."

"It would be just plain crazy," echoed Disraeli.

"Let's put it this way," Romulus clarified, "Things have been more or less OK, but we have not been operating at our best. Things could be better."

This was a buzz word designed to bring Katella Beach on board, and it worked its magic. "Yes," she agreed. "Things could certainly be better around here. Perhaps a new chairman could make things even better. Higher salaries, fewer classes, a freight elevator in the building, and a sun deck on the roof. Those would be good improvements."

"No they wouldn't," countered Bobkov. "Salaries cannot be hiked up just because more money is better than less. There have to be standards for promotion and for salary increases, and we have had such standards."

"Why?"

"Why not? We have standards because we have standards, and that's that."

"What about a freight elevator?"

"Our building consists of just three floors, and you need a freight elevator?" demanded Bobkov. "What are you planning to haul up to your office, for Christ's sake? I've seen a few three-story buildings with freight elevators back in Omaha, and we even had one in Lincoln, but we have a regular passenger elevator in our building and that has been sufficient up to now." He paused for a brief moment and then added, "If we are going to vote on installing a freight elevator, I'm voting 'no'."

The Judge raised his head to mutter, "I'm thirsty."

"We are all thirsty," said Romulus. "Thirsty for water, thirsty for justice, thirsty for – "

" – whiskey!" said the Judge, filling in the blank.

"We are thirsty for water," said Romulus, "and we have not been getting the water we need."

"Let's put it to a vote!" said someone.

"Put what to a vote? There isn't a motion on the table so far."

"I move that we adjourn," offered Pestalozzi, who seemed to be very upset about how things were developing.

"Vote! Vote! Vote!"

"I move that Professor Joe Friday resign immediately as chair," said Romulus, "and that elections be held for a new chair."

"I second the motion," declared Bart Maverick-Holloway, who was always "smooth as a handle on a gun."

"OK," said Friday. "Let's vote. All in favor of the motion that I resign raise your hands." Voting for the motion were Romulus, the Maverick brothers, Beach, Carver, and Brookhurst. Romulus glanced over to Pestalozzi's hologram, but just then Pestalozzi apparently turned off his hologram, which disappeared before the votes could be counted. "All opposed to the motion raise your hands." And, in addition to Friday, there were five additional votes supporting Friday – from von Kletten, Disraeli, Cleary, Bobkov, and Haldor MacGrory, who shouted "Long live Friday!" as he raised his hand. This was a 6 to 6 vote -- a tie, thanks to Pestalozzi's abstention. Friday kept his chairmanship – at least for the time being.

Aztec Gold

The celebrations of the founding of Uptown were a highpoint in the history of this small community. There was so much singing in the streets that, as the reporter from *The Uptown People's Gazette* put it, you might think the entire town was participating in a great musical. Locals brought in a carousel for the kids, as well as a shooting gallery (no real bullets, of course), a cotton candy booth, and even a fortune teller from Iowa. The fortune teller, some dude by the name of Brad, was very smart and everyone came away from his kiosk with a huge smile. It looked like everyone had a bright future to look forward to. The don't-feed-the-llama contest was also a big hit. This was limited to children between the ages of 8 and 14 and what they had to do was to carry around open bags of high-quality grass, with a little grain added, and see how close they could get to the llama without the llama getting the food. In fact, the llama always ended up getting the grass, and when he (or she) did, the locals who had gathered to watch the event cheered. But probably the most exciting event at the celebrations – at least for members of the political science department – was the ostrich race since, among the 12 contestants, each riding his or her own ostrich, were none other than Professors Friday and Romulus. The contestants had to ride around the course three times. At first, Friday and Romulus were pulling up the rear and, to everyone's surprise, Big Bill Tarton, the town drunk, was in the lead, sitting atop a pink ostrich. But Big Bill was drunk as a drunken sheepdog and swaying badly. Soon after finishing the first stretch, he fell off his ostrich and into the ditch. Everyone roared with laughter, as people are apt to do when others suffer small accidents. Meanwhile, Friday and Romulus were catching up with the others and, after finishing the second round, Romulus was in the lead, shouting what sounded like jibberish – at least that is how it was reported in the local newspaper, *The Uptown Lighthouse.* But then Friday said some sweet things to his ostrich and tore into the lead, holding it and finishing in first place. Friday's supporters cheered wildly, as did almost the entire town, since they remembered that it was Friday who had published an article in *The American Political Science Review.* Romulus and the Maverick brothers looked downcast. As for Pestalozzi, or rather his hologram, he was riding the carousel at the time, and starting to look a bit dizzy.

Of course, every anniversary celebration has to have a speech and who could have been better poised to present the anniversary speech than the town's unelected mayor. But Old Man Marlowe had a big surprise for the people of the fair town of Uptown. "Fellow Americans, fellow Nebraskans, it is a glorious day for us that we can celebrate 55 years of freedom here in Uptown and 43 years since I opened the Fancy Turtle Saloon. Today, it is my great pleasure to announce that, beginning next week, we shall be opening a full-fledged restaurant right here in Uptown. The sheriff, the pastor, and I have pooled our resources but we couldn't have done this without a small investment from a businessman in Omaha. Now I can announce that, next Monday, you will see the opening of the Steakholders' Steakhouse, Bar and Grill. We're gonna use the finest beef that Nebraska has to offer, and you can all come on 'round and chow down."

"What about okra?" someone shouted. "Are you gonna serve okra?"

"Well, of course," Old Man Marlowe said, in a reassuring tone. "There are many things you can do with okra. And speaking of okra, we all have our annual okra festival to look forward to." And upon hearing those words, looks of complete rapture came over the crowd, in anticipation of having an entire festival devoted to their favorite delicacy.

But just then, while all the events of the town's anniversary celebration were still going on, a young boy ran up to where Old Man Marlowe was standing, shouting, "We've found Aztec gold nearby! There's Aztec gold in the hills! Aztec gold!" The youngster was nearly out of breath, probably not so much from running all the way to downtown Uptown, as from sheer excitement. But the crowd was so focused on okra, that they could barely take in the notion of gold. Indeed, some of them were still murmuring "hmmn, okra, okra" lovingly.

But Aztec gold was not something one could ignore for long. And soon there were selfless, self-appointed archeologists rushing out to the nearby hills, looking for gold. Soon enough, some people came back to town carrying bits of gold-colored rock, which everyone assumed was gold. A committee was appointed to talk about this with all those who might be interested in the Aztecs. The not-yet-opened Steakholders' Steakhouse was a lot bigger than the saloon. So it was decided to convene a town meeting there, with three invited experts to serve on a panel of experts: Bruce, the gas station attendant, who was an independent scholar and self-taught archeologist; local geologist and surveyor Handsome Harry Harrigan, best known for having prepared a geological map of western Nebraska; and Professor Eustadiola von Kletten, the university's newly arrived specialist in Aztec history. Needless to say, Old Man Marlowe served as chair and master of ceremonies.

Bruce (no one knew his family name) was the first to speak. "I've always suspected – no, I've always known that there was Aztec gold in those hills," he started, nodding northward, where the gold was supposedly to be found. As he did so, the roughly 300 people who had packed into the steakhouse looked in that direction, oblivious to the fact that they were in a steakhouse and that the walls of the steakhouse obstructed their view of any hills. "I heard about it from my pappa, when I was a small boy. He said that the Aztecs had their regional capital right here on this land where we are now living." Sounds of hushed excitement, and perhaps of nervous energy. "The Aztecs were a great people – some say, the first Americans. And, as Americans, they built a great city. They worked hard and were paid in gold. At first they put their gold in banks, but when the Spaniards arrived, they realized that the Spaniards would be making withdrawals from the banks, and so they moved their gold to the hills, and buried it. I know this because my pappa told me." This was followed by applause. Some people were raising their hands to ask questions, but Old Man Marlowe told them that they should wait until they had heard all three speakers.

Handsome Harry Harrigan was the next to speak. He was certainly handsome, and the ladies loved to look at him and watch his lips as he moved them to form words. They loved to listen to his mellifluous sentences, flowing from his mouth out into the room. The men too were captivated by his charismatic presence. "As you all know," as he said that, everyone started nodding, "I mapped this area a while ago. I collected a nice fee from the U.S. Geological Survey for my work, enough that I was able to buy a brand new Chevy. Driving around in my Chevy is a great experience, and I've even driven out to the hills north of here. What you see in the hills is mainly buttonweed, Russian knapweed, goatgrass, pigweed, ragweed, brush, tumbleweed, dirt, and, after it rains, mud. All of this looks pretty unhospitable for Aztecs. But remember that the Aztecs were here more than 500 years ago, and the climate and vegetation were different then. So, it is very likely that they wanted to put their gold in those hills. Best places to start to look would be in caves and pits, but since there aren't any, that won't be the best after all."

"I also drive a Chevy," someone in the audience called out. "One of the best buys I ever made."

"Bet it doesn't get as good a mileage as my Ford pickup," called out someone else.

"Hey, what does this have to do with gold?" complained yet a third person in the audience.

"Jake's right," said Old Man Marlowe, now identifying the third man as someone other than Harry Lime. "What we want to learn today is about Aztec gold and now it is a great pleasure for me to introduce our own local expert on Aztec gold, Professor Eustadiola von Kletten, who has just joined the faculty at the department of political science at UWU. She has no less than two Ph.D.'s -- one in political science from the National Autonomous University of Mexico in Mexico City and one in archeology from Yale University. Some folks say that Yale has the best archeology department in the world! She speaks German and English, as well as Mexican and the Aztec language. And here she is to tell us all about Aztec gold." People spontaneously clapped, looking at this still youngish professor with intense interest.

"Thank you, Mayor Marlowe, for your kind introduction," von Kletten began. "Before I turn to talking to you about Aztec gold, let me first tell you about some of my digs in southern Mexico. It was while I was doing my doctoral work in political science in Mexico City that I became interested in the Aztecs. I took advantage of my time in the land of mariachi to learn Nahuatl – " Since everyone looked puzzled at this word, she immediately clarified: " —that's the Aztec language. I did a few digs around Mexico City already then and after I entered the doctoral program in archeology at Yale, I returned for two years of fieldwork, during which I took part in digs at Templo Mayor, which had been the main temple complex at the Aztec capital of Tenochtitlan, as well as at Cihuatlan and Tochtepec. At Templo Mayor I was able to inspect the then-recently discovered stone disc with an image of Coyolxauhqui, the Aztec moon goddess and, some say, goddess of the Milky Way."

Some of the people in the saloon were finding all of this intriguing, even if all of these Aztec words were impossible to remember. But some of the locals were getting bored, and a few of them were starting to look around the room, as if looking for a swarm of Western Meadowlarks. "What about the gold?" someone at the back of the room shouted.

"I'm getting to that," the professor answered. "But I thought that you should know a bit about my background before we start going into details. As most of you probably know, the Spaniards conquered the Aztecs in the early sixteenth century, taking Tenochtitlan in 1521. They immediately demolished the Aztec capital and built a new city on top of the ruins. That new city is today's Mexico City. For the Spaniards, there were three prizes in conquest: land, gold, and the opportunity to spread Christianity. What happened to the Aztec gold? Most of it was taken back to Spain, where it was used to adorn cathedrals and palaces and to pay for more conquests. Some of the gold stayed in Mexico, of course. But the Aztec empire never covered more than the lower third of what is Mexico today, and no gold was ever taken far out of that region. Archeologists agree that there is no Aztec gold in the USA."

This provoked shrieks of horror and outrage throughout the saloon. "What about the Lost Dutchman's mine?" Jake shouted.

"Actually," the professor clarified, "the so-called Dutchman was Deutsch, which is to say German. He was not Holländisch. But whatever the truth about gold found by the Dutchman, it could not have been Aztec gold, because the Aztecs never made it to either Arizona or New Mexico, or for that matter Utah."

"We don't care about those foreign states," chimed Mabel Newberry, proprietor of Newberry's "What You Need" shop, which included such things as chocolates, flowers, hotdogs, and alcoholic beverages. "What we want to know is about the Aztecs who came here to Nebraska!" The entire room was hushed now, with everyone looking very intently at Eustadiola von Kletten. She looked intently around the saloon, and knew of course that she should weigh her words carefully. Should she tell the truth, the whole truth, and nothing but the truth, or tell some pleasant fibs, or tell just a bit of the truth but do so in a confusing way? She was a professor and for her this meant that she had to tell the truth.

"There have been stories circulating," she began, "about Aztecs coming to Utah or to Nebraska and burying gold in one place or another." Looks of anticipation now. "But if the Aztecs did come to this part of the country, did they just make a drop-off and then head back to Mexico? Or did they build a city around here? Or did something else happen to them?"

"They built Uptown," someone offered.

"So far," she continued, "no one has come up with any evidence to substantiate that claim and no archeologists have been willing to start excavating in Uptown. I have talked with the people in our archeology department, who are specialists in Egyptian, Babylonian, and ancient Roman archeology, and none of them have any interest in digging in your town. My own research strongly indicates that no Aztecs came even as far as Arizona or New Mexico, let alone as far north as Nebraska."

"I've heard that the Aztecs were extraterrestrials," an amnesiac taxidermist shared. "I'd like to know where their main landing sites were."

"This not serious," the professor replied. "No one seriously believes that the Aztecs were extraterrestrials."

"I do," the amnesiac responded, "and I think that their descendants are still living in the USA, probably underground."

"What about the curse of the Aztec dummy?" someone in the back of the room shouted.

"Again there have been stories and rumors," von Kletten responded, "but there does not seem to be any more substance to those stories than there is to the notion that the Aztecs buried gold in Nebraska!"

At this point, people started to shout, stomp their feet, and throw paper napkins around. Then out came the water pistols; apparently nearly everyone in Uptown possessed at least one of these hydraulic handguns. People started shooting at von Kletten, who of course wasn't packing a piece. But pretty soon it became a free-for-all, with people firing water at each other, while Old Man Marlowe almost sobbed as he reminded them, "no water pistol fights on the premises!" Friday came over to von Kletten as fast as he could and shielded her from most of the water being fired in her direction, while using his own large water pistol to shoot the main offenders. The water pistol riot only stopped when the water pistols ran out of water and, by then, just about everyone was drenched. At that point, people swarmed out of the saloon shouting and, as they did so, one could hear shouts of "I'm gonna get my shovel," "There's gold under Uptown – that's for sure," and "Who does that professor think she is, telling us that there's no Aztec gold in Nebraska?"

The next day, the local (weekly) newspaper, now appearing as *The Uptown News Daily & Every Advertiser's Dream*, known among locals by its acronym, *The UNDEAD*, ran a five-column headline: "Panel confirms Aztec gold under Uptown":

"A panel of experts on Aztec gold presented their findings to local citizens in a town meeting at the Steakholders' Steakhouse yesterday. Professor Eustadiola von Kletten, who has written a book about Aztec gold and speaks Mexican, confirmed that there was gold in the area. Handsome Harry Harrigan, the internationally renowned map maker, indicated that Aztec gold would most likely be found in local caves and pits. Local scholar Bruce recounted local traditions and offered that Aztec gold might even be found under the streets and buildings of Uptown. People were ecstatic at hearing all of this, and celebrated by firing their water pistols in the air. Mayor Marlowe later said that he hoped that people would be encouraged to take up the search for Aztec gold in earnest."

Some might say that this news account did not entirely reflect what had transpired at the meeting but, since only a fraction of the town's population had been able to jam into the saloon, most of the rest of the town had to rely on a combination of the report in *The UNDEAD* and the various, often conflicting, rumors circulating. And once people had read the news article, scores of them grabbed shovels and other implements and started to dig – under their own houses, in the streets, even under shops. There was only one bull-dozer in town and that was owned by Pastor Grace, and he was not about to let it leave the Church premises. But folks with snow plows found ways to adapt their plows to the excavation, and soon people were digging up Uptown. Some folks wanted to dig under the saloon, under the new steakhouse, which had not even officially opened, under the church, under the gas station, and even under the sheriff's office/barber shop. Needless to say, the proprietors of these establishments put a stop to these efforts, with the sheriff brandishing a real rifle, with real bullets not just water, and the pastor holding up a crucifix, telling people to respect the house of the Lord. Bruce warned people that digging under his gas station could result in gas escaping onto the streets, with all the risks that that posed, and Old Man Marlowe brought out a fearsome-looking water rifle, loaded however with whiskey, and started squirting whiskey at the folks who were beginning to undermine the founda-tions of his saloon. But there was no manpower to stop people from digging up Main Street, which someone suggested might have been the main boulevard in the ancient Aztec town which some people wanted to believe had been situated right there where Uptown was now situated. Mayor Marlowe thought the thing to do was to call out the National Guard but, to his disappointment, when he called the National Guard Office in North Platte to ask for assistance, he was told that the office had no record of there being a mayor in Up-town, which was apparently listed as an outlying district of North Platte. The Sheriff tried to seek assistance from the state police, but was told that there was no record of there being any district or set-tlement called Uptown, let alone a town, and even when the Sheriff told them that it was located near the lush Okra Stream, the only reply was that their maps showed no record of any stream called Okra. Apparently, the state police did not have Handsome Harry Harrigan's definitive maps. The digging went on for more than a week, with some folks who fancied an easy dig turning to the city park. Pretty soon the once lush green lawns and multicolored flowerbeds of the city park were full of deep holes, with brown earth carelessly flung over the flowerbeds. One of the diggers managed to crack the water main, another caused his own turreted house to tilt, allowing locals henceforth to compete with Pisa, by boasting of their own "Leaning Tower of Uptown", although it was more a turret than a tower. Yet another digger "excavated" a large hole in his driveway and, after a cave-in, found himself temporarily buried up to his neck, until his neighbors set aside their own excavations to come over to help. Over at UWU, some of the students from the archeology department grabbed shovels and started digging up the university quad and, when stopped by the campus police, they claimed that their professors had offered them extra credit if they participated in the quest for Aztec gold. The professors took pains to deny this.

Finally, after University President Floorboard phoned the governor's office in Lincoln, the National Guard was finally dispatched and put an end to the digging. There was room in the town jail for as many as four prisoners. So four persons, apparently picked at random, were identified as "ring-leaders" and jailed for three days. But just as calm was being restored to Uptown, Jimmy the Shimmy, a local dance entertainer, drove into town in his bright blue jeep. He was grinning ear to ear and, as he set the brake on his car in front of the saloon, held up a brown paper bag and shouted, "This here bag is full of gold! Gold from the hills of Uptown! Gold not far from fields of Okra!"

Hearing the word "gold" was exciting enough, but to hear the words "gold" and "okra" in the same sentence was more than the crowds milling around in front of the saloon could handle. Some of them fell to their knees crying, others threw their hats 30 feet into the air and tried to catch them as they fell back down, others shouted "Hurray for Uptown! Hurray for the people! God bless America!" And still others started to sing this old cowpoke song:

I'm whistling a song that ain't so old,

I'm thinking about a mountain of gold.
If I find that mountain, I can build a new home,
and till the lush and fertile loam,
while I sing yippie yi yi yay,
while I sing yippiie yi yi yay.

People inspected the "gold" and, of course, were eager for an appraisal. With nervous excitement, the sheriff-barber phoned over to the geology department at UWU and asked if they could send someone over to appraise the value of the gold, since Jimmy the Shimmy had quite a bagful. Even before the geologist could arrive, some locals were already packing into their convertibles and hatchbacks and driving over to the nearby hills, without even waiting to find out exactly where Jimmy the Shimmy had found his "gold". Some people who had been in the saloon for the panel discussion were now saying that this proved that Professor von Kletten was completely wrong and should stop talking about things she didn't know about. Others, who had relied on the *Uptown Weekly Race for Truth* as their source of information, were saying that this validated von Kletten's credentials and that she had been right all along.

Eventually, the geologist arrived – a professor with the appropriate name Goldie Rock – got out of her BMW and came over to the saloon to look at Jimmy the Shimmy's bag of goodies. She was wearing a tight-fitting T-shirt and a loose bright red jacket, short skirt, a geologist's hat, and of course cowboy boots made "right here" in Nebraska. Jimmy the Shimmy had taken his rocks into the saloon and was sitting at a large round table with the mayor, the sheriff, the pastor, and two or three other personages. Before the geologist was even shown the rocks, the pastor said a short prayer: "Let us give thanks to the Lord our God for this blessing, and may it bring even more prosperity to our small town." Old Man Marlowe gave a sign to his assistant to fetch the fireworks he kept on hand, so that they could celebrate their "gold". But as Professor Goldie Rock picked up the rocks, turning them over with a dismissive smirk on her face, she announced: "These rocks are pyrite – fool's gold. They are worthless." It would be difficult to imagine a harder blow to people who had already started dreaming of buying motorboats (even though the nearest lake was 300 miles distant) or of putting bright new tiles on their roofs or of taking a vacation in Oklahoma. Some of the people who had been throwing their hats into the air just a short while earlier, were now falling to their knees crying, while some of those who had been on their knees crying for joy earlier, were now throwing their hats – not into the air, but onto the ground and stomping on them.

The Great Okra Festival

Fortunately, there was the Great Okra Festival to look forward to. There are so many things you can make with okra, such as fried pecan okra, pickled okra, okra-and-corn maque choux, okra rellenos, okra creole, fried okra salad, shrimp-and-okra hush puppies, and baked polenta with cheese and okra. And though the Civil War, which tore apart this great country of ours, took place more than a century and a half ago, some folks in Uptown still talk about a recommendation published in the *Nebraska Farmer* in March 1862 that one could make "coffee" using okra seeds instead of coffee beans. Coffee beans were hard to get in those times, but there was okra everywhere, great expansive fields of okra, and everyone liked okra in those days, including the buffalo, the Western Meadowlark, and all manner of scavengers. Not to forget, okra was and still is a favorite with the Great Plains Toad and the Northern Leopard Frog and some folks said that okra was or should be the state vegetable. Actually, only a few states have official state vegetables. In Arkansas, for example, it is the South Arkansas vine ripe tomato, in Louisiana and North Carolina it is the sweet potato, and in Washington state it's the Walla Walla sweet onion. But okra was not honored in any of our 50 states and – no surprise here – there were strong feelings in Uptown that okra should be declared the official state vegetable for Nebraska, which up to now had not had a state vegetable. Old Man Marlowe, Uptown's very own self-appointed mayor, realized that, with the disappointment over the discovery of pyrite in the hills, locals needed something to reenergize themselves, and what could be better than a movement to promote okra as the official state vegetable of Nebraska. So, amid horse-drawn carriage rides through the okra fields, children playing games with okra on the railroad tracks, fishing events at the nearby Okra Stream, and an okra yodeling contest, with locals doing their best to yodel while eating okra, this conscientious but unpaid mayor brought as many people as he could to the city park, and talked to them about the civilizational value of okra. Some people said that "civilizational" wasn't a real word and that it made more sense to say simply that okra tasted real good. But the mayor wanted to make a grand statement and, if okra was important for human civilization, then it surely should be honored as the state vegetable. Besides, whether "civilizational" was a real word or not, everyone in town was enthusiastic about this idea and even more enthusiastic when it turned out that the petition which Old Man Marlowe had prepared for their signatures promoted not just okra, but Uptown Okra, to be chosen as the state vegetable. Soon, with the exception of a few infants who had not yet learned how to write, the entire population of Uptown had signed the petition.

Taking the petition to the Governor's Office would have to wait for a few days, however, because the grand opening of the Steakholders' Steakhouse had been scheduled to coincide with the opening of this year's okra festival. And what an event it was. The school band arrived at the steakhouse to play a few marches to celebrate the big event, while fireworks were bursting in air in the sunlight. And whenever Uptownians were feeling especially happy, out came the water pistols. Only this time, they were not squirting each other, but firing their water pistols into the air. There was even a small contingent of uniformed band members who gave a 21-water pistol salute. There were also speeches about okra, recipes were exchanged, and the so-called "bookstore" announced the publication of a book on the history of okra. Old Man Marlowe also provided free okra beer (prepared according to his own special recipe) throughout the three days of the festival and by the time the festival had come to an end, people were once again feeling joyful, although a small minority had gotten themselves totally drunk and needed a couple of extra days before they could once again feel joyful.

It was decided that it would be best if the mayor, the pastor, and the sheriff – as the three most important persons in the town – would drive the 240 miles to the Governor's Office together. Old Man Marlowe had only an old jalopy, Pastor Grace had a fine vehicle with the words "Jesus saves" painted in large letters on one side and "Buddha saves" on the other and, of course, his bulldozer, and Sheriff Dorbin had two vehicles – her squad car and a somewhat fancier "barber-mobile". Given the choices, it was decided that they would drive to Lincoln in the squad car. This, of course, had the advantage that they could turn on the siren whenever the traffic got a bit heavy. And so it was that, after driving for less than four hours, with a large sack of okra in the squad car, they arrived in the state capital and approached the Governor's Palace.

Situated atop a hill overlooking the entire city of Lincoln and with a surveillance tower to keep an eye on the intellectuals working at the university, the Governor's Palace was, of course, made of fine Florentine marble, and had 16 Doric columns, 17 gargoyles adorning the yellow fluorescent roof, and guards dressed in Renaissance costumes and carrying halberds, standing guard at the entrance. The palace was huge, probably bigger than the U.S. Capitol, and just to the left of it, in the Garden of Wonders, there stood a 20-foot high replica of the Statue of Liberty. As the mayor, the pastor, and the sheriff saw all of this for the first time in their lives, their hearts raced. But they marched up the stairs, with the mayor and the sheriff carrying the sack of okra, while the pastor marched ahead, holding up the Holy Bible in front of himself. Normally, one would think that one could not just march in to see the Governor without an appointment. But these three were dressed in their Sunday best, and looked so official that they were immediately ushered in to see the Governor. They ascended the spiral staircase, taking in the various paintings of Indian chieftains, and finally reached the second floor. Here they were stopped by yet another Renaissance guard who inquired as to their business. "We want to see the Governor," announced the pastor. "It is about okra, and God is with us."

The guard was taken off guard by this remark and momentarily looked around, as if he might see God somewhere. Then he remembered that God does not usually make Himself visible, collected his wits, and responded, "What's this about okra?"

"It should be our official state vegetable!" the pastor replied.

"Ah, a noble cause," the Renaissance man replied. "Come this way." And he led the threesome straight into the Governor's office, announcing to the Governor: "These men have come to talk with you about okra."

"Why welcome, partners," said the Governor Eddie Fitzerback with a vaguely Southern-sounding accent. Perhaps he wasn't born in Nebraska. "I love okra. It is my favorite vegetable. My mother prepares it for dinner at least once a week. So, what can I do for you, fellow okra-lovers?"

"We would like it to be proclaimed the official state vegetable of Nebraska," the three okra-lovers replied in unison.

"That's a great idea!" responded the Governor with unrestrained approval in his eyes. "I'll get on this right away."

This took the threesome by surprise. "Right away, your Excellency?" said the pastor timidly.

"Why of course, my good citizens of Nebraska. At last we can make progress on something serious around here. The state senators have been making a lot of noise about something I just don't get," the Governor began. "They say that they don't like driving north only to enter a state called '*South* Dakota' and figure that, if it lies to the north, it should be '*North* Dakota'. They say that the two states should be switched around, with all the cities and industries and farms and people in South Dakota moved to what is now North Dakota, and vice versa, and then we would have North Dakota close to us, and South Dakota pressing its bosom up against Canada. I don't know about the bosom, but I can tell you this: it ain't gonna be easy to move Mount Rushmore."

"That sounds tough, real tough," said the sheriff, doing her best to display maximum empathy.

"And it doesn't stop with that," the Governor continued. "Some senators want to introduce accelerated education in elementary schools, so that at the age of 13 the graduates can go straight into the University of Nebraska or any of a number of our other great universities and colleges in this great state. This, in turn, would allow local communities to close their high schools, saving a stash of cash that they could then use to build theme parks. They believe that having a theme park in every town would be a great thing, a great thing. They even have a slogan: 'A theme park for every municipality.' What am I going to do about this endless lunacy?"

"Yes," Mayor Marlowe offered, "you've got quite a dilemma."

"And meanwhile," the Governor added, changing the subject, "I've been commuting from home to work in a hot air balloon and all I'm asking is for the legislature to pay the costs of my commute. But they say that no other governors are commuting to work in hot air balloons, so why should I have to do this? My answer: I like getting high."

"Yes, your Excellency," said the pastor. "And here is our petition." The pastor pulled the petition out of the Holy Bible, where it had been marking the Book of Ezekiel, and handed it to the Governor.

"Thank you," the Governor said, "I'll get on this right away... How about a tour of my Garden of Wonders? Would y'all like that?" And so they left the building, escorted by the Governor himself, who gave them a tour of his Garden in which, in addition to his miniature Statue of Liberty, one could also find miniature models of the Golden Gate Bridge, the Alamo, Mount Rushmore, the Grand Canyon, Niagara Falls, Old St. Patrick's Church from Chicago, the cowpoke town of Tombstone, and much much more. It was a tribute to all things American. It was a heady experience. Two weeks later, came the good news that, with the assent of the senate, the Governor had proclaimed Uptown okra the official state vegetable of Nebraska. Not just any old okra, but Uptown okra – what a great day for the people of Uptown! It was not surprising that when the citizens of Uptown heard the news, they starting waltzing in the streets. The band caught the beat and played the waltzes of Johann Strauss.

The Aztec Urn

Romulus could not care one way or the other about okra, prefer-ring "real beer" as he called it, over okra beer. Well, to each his own, local citizens said. But his mind was on other, grander for him at least, ambitions. What he wanted was to be head of the political science department, which looked to him like a position of power and prestige. Besides, as head of the department, he would receive a 10% boost in his salary and, within the university setting, he could also dream of being selected "departmental head of the year" – a most enviable honor which, he was sure, would guarantee him access to the halls of power in Lincoln. He was sitting in a cor-ner in the Fancy Turtle Saloon, stirring his "real" beer and thinking, when the Maverick brothers, accompanied by Pestalozzi – well, Pestalozzi's hologram – entered the saloon. They sat down at the table with Romulus. They could see that he was deep in thought and a few minutes passed before anyone said anything.

"I've been thinking," Romulus said finally. That seemed to the brothers like a good start and certainly an ice-breaker. "I've been thinking about what to do about our department."

"Yes," said Bret, the smarter of the two brothers, though, for a professor, he was not particularly smart. "It was a close vote."

"That's right," brother Bart agreed. "That's right. It was a close vote. That's right."

Romulus looked at Pestalozzi's hologram, clearly wanting him to show solidarity. "Yes," the hologram agreed. "These are indeed difficult times."

"The question is what are we going to do," Romulus said in a hushed tone. "How shall we get Friday out of power."

"Fountaingate almost worked," Bart noted quietly. "Perhaps we can try with that again."

"Don't be an idiot," Romulus snapped. "We are not going to be able to get people worked up about that again."

"If you did something truly spectacular," the Pestalozzi hologram pointed out, "you would instantly become a local hero."

"That's an excellent start, but what precisely?"

"Locals are obsessed with the Aztecs," the hologram continued in a murmur, so that Old Man Marlowe, who was at the bar, would not overhear. "If you revive people's faith that the Aztecs were here, with or without gold, then both Friday and von Kletten will be completely marginalized and you will be carried to the chairmanship of our department in a gush of enthusiasm. You will be a hero!"

"Excellent, Pestalozzi! Truly excellent! What about you two, Bret and Bart, what do you think about this? Is this a good idea?"

"Yes, it is a good idea, an excellent idea," the brothers chimed in unison. "That's right, yes it is. That's right, yes it is..."

"Stop that! We need to think up a plan," Romulus announced.

"If you can present some Aztec find," Pestalozzi suggested, perhaps not as wisely as one might think, "this might work quite well. Rob a museum, for example in Mexico City, and bring back the artefact and tell people that you found the artefact right here in the Okra Hills."

"Well, I'm not a hologram, and the Mexican police are, by reputation, no fun. I for one am not going to try to steal a valuable artefact out of Mexico's National Museum and see if I can smuggle it across the border. I know for a fact that security is very tight at that museum as well as at the border. So, that's a non-starter."

"The museums in Nebraska have loose security," Bret pointed out. "Bart and I can break in and steal an Aztec artefact."

"Our museums in Nebraska don't have any Aztec artefacts. How do you propose to steal something which does not exist?"

"We'll steal something else and paint it with Aztec images," Bret announced, looking very very proud of himself for coming up with this idea. "And we have the Museum of Grecian Archeology in Omaha. We can find something suitable there and 'fix' it."

Somehow, this rather implausible idea appealed to Romulus and to brother Bart; in fact, the latter started clapping enthusiastically and smiling so broadly that Old Man Marlowe, who could not hear this hushed conversation, knew that something was up. "Can I get you boys some okra beer?" he asked. They shook their heads.

"Whiskey!" the threesome clamored. Holograms don't drink; so Pestalozzi kept silent. The mayor brought them whiskey and, as they gulped it down, they began to hatch their plot. The idea was that the brothers would drive to Omaha, break into the museum, steal an urn, repaint it with Aztec motifs, and bring it back to Uptown. It would then be presented to the local and university public as a discovery made on Romulus' initiative. The Maverick brothers headed down to the cafeteria, and sat around drinking coffee for hours on end. They knew that this could be their big moment in life. Brother Bart wanted to take the train from North Platte to Omaha, but Brother Bret pointed out that it would be easier to hide a stolen urn in the trunk of their car. Bart made a fuss about a dining car, but Bret promised to take him to a first-class diner if he would agree to drive to Omaha by car. Bart then came up with the idea of a hot air balloon, since he thought that that would afford them many beautiful views of Nebraska's landscape. Brother Bret had to remind his brother that this was not a pleasure trip, and insisted on their driving by car. Finally, Brother Bart gave in and, the following day, the brothers set out, "early" in the morning – meaning by 11 a.m. – for Omaha. The brothers, of course, knew it would be best to break in at night, when there would be only one night watchman. They thought of almost everything. They brought along flashlights (of course), laughing gas, in order to neutralize the night watchman, wire clippers to cut the alarm wires, and magnets (just in case). As they approached the museum, they checked the grounds to make sure that they would be able to escape without any problem, with Brother Bret even shining his light into the illuminated pool in front of the museum. Unfortunately, they were foolishly wearing boots with taps, so that they made a lot of noise as they walked through the museum. In spite of all the noise they made, they eventually pulled off the heist successfully. They cut the alarm wires, left the night watchman sitting in his chair laughing uncontrollably, smashed open a glass case, and walked out car-

"As they approached the museum, they checked the grounds to make sure that they would be able to escape without any problem, with Brother Bart even shining his light into the illuminated pool in front of the museum."

rying an exquisite Grecian urn from the sixth century BCE. They were so pleased with themselves that they lifted the urn up over their heads triumphantly as they literally marched down the steps of the museum to get into their car. Since it was 3 a.m., most citizens of Omaha were asleep, but, by the time they left the museum, there was a crowd of pot-smoking youth hanging around, and, as they saw the brothers carrying out the urn, they started cheering. One of them even shouted "Power to the people!" Another shouted "Long live urns!" A third one, less imaginative, smiled from ear to ear and exclaimed, "Look at those dudes with the urn!"

"We are not 'dudes'," Brother Bart informed them. "We are professors from the University of Western Uptown!"

"Shut up, Bart," Bret said. "You don't have to put us on the suspect list!"

Fortunately, no one in Omaha had ever heard of the University of Western Uptown and the next day's *Omaha Prairie Bison*, the city's most important newspaper, carried the headline "Two dudes steal Greek treasure from Omaha museum".

Meanwhile, the brothers wrapped the urn in bubble wrap and drove it to Loup City ("Here we go, loup de loup"). With a population of just over 1,000, Loup City nonetheless boasts the famous Loup City Diner, serving up great chow since 1952, but more to the point, the Loup City Arts & Crafts Center, where local craftsmen are ready to help would-be artists produce works of fine art. So, when the brothers arrived in Loup City, the first thing they did was to head over to the diner for some grub. They put a quarter in the jukebox and ordered some BBQ spaghetti and meatballs – finger-lickin' good. Then, after giving the waitress a large tip, they headed over the Arts & Crafts Center, carrying in their prize, still enclosed in bubble wrap. The proprietor, a man calling himself Tar Vardon, welcomed them and, when they told him that they had some junk urn and wanted to fix it, he seemed dubious at first but then told them that this could be done for a flat fee of $3,000. Fortunately, Brother Bret had come along with plenty of cash, put the bills on the table, and said "Let's get to work."

So it was that this ancient Grecian urn was sandpapered down to eliminate the original art and, with Vardon's help, the two brothers painted images of Aztec maidens chasing chickens and goats, and Aztec men plowing their fields and herding sheep. The art looked relatively convincing, at least to an untrained eye – and the three craftsmen at work on the urn were certainly untrained in Aztec art. When the artwork was finished, Brother Bart etched in the words "Viva Mexico!" in a prominent place.

"I don't think that the Aztecs spoke Spanish," Brother Bret offered. "They had their own language, which they called 'the Aztec language'."

"That don't sound right to me," Vardon said. "Why don't we check this on Wikipedia."

Well, it turned out that the Aztec language was called Nahuatl (just as Eustadiola von Kletten had explained), and that it wasn't written in the Latin alphabet but used pictograms. And it wasn't Spanish. So, Brother Bart, sandpapered away "Viva Mexico!" and copied some lines in Nahuatl that he found on the internet onto the urn. Now the newly minted 'Aztec urn' looked great. The brothers were so pleased with this result that, after packing the urn up once again, and stashing it in the back seat of their car, they headed back to the Loup City Diner for more victuals. They ordered and wolfed down (in honor of Wolf Romulus) a pair of seven-decker burgers with French fries, which they doused in ketchup, and ordered half a dozen Nebraskan Reuben sandwiches for the trip. Turned out that the Loup City Diner also offered a local cola, Loup City Cola. The twosome bought a couple of six-packs of the cola, headed out to their automobile, and pressed the accelerator to the floorboard. They zoomed off ("riding the trail to who knows where"), giving proof that the seven-decker burger was packed with nutrients. As they started on their roughly three-hour trip back to Uptown, they grabbed for the colas and began drinking. After going through about four colas each, they were getting very jolly and Bart's driving was becoming very erratic. As he drove the car back and forth between the lanes, he and Brother Bret suddenly heard a siren behind them. They pulled over, and Sheriff Goodman swaggered up to their car and asked them, "What have you two been drinking?

"If the brothers had been content to drink rain water off the streets, well, they would not have been pulled over."

You are as drunk as a couple of pigeons." Whether pigeons actually get drunk is another matter and, in fact, there is little to substantiate that suggestion, since pigeons prefer to drink rain water off the streets. If the brothers had been content to drink rain water off the streets, well, they would not have been pulled over.

"Just cola we purchased in Loup City," answered Bret, "nothing alcoholic."

"Aha," the sheriff replied. "Here we go loup-de-loup. Well, you two should have checked the small writing on the cola you've been guzzling down. Loup City Cola has an alcohol content of 15% -- the second highest in the country. Among beers, only Sam Adams beer has a higher alcohol content – that's 17.5%, in case the two of you like getting plastered. Now, get out of the vehicle and put your hands in your pockets."

As they did so, the sheriff became upset. "No, I mean place your hands on your knees."

So the twosome bent over to touch their knees. At this point, Sheriff Goodman realized that his own brain was a bit fried, possibly from smoking okra cigarettes all morning. He did not want to embarrass himself anymore and simply told them, "Get back in your car and do your best to stay in one lane. If I have to pull you over again, I may have remembered by then where you are supposed to put your hands when I want to arrest you. Sayonara, baby!" The brothers thought that it was strange to hear this Anglo sheriff say "Sayonara, baby!", but perhaps he had picked it up from one of Arnold Schwarzenegger's movies.

The brothers decided that caution was the best policy and drove only as far as Rawhide, a town of just over 8,000 inhabitants, which lay just four miles due West of where they had been stopped. Among Rawhide's highlights are the Cowpoke Steakhouse and the famous Gunslinger Motel. They headed over to the motel, paid for a room for two in cash, and nodded off to sleep. Being a cautious pair, they brought the urn into their room and stashed it in the closet. They must have slept for at least 12 hours but, the next morning, after eating a breakfast of grits in gravy and enjoying the motel's own special blend of nonalcoholic coffee – yes, they checked about potential alcoholic content in the coffee before drinking it – they headed over to the Cowpoke Steakhouse where they devoured two of the most delicious steaks they had ever eaten. Then, they returned to the Gunslinger Motel, packed up their things and began driving – this time, without enjoying the refreshing, finely brewed Loup City Cola. They were about 20 minutes down the road when Bret suddenly remembered, "Hey! We left the urn in the room!" A look of panic crept over both of their faces as they turned the car around and returned to the Gunslinger Motel. When they arrived and told the clerk that they had left something in their room, they encountered yet another difficulty.

"Yes," the clerk said. "We found a big pot in the closet. It looks valuable. I was just about to call the police."

"You don't need to do that, ma'am," Brother Bret explained, flashing a winsome smile. "It's a gift for our mother for Mother's Day!" Mother's Day was several months off, but the clerk looked at the two brothers and decided that it was less work and less bother to take them at their word. So, she reached under the desk, retrieved the "pot", as she called it, and handed it over to the brothers. And with that, they were once more on their way, arriving in Uptown just in time for dinner at the Fancy Turtle.

The Rise of Romulus
and the Reign of Error

Another day, another faculty meeting at the department of political science. In fact, at UWU only the physics department had more faculty meetings than the political scientists since the physics profs had a faculty meeting every day (!), even when there was no new business to discuss and very little old business. The physics professors talked mostly about Nebraskan beef and corn, and about the departmental chair's pet goat, which he called Newton – a bit predictable, perhaps, but better than calling his goat Goat, as was the chair's original idea. But Newton the goat had no discernible talent for physics and left this to his master, Professor and Head of the Physics Department Eugen Klemens Krüger. Some people said that that was a funny name, others said that it had a proud heritage, still others did not care about his name or about his goat, and still others wanted to have more faculty meetings at the department of physics.

Meanwhile, back at the political science department, Romulus let it be known that he and the Maverick brothers had a big and exciting announcement they wanted to make – specifically, that they had found an important Aztec artefact not far from Uptown. A faculty meeting was called and was opened to the general public. Some professors from other departments at UWU, especially from the departments of physics and archeology, came over, as did many townsfolk. So many people came to hear what Romulus had to say that the meeting had to be moved to the Millard Fillmore Auditorium on campus. President Floorboard, that dapper man of action and cosmopolitan dead-ringer, looked positively embarrassed as he addressed the crowd of perhaps 500 people.

"My fellow Uwuans, citizens of Uptown, patriotic Nebraskans, my fellow Americans!" he began, turning an inspired phrase. "Today it is my pleasure – " he winced a bit here " – to welcome Professor Wolf Romulus to the podium, where he will reveal what he says is an important Aztec treasure found in our very own backyard." With that, President Floorboard retreated to his seat in great haste and started staring at his shoes. Meanwhile, the crowd roared with nervous excitement and gave Romulus a loud applause.

"You won't be disappointed," Romulus began. Cheers and applause. "I can confirm positively today that the Aztecs did come as far as Nebraska – " increasingly frenetic cheers, " – and that we have brought an artefact straight from the Okra Hills to show you. Brothers Bret and Bart, please bring the urn to the stage."

The two brothers had placed the urn in a large box, tied with a ribbon. As the two brothers ceremoniously brought the box to the stage, the excitement mounted. Then, as the brothers held the box forward, Romulus reached inside and pulled out the urn. He held it up and people started to swoon. There were moans of joy, which sounded positively orgiastic, sounds of laughter such as one hears only when people are in high ecstasy, and vague gurgles, which were almost surely gurgles of approval and gratitude. "This," announced Romulus, "is an ancient Aztec urn, with authentic Aztec inscriptions. We have already had it carbon-dated and I can verify that it is very old." And as he held it up above his head, the audience started to chant, "Aztec! Aztec! Aztec!" and "Romulus for department chair!" People then gave Romulus a stormy and prolonged applause, transforming itself into an ovation. People stomped their feet, shouted their approval, and clapped for more than 30 minutes. All, that is, except for Floorboard, Friday, von Kletten, Bobkov, Disraeli, Marlowe, Sheriff-Barber Dorbin, and a few other supporters of Friday and skeptics about Romulus' claims. As the political scientists left, they gathered in the moss garden and talked about the department. Although they were still divided, there was now a slim majority in favor of ousting honest Joe Friday as chair and replacing him with Romulus. A week later, it was a done deal.

Friday was replaced by Romulus, and Pestalozzi took von Kletten's place as deputy chair of the department. As Romulus came to his first faculty meeting as chair, he wore not his usual cowboy outfit but a toga and had placed a laurel wreath on his head as a sign of victory. As he came into the room, Gabe Carver shouted "Hail Caesar!" Professors Bobkov, Cleary, and Disraeli wrote a public letter protesting the coup in the department, and managed to get it published in Uptown's weekly newspaper, *The Uptown Weekly Urn*. His appearance in a Roman toga gave rise to some gossip, with some people speculating that he had a multiple personality disorder although, since the "evidence" for this was that he occasionally wore a Roman toga and usually dressed in what locals called "Nebraskan cowboy" attire, it was not obvious that having *two* rather different outfits qualified either as "multiple" or as a personality disorder. Everyone agreed, however, that Romulus was a flamboyant personality.

Romulus' first act as chair of the department was to issue an *ordo* (Latin for order), as he called it, declaring that he was going to install twelve more drinking fountains in the department, including in both washrooms. This "ancient Roman"-cowboy also announced that he was authorizing the purchase of 32 paintings on velvet of scenes of Nebraska, and planned to hang one in every office and wash room and meeting room in the department. These announcements came by email, even before the first faculty meeting under his leadership.

Romulus thought that Monday was the best day for a faculty meeting since people might still be recovering from their weekends and ready to agree to his all-too-reasonable proposals. So, the Monday following his ascent to power, Romulus called the first faculty meeting and the first order of business was his title. He was not satisfied with the title "chair of the department". He wanted to be called "the Commander". There was a lot of resistance to this, even from his erstwhile allies – though not, of course, from the Maverick brothers, who lapped the milk from his saucer.

"Whaddya want with being our 'commander'?" asked Cleary. "Are you planning on giving us commands?"

"When necessary," said Romulus. "When the department cannot make a decision or does not want to make the right decision."

"Do you think this is how it is done in other departments, or at other universities?" Bobkov challenged. "I've never heard of any department being headed by a 'commander'."

"This is a really good idea," Bart Holloway interjected, "a really good idea."

"And I like it too," chirped brother Brother Bret.

"Well, it might be a good idea, but it might not," said the ever-hesitant Brookhurst. "We could ask around in other departments, such as the physics department, and see what others think. I like it, but at the same time I don't like it. Or, to put it differently, I don't like it, but at the same time I like it."

"I object to this idea strenuously," declared Katella Beach. "The idea of having a commander!! Departments are supposed to operate according to democratic rules."

"There is nothing wrong with having commanders in democracies," Romulus explained. "Surely no one will deny that Dwight D. Eisenhower was a great American president, loyal to our democracy. But he was also Supreme Commander of the Allied Expeditionary Force during World War Two. I am not asking to be designated 'Supreme Commander' of this department, only 'Commander'. Besides, I have already allocated considerable departmental funds to purchase new stationery and a new desk pieces, identifying myself in this way. And again besides, sometimes only a commander can sort out the tangled knots of intradepartmental politics."

The wrangling went on for more than an hour and a half. As it continued, some of those originally present had to leave for other engagements. Eventually, most of those who were dead-set against this apparent usurpation of presumed power had left, with enough professors remaining in the room to make a quorum and most of them prepared to indulge Romulus, if not frenetically enthusiastic about having a commander. With seven of the 13 professors still present, counting the Pestalozzi hologram, Romulus called for a vote, and was accorded the title he craved by a vote of 4 to 3. Henceforth, he was to be addressed as "Commander Romulus".

But that first faculty meeting was not yet over, as Romulus had a second order of business. Some funds had been allocated to hire a specialist in Latin American politics. But since the search had not yet started, Romulus wanted to reallocate the funding to hire someone specializing in crime and politics. He claimed that this was a "hot" new field and that it was highly relevant. Once again, the vote went 4 to 3 – although this time the hologram was opposed to Romulus – and Romulus announced that a search would begin. Ads were placed in the appropriate places, including in the town's newspaper, *The Uptown News Reporter & Extraterrestrial Alien Loveship* (known among locals by its acronym, The UNREAL), as well as in the campus newspaper. The opening was even announced on KNOP-TV News, broadcasting out of North Platte. Soon applications were streaming in and, by the time the deadline had arrived, there were more than 300 applications – some from schoolteachers, some from gas station attendants, some from dentists, some from professors, some from police, and, inevitably, a large number from persons who were probably –who knows for sure? – associated with the criminal underworld.

Romulus appointed a committee to review the applications and propose three candidates to be interviewed. The members of the committee were Romulus himself, the Maverick brothers, and Joe Friday. Although he expected to be marginalized on the committee, Friday agreed to serve on it, so that his voice of reason could at least be heard. After the committee had conferred, it presented its recommendations to the faculty as whole. The majority report proposed to interview three candidates: a professor of criminal law who had been teaching at a small college in neighboring Iowa, known to his friends as Professor Dean "the brick" Boring and, to his enemies, as Professor Dean "the bore" Boring; a retired police chief named Marcus Remus (rumor had it that his name reminded Romulus of someone); and a mafia boss, called Micky "the wrench" Rossini (no relation to the famous Italian composer Gioacchino Rossini, who composed the "Lone Ranger" theme). Friday presented the minority report, proposing to bring in Professor Henry Gordon, an internationally renowned professor at Harvard University, who had written five books about the politics of crime. After the faculty considered these options, the vote went 7 to 6 to bring in those recommended by Romulus and the Maverick brothers.

So the day arrived when the first of these candidates was to present his talk: Professor Boring. It was an overcast day, and the mold on the walls of the faculty meeting room seemed to be a brighter green than usual. As the professors took their seats, with the full professors at the center table, and the associate and assistant professors sitting around the walls, the secretaries arrived to serve three-day-old coffee and two-day old donuts. Everyone was feeling good, probably because it was a Monday. Carver looked very hung over from his weekend drinking bout, Disraeli was staring around the room as if looking for flies, Brookhurst kept bending over to untie his shoelaces and retie them, MacGrory was talking to himself, Friday and von Kletten were whispering to each other and looking very sensible, Beach was preening herself in her mirror, and the rest were sitting in great expectation of the first speaker.

After he was introduced, Professor Boring began, "Hello. I am Dean Boring, and I want to talk to you about crime. As you all know, crime is a problem, not only for those directly affected but also for the communities in which they live, and for that matter for the nation as a whole. To tackle crime, you have to get at the root of crime and the root of crime is bad manners. If people would just say 'please' and 'thank you' and 'excuse me' and 'pardon me' on a regular basis, they wouldn't be so aggressive. So we start with training young people to be polite, and to greet everyone they see in a friendly way. What is so difficult about that?..." He was saying all of this in a complete monotone, and soon half of those present were nodding off to sleep and, by the time he had finished, even Romulus was having trouble keeping his eyes open. In fact, Boring did not actually finish – he was cut off by Romulus after at least five of the other 12 professors in the room were snoring loudly.

"Thank you, Professor Boring," Romulus virtually shouted, "for a truly thrilling and inspiring lecture. Now, are there any questions?"

"Sure," said Bobkov, shaking himself awake. "Do you actually expect us to be impressed with the rot you have disgorged?"

Boring muttered something no one bothered to listen to, Romulus ushered him out of the room and took him on the mandatory tour of the campus. No one wanted to join Romulus and Boring at dinner, and by the next morning Boring had been packed onto a plane, two days ahead of schedule, and sent back to Iowa.

A week later, it was the Police Chief Remus's turn. His idea of politics was that he had constantly had to fight with the mayor and city council of his town to get more funds for the police force and to renovate the city jail. Then it was time for questions.

"What do you think of Henry Gordon's classic work, *The interpenetration of the criminal underworld and the political estabilishment?*" came the first question.

"Sorry, I have never heard of it."

"How about P. J. McKinley's book, *Politics, crime, and social decay?*"

"Sorry, that's another book I haven't heard of."

"So, what book would you cite as the most influential for you in your work as a police chief?"

"That would be *The Police Manual.*"

Giggles all around. Then someone asked, "Have you ever arrested a professor?" More giggles.

The chief shook his head and said, "Not as far as I can recall."

"What about haircuts? Our sheriff also runs a barber shop and she gives great haircuts. Can you give haircuts?"

"Give me a pair of scissors and I'll give it a shot," the chief replied. There were more giggles. And then he added, "Do you guys have a good ice cream parlor in town? I really like milk shakes."

And so it was that, after his talk, the entire department joined him at the local ice cream parlor, where it was milk shakes all around. No one in the department, except for brother Bart, thought that the police chief could conceivably work out, although some of the faculty got out their cameras to take photos of Romulus and Remus standing together. So all hopes were pinned on the mafia boss, set to arrive the following week.

The arrival of the mafia boss was of course big news, and was picked up by local radio stations. Realizing that this job talk could attract a big crowd, Romulus wisely moved the talk to the Millard Fillmore Auditorium. To say that the crowd was huge would be an understatement. Not only were all the seats taken, both in the gallery and in the balconies, but there were people sitting on the steps and on the stage, and even a few youngsters hanging from the rafters. Members of the departments of political science, physics, economics, animal husbandry, automobile safety, archeology, entomology, and others were all present, as were many of UWU's students, local townsfolk, schoolchildren from the Uptown Elementary School and their teachers, and of course a reporter from the *Uptown Herald*. As Commander Romulus strode to the podium in full cowboy regalia, including black leather cowboy hat and matching water pistols in his holdsters, the crowd broke out into thunderous applause – not for the commander, of course, but in anticipation of hearing a lecture by a notorious mafia boss.

Romulus raised his right hand in something that looked a lot like a salute and the crowd hushed. He leaned toward the microphone, pausing for a moment, and then began: "Ladies and gentlemen, scholars and students, citizens and patriots, fellow Nebraskans and visitors from other countries, greetings and welcome! Today it is a great pleasure for me to introduce our final candidate for the professorship in politics in crime. Micky 'the wrench' Rossini (no relation to the famous Italian composer Gioacchino Rossini, who composed the 'Lone Ranger' theme), is the head of the powerful Little Bologna Syndicate, which has brought law and order to New York and other cities in the east. He is widely respected and is considered highly knowledgeable about crime in America's cities."

Most people in the audience knew what these lines meant, and were intrigued. They gave Rossini a thunderous welcome. Some people started to sing the theme from "The Lone Ranger", even though it wasn't *this* Rossini's work. Eventually, the entire audience was singing the "Lone Ranger" theme, some of them even slapping their legs to the beat.

Rossini strode up to the podium, his piece bulging in his hip pocket. "Fair ladies and gentlemen," he began, "it's lovely to hear that theme, though, as far as I know, I am not related to my second favorite composer. I am, of course, my own favorite composer. I've composed a little music in my day, but it has been mostly chin music. I thank Professor Romulus for his warm invitation and introduction, but note this: I am a simple businessman. As a businessman, I benefit from the great freedom in this country – "

Cheers throughout the auditorium at the mention of freedom.

" – and I never cease to thank the day that I was born in this country, in the US of A. I am a New Yorker, but I have visited Nebraska many times, mainly in connection with my business ventures in Omaha, but also to visit your great parks – the Homestead National Monument and the Nebraska National Forest. New York

"I am in the business of providing services," Rossini continued. "Me and my wise guys, we offer protection. Every knucklehead needs protection, 'cause this is a dangerous world. You need protection? You come to us, or more often we come to you and we offer you our services. You pay us a fee and we provide protection.

might be the greatest city in the world, but Nebraska is the most beautiful place in the known universe."

More cheers. Rossini was clearly an accomplished people-pleaser.

"I am in the business of providing services," Rossini continued. "Me and my wise guys, we offer protection. Every knucklehead needs protection, 'cause this is a dangerous world. You need pro-tection? You come to us, or more often we come to you and we offer you our services. You pay us a fee and we provide protection. That's how it works. We don't like to see mugs and their molls be-hind the eight-ball, but sometimes they're gonna be wanting a little of the Broderick so they can remember how protection works. I'll tell you this: I too need protection, and that's why I pay protection money to a lot of senators – yeah, US senators – and they protect me. That's what life is all about, paying for protection and getting it. And if some chump gets in your face and you have paid for protection, we'll send down our chopper squad and make a mess of his beezer, we'll stick a drainpipe up his ass, and send him on his way.

"I done a bit in the slammer, I'll admit it, but that was like school, and it was before I started paying protection money to the senators. Now I don't go to school no more. Now I'm a service provider, and I provide a range of services. You want some ice? – I can get it for you at a discount. You want to relax? – I got can houses where you can have a good time and throw back some eel juice. You want a couple of brunos to teach someone to sing for you? – I can arrange that. But don't pay me with no orphan paper or you'll find yourself sleeping in a Chicago overcoat. I don't cozy to no flimflammers.

"I work closely with law enforcement and am always ready to help the men in blue down at the clubhouse. Just the other day, the chief at one of the precincts that I call home phoned me. He had some mug in custody who'd been socked in the beezer, and this chump was fingering a friend of mine as the wise guy who'd fixed his face. Well, I went down to the precinct station, gave this chump some muggles and greased the palms of the men in blue and got the charges dropped. This is just one example of my active cooperation with the police. The cops provide protection and so do I – so it is only natural that we cooperate. We're all in this together.

"Now, if there are any questions, I'd be happy to see if I can answer them."

The audience looked a bit stunned, and not only because Rossini's vocabulary included a lot of words and expressions being used in unfamiliar ways. Finally, after a few minutes, an elderly man in the back of the auditorium raised his hand, stood up, and said: "I have worked for much of my life in law – first as a defense attorney and later as a prosecutor. I can see that you have some direct experience in the area of protection and enforcement, and have connections in the police and in the senate. What I want to know is, what would you plan to teach our kids here at UWU, and why do you think that your experience makes you the right man to teach as a professor at our university?"

"I'll start with your second question," Rossini smiled. "You got two kinds of teachers in the world, those who learn from books and those who learn from life. Reading is a great thing. Why I even read a couple of books in my time! But when you read you are only getting someone else's experience and knowledge, it's all second-hand. You wanna really know something? Then do it! You wanna know how law enforcement works? Get yourself booked for a bit or, better, fix some enemy of yours to do time in the joint! You wanna know what it's like to chill off someone? Have your goons plug some heel! Or do it yourself! That's life, that's what it's all about!"

"And my first question?"

"I'm getting to that. Don't rush me," Rossini replied in a slightly threatening tone of voice. "You wanna know what I plan to teach the kids out here at, what's the name of your school?"

Shouts of "UWU" and "the University of Western Uptown!"

"Yeah, the University of Western Uptown," Rossini snarled. "I've heard of it. I'll teach your children that this is a dangerous world, that you gotta get protection and that you gotta pay for it. If you don't get protection, you're gonna be in a whirl of shit, and if you sign up for protection but don't wanna pay, then – well, the answer is duck soup. Listen, I don't get no kicks from blipping off losers. But if you get services, you gotta pay. That's what I plan to teach the students out here at UWU."

With that, Romulus rushed nervously to the podium, and, though there were at least 60 persons waving their hands now and wanting to ask questions or perhaps to protest, Romulus declared that the speaker had already answered enough questions and that it would not be right to tire him out. Romulus then thanked the mafia boss for his talk and a few of his closest allies in the audience joined him in clapping. Of the more than 800 people crammed into this auditorium, with a legal limit of 600 as set by the fire marshal, only about a dozen were clapping at first, until they were joined by the members of the physics department, who did not understand a word of what they had heard but figured that it was probably deserving of an applause.

Where Romulus and his closest associates took Rossini for dinner was a closely guarded secret. What soon became public knowledge, however, was that Rossini was being offered a full professorship in the political science department, with responsibility to teach classes on the interpenetration of the criminal underworld and the police and political establishment, a subject about which he had already displayed a certain knowledge.

Rossini did not, however, immediately accept the offer. He had two stipulations. First, he wanted to move in immediately. That was not a problem, as there was an office available – an office which had once belonged to Professor Jason Andy "Argonaut" Perkins and which had been vacant ever since Perkins had committed suicide in his office six years earlier. Second, he wanted to bring along two 'research assistants' of his choice and put them on the UWU staff, with full medical benefits. That was a bit more complicated and had to be run past University President Floorboard, who was ill disposed toward Romulus.

"OK, let me get this straight," said Floorboard upon hearing Romulus' request. "Not only do you want to hire this Rossini, who did not even finish college, let alone earn a doctorate, to teach at UWU, but now you expect me to authorize hiring also two friends of his and dress them up as 'research assistants'. Is that right?"

"I can explain that."

"You can explain that?"

"Let me point out Rossini's superb qualifications," Romulus clarified. "Rossini is an old friend of mine, he's charismatic, and he's a great teacher. He has taught a lot of people lessons they'll never forget."

"I'm sure of that," Floorboard countered, "but the kind of lessons Rossini has taught people in the past are not likely to be the kind of lessons we need taught around here. I cannot see any way to approve this hire, let alone to bring in two additional staff. Did the members of your department vote to hire Rossini?"

"Not exactly," Romulus conceded. "But they elected me Commander of the department and, as Commander, I have the authority to make unilateral decisions on matters of hiring, consulting only the brothers, Bret and Bart Holloway."

"The Maverick brothers."

"Right. They are very sharp, you can't put anything past them. Sharp as a needle."

"Well, I'm not sure I agree with that either."

"The most important point, however," Romulus now played his trump card, "is that the salaries of Rossini and his research assistants will be covered by a grant from the United States Senate. A few US senators who admire Rossini and his work have agreed to pay his salary and the salary of his research assistants and, if we hire them, to pay for the installation of a duck pond on campus, the construction of a new and enlarged library, and the erection of a 420-foot high campanile on campus. That would be almost 100 feet higher than the campanile on the University of Northern Iowa campus. As you know, we don't have a campanile at UWU and many people have told me that they yearn to have a campanile on campus."

"They yearn?"

"Yes, they yearn."

"What about more books for our library?"

"I am sure that that can be arranged. The senators admire Rossini greatly and are prepared to authorize considerable funding for our university if he is hired."

"OK, then. Hire him. But I want all of this written down, in the form of a contract. No campanile, no Rossini. No enlarged library, no Rossini. Understood?"

"Understood, boss," said Rossini, adding, "And now we can use the funds allocated to hire a Latin Americanist."

"We'll have to see about that," Floorboard replied. "The enrollments in political science are not that high and the university budget is tight. And you have just added this Rossini to your teaching faculty."

"Yes, that's true," Romulus conceded. "Rossini will be a great addition."

"Do you have an office for him? I thought that all the offices at the department were filled."

"We have Perkins' old office available – "

"Isn't that haunted?"

"Only a little…"

"Only a little haunted? What does that mean in practice?"

"In practice, that means that Perkins is sometimes visible, sometimes not. He moves around items in the office, sings bawdy songs, and sometimes goes for a stroll on the second floor, though that is usually after dark."

"Fine," said Floorboard. "Give him that office. Perhaps the ghost will be more afraid of a mafia boss than the other way around."

A week later, Rossini arrived in Uptown, where he purchased the old Granger House, the most magnificent house in town, built in 1882 and restored twice since then. Now Rossini was planning to give it yet another makeover. He arrived with three truckloads of Louis XIV furniture, high-tech computers, surveillance equipment, and an armory of weapons which, of course, he did his best to conceal from the local citizens. Once he had his house arranged, he invited the entire political science department, several Nebraska state senators, the two US senators from Nebraska, plus Floorboard and a few physicists, to come to his house for a gala dinner. Counting also wives and husbands, there were a total of 38 guests. Needless to say, Rossini had already hired a full-time staff consisting of three cooks, two maids, a butler, and what looked like a sergeant-at-arms. Rossini and his guests took their seats at a long dining table in the Great Hall, which was adorned with fifteenth-century English and Italian tapestries, showing various scenes of courtly love, hunting parties, and sieges. Here, in the Great Hall, his guests were served a seven-course culinary experience. Rossini had also hired two harpists for the occasion, borrowing them from the Lincoln Symphony Orchestra. The host showed a fine sensitivity for local tastes and traditions, and included okra/garlic soup and okra salad on the menu, alongside hummus, baba ganoush, a selection of hors d'oeuvres (including cheeses from seven countries), orange and olive salad (following a recipe developed in North Africa), roast lamb studded with rosemary and garlic, fresh Norwegian salmon which he had had flown in from Norway that morning, pampushki, penne with swordfish and eggplant, asparagus with fried eggs and parmesan, Ukrainian barley bread, and an assortment of desserts, including Black Forest cherry cake, Rigó Jancsi, baklava with pistachio, and peach sorbet. This was a dining experience to remember!

None of his guests, except perhaps for the two US senators, had ever enjoyed such gustatory thrills in their lives, and the next day, when Rossini reported for work for the first time, he found everyone at the department, including Friday and von Kletten, smiling appreciatively at him. How could one not appreciate the generosity of spirit which he had shown them and the excellent taste he had displayed. Upon arrival, by chauffeur-driven limousine, at the department, Rossini immediately went up to Romulus' office. Romulus had a large picture of Joe Friday on his wall and was amusing himself by hurling darts at the picture, scoring a few bull's eyes on Friday's nose. As he saw this, Rossini raised his eyebrows and wondered to himself about Romulus' sanity. He was not the first to wonder about this, and some people were already calling Romulus "the crazy professor". But this was not the time for psychoanalysis. It was the time to get his office assigned.

Romulus stood up from his desk and handed Rossini the keys to the department and to the office he was being assigned, and walked him down the corridor so that he could see where he would be headquartered. As they entered Rossini's new office, they saw a professor sitting in the office. Rossini was surprised at this and asked, "Who's that mug?"

"Oh, don't worry," Romulus answered. "That's just Professor Perkins and he's been dead for six years. His ghost hangs around on some days, but he won't bother you. Just tell him to vacate your seat and you can make yourself right at home."

"I don't remember being told that I would be assigned a haunted office!" Rossini grunted, glaring at Romulus. "Don't you have anything else available?"

"Not at the moment."

"What about *your* office? I could take that, and you could move into this office."

"No," Romulus protested. "That wouldn't do. The Office of the Commander is the biggest office in the building and I, as the Commander, should occupy it – not a newly hired professor. Not even yourself..." After a moment, he added, "Sorry."

Then, turning to the ghost, Rossini shouted, "Get out of my chair and out of my office, or I'll blow your brains out!"

"I've already done that to myself," the ghost of Perkins replied, turning his head so that Rossini could see the gaping head wound. "Not much to improve on that score." But just then, the ghost disappeared – pfiff – into thin air. Rossini looked at Romulus, Romulus looked at Rossini, and Rossini sat down in his chair, which seemed unusually cold. The smell of roses was in the air.

The Haunted Office

It was now June, and Nebraskans everywhere were bringing out their June poles, to celebrate the arrival of spring. They used to celebrate in May with May poles, following an ancient Swedish tradition to celebrate the return of vegetation. But, as the proportion of Swedes in Nebraska has steadily declined and as other ethnic groups have made gains against the Swedes, many people thought that it would be better to celebrate the arrival of spring after school was out – and that meant that it had to be in June, not May. Some Nebraskans still call their poles "May poles", but these are probably Swedish-Nebraskans. Most Nebraskans call their June poles "June poles" and are happy with that. Since most Nebraskans think of them as "June poles", these poles can mean anything that people want to believe. What is important is that there is lots of music, dancing, fun, and Nebraskan beef, corn, and okra beer. Uptown shared in these festivities with Pastor Grace presiding over the local June pole festivities. Some people said that he tried to give it a Christian interpretation. Others said that he was acting like a pagan. Some people had no opinion. Some said that they didn't care one way or the other. And, when queried by a reporter from the *News from Uptown Now* (also known by its acronym, NUN), some people said that they were not going to say what they believed, since it was nobody's business.

While June pole celebrations were bursting out all over Nebraska, construction began on the new library and the campanile and, of course, the installation of the duck pond, complete with Mandarin ducks, Muscovy ducks, and just plain ordinary duck-type ducks. At Romulus' direction, the new library was constructed as a look-alike for Hadrian's tomb. The campanile was the spitting image of the Tower of Hercules. And – in this context, not surprisingly – a giant replica of the Colossus of Rhodes was set in place astride the duck pond. In fact, the entire UWU campus was being reconstructed to look like an ancient Rome theme park. Thus, the old Student Union was torn down and a new one arose, modeled on the Pantheon. The Quad was renovated to look like the old Roman forum (although in much better shape than the original). When it came to the political science building, Romulus had in mind a mock-up of the Parthenon. Rossini pointed out that the Parthenon was Greek, not Roman, but Romulus remembered that, in ancient times, the Roman Empire had swallowed all of what had been the glory of Ancient Greece, including the Parthenon. Thus, as far as Romulus was concerned, the Parthenon could be claimed for Rome. With the political science department encased in a life-size Parthenon, the folks at the administration started to ask what grand edifice would be theirs. They did not have long to wait, although they were surprised when Romulus, with Rossini's endorsement, decided that the entire administration of UWU (numbering approximately 4,000 administrators, for a ratio of more than 10 administrators for each professor) should be moved into a full-size replica of the Colosseum in Rome. President Floorboard was consulted, as a matter of form, but he barely took any note of this, except to insist that the building in which his office was located (which sat next to the administration) be redesigned to resemble the Temple of Jupiter Optimus et Maximus (the Temple of Jupiter, the best and the greatest). Romulus also organized a referendum on campus concerning whether to rename the university's small stadium. Thanks to his brilliant campaign, the stadium was renamed Circus Maximus, in honor of the famous stadium in ancient Rome. In fact, although Romulus was only the political science chief, he was able to stoke such enthusiasm for his project that every single building on campus (with one exception), including the student dormitories, the Faculty Club, the cafeteria, and all the other departments were quickly remodeled ancient Roman style. The exception was the Millard Fillmore Auditorium, named for Nebraska's most beloved president. By the time the construction work was finished, all paid for by the ever generous Rossini, the entire campus was attracting worldwide attention, and drawing tourists to the campus. Rossini asked for and received a franchise to build a souvenir shop on campus, where visitors could purchase statuettes of the gods and goddesses of ancient Rome, miniatures of the "Roman" buildings on campus, postcards, scarves decorated with ancient Roman motifs, and much much more.

Rossini and his senator friends arranged for the importation of fine Florentine marble for the campanile and, as it rose, layer by layer, to the heavens, students and faculty alike were coming outside to sit by the new duck pond and stare at this new marble edifice. The library, too, looked to be an impressive construction, and it was a good thing that there were some empty fields immediately adjacent to the UWU campus. The old library had had a capacity of just 300,000 books, although there were said to be tens of thousands of uncatalogued books lying around in the basement of the library. The new Micky Rossini Library (informally known as the Mafia Boss Library) would have a capacity of two million books, putting the UWU library in the same class with libraries at Ivy League universities, at least in terms of capacity. Of course, there was still the matter of filling the shelves, but this task was assigned to Rossini's 'research assistants'. Their plan was to contact used book dealers around the country and just buy up books in quantity – without wasting time on checking what they were buying – and send the bill to the U.S. Senate. The result would prove to be a very large but also very unusual collection. Truckloads of books were being delivered, even before the library construction was completed and, as the books went up on the shelves, students found such titles as *How to build a better dog kennel*, *Getting rid of pimples forever*, and *A guide to successful dating*. But there were also very serious books brought to the library, including some first editions and even some rare and valuable books. By the time Rossini and his assistants had finished their book purchases, the library boasted more than 1.8 million books.

But there was still the problem of the office. Newly minted Professor Rossini decided to see if he could get his way with the ghost the same way he had gotten his way so many times with living people – meaning a combination of flattery, threats, bribes, and beatings. The problem is that ghosts don't respond to threats and have no use for bribes; after all, what can you give a ghost that he would consider desirable. Well, there is the office, of course, but Rossini was supposed to be getting that. He did try flattery, but Rossini was more adept at flattering the ladies than at praising men and when he praised men, it was usually because they had clipped someone or given someone a little chin music.

So that left some form of physical punishment and, one evening, after it had gotten dark, Rossini returned to his office with his two 'research assistants' because he had already seen for himself that, once the sun went down, the ghost of Perkins was apt to make an appearance. And so it was that, one Wednesday evening, as the threesome approached Rossini's, or rather Perkins', office, they could hear the dead professor singing a bawdy seafaring song. It went something like this:

I'm sober each morning 'til quarter to ten,
but by then I've indulged in a bottle agen,
I'm thinkin' of ladies I've known in the past,
especially the ones that I pinched in the ass.
Oh, bonnie dear Suzie, queen of the sea,
why wouldn't you come to be livin' with me?
I've got a soft belly and cash in the bank,
I've got a good brain but my old rowboat sank.

After standing in the corridor as they listened to these lines, Rossini and his assistants unlocked the door and entered the office. Perkins, or his ghost, was standing on the desk, wearing what looked like a pirate captain's cocked hat, waving around a ghost-sword and, as the three wise guys entered, Perkins first increased the volume of his singing, then stopped abruptly and challenged them: "Ahoy, me hearties! What brings ye to this port of call?"

"This is my office, ghost-man," Rossini replied. "Pack your things and get out of my office now."

"Or you'll do what to me?" Perkins replied in what sounded like a fake Irish accent, but definitely fake, since Perkins was not Irish, whatever you make of his name.

"We'll give you a drubbing you won't soon forget," came Rossini's retort. "Time for you to dust out! Or do you want to die of lead poisoning?"

"Oh yes," the ghost replied, "die of lead poisoning. How droll! When the dead can die, then all small fry, can quake in their shoes, to hear this news."

"OK boys," said Rossini to his wise guys. "I don't like rhyming. This ghost is rhyming. It's time to teach him a lesson he won't forget."

And with that, the two 'research assistants' pulled two very large machine guns out of their deep pants pockets and opened fire. The bullets went straight through the ghost, who just kept laughing at them the whole time.

"OK, buster," said an increasingly exasperated Rossini, "how about some lettuce. How much we gotta pay you to leave?"

"How much is it you gotta pay, to have things settled just your way? Well, start counting, get to nil, 'cause there is nothing good or ill, that you your friends can do for me, except to leave me alone and free."

"I hate ghosts that talk in rhyme," muttered Rossini, who stormed out of the office, with his 'research assistants' following him.

The next day, Rossini turned up at Romulus' office, just in time to see the Commander affixing a huge portrait of himself on his office wall. Romulus turned around and gave Rossini a warm, even loving welcome: "Dear Rossini, so good to see you. How is everything? How is your office working out?"

Rossini installed himself in the large leather chair intended for guests with a scowl on his face. "My office is haunted," he announced.

"Yes, we already discussed that."

"This is not acceptable. Perkins stands on his desk, dressed like a pirate and sings stupid songs from some by-gone century. I won't stand for it. What else you got for me?"

"Well," responded Romulus thinking carefully. "All the offices are taken. But we have a seminar room and we have two restrooms. Perhaps we can convert one of the restrooms into your private office. It would involve some renovation, but you would end up with the largest office in the building, even larger than mine. What do you think of that?"

"And I'll have to pay for the renovation, right?"

"Could you please?"

"OK, but I get to pick which restroom I want to convert and I'll do it my way."

"Yes, like Frank Sinatra."

Rossini glared at Romulus as if he did not catch the allusion but then said: "I'll remove all the toilets except one, all the sinks except one, redo the windows, have wall-to-wall carpets laid, and bring in the furniture I'll need."

"Done."

And with that, Rossini stormed out of Romulus' office. But Rossini was nothing if not a mover and a shaker and, within less than a week, a construction crew was on site, working on the restroom on the second floor. As promised, all the toilets were removed, save one, as well as all the sinks but one. The one remaining toilet, now fixed with a platinum toilet seat, was then enclosed behind a finely sculpted gold partition, with the knob connected to a music box, so that, whenever anyone entered or left the toilet booth, one would hear the music box play John Philip Sousa's "Stars and Stripes Forever". The remaining sink was then given a platinum coat to match the toilet seat, and topped off with gold taps. The small, opaque windows were replaced with large stained glass windows which may or may not have been stolen from a medieval cathedral in France. A pure luxury 100% wool carpet was installed, wall-to-wall of course. The walls were redone and were decorated with six paintings by seventeenth-century Dutch masters. Finally, there came the maroon satin curtains, the marble desk, and the various Thomas Chippendale chairs and tables, plus a cabinet with a Victorian tea set and another cabinet full of some of the finest whiskeys and cognacs the world has ever produced. When it was finished, not only did Rossini have an office with which he could be satisfied, but he also had his own private toilet. All of this was done without the foreknowledge of either President Floorboard or ex-chair Friday, and protests from Friday, von Kletten, and others were unavailing.

What about a second restroom for the rest of the faculty? Well, Rossini had thought of that, and – with Romulus' go-ahead but again without the foreknowledge of Floorboard or, for that matter, of anyone else besides Romulus – he orchestrated the conversion of Perkins' haunted office into a haunted restroom. Let the ghost of Perkins dance and sing on the toilet seat, Rossini said to himself.

It was not long before there were complaints about this situation. There was, of course, a restroom on the first floor, but those with offices on the second floor – among them, Commander Romulus – were more inclined to use what had been Perkins' office and, with only two toilet seats installed in that office/now-restroom, there was often a queue outside. Once inside, of course, there was the ghost to contend with and now, with his office converted to a restroom and his desk replaced with toilets, the ghost of Perkins was often in a bad mood. People would come in, just wanting to make a deposit, and while they sat there, they had to endure the Perkins-ghost's endless complaints, accusations, lamentations, jeremiads, and temper tantrums.

It was about that time that Romulus decided to put Bart Holloway, an untenured Assistant Professor, up for promotion to tenured Associate Professor, a rank already attained by his slightly more accomplished brother Bret. In fact, Bart did not have a single publication to his name, not even an article in the recently launched *Romulus Journal for the Rational Study of Reality*, which had already brought out its first issue consisting of four articles, all by Romulus himself (certainly a great thrill to his admirers). When the faculty assembled to consider Romulus' proposal, Friday, who remained Romulus' biggest challenger, objected that no one, in the history of UWU, had ever been granted tenure without some publications to show – except in the music therapy department, where the composition and performance of a critically acclaimed symphony or piano concerto was considered adequate. Romulus countered that Bart had been critical in the discovery, together with his brother Bret, of the Aztec urn, still on display in the political science department, and that this certainly warranted the grant of tenure. Calling him Bart Maverick, Romulus contended that the younger Holloway was a valuable asset to the university. But when it went up for a vote, only brother Bret and Micky Rossini backed Romulus, and the motion to promote Bart "Maverick" Holloway failed. "Ridiculous," MacGrory muttered as he stomped out of the seminar room in disgust that they had had to waste time on such a preposterous notion. Romulus was, by now skating on thin ice, but he seemed barely aware of it.

The Grecian Urn

Driven from their positions of responsibility, Friday and von Kletten were increasingly spending time together at the new duck pond, at the Fancy Turtle Saloon, or in the town park. Both of them were disgusted by Romulus' coup and fed up with how he was running the department. In addition, von Kletten was furious that her husband had not used the power invested in his position as president of the university, to defend her when Romulus ejected her from the post of deputy chair and, for that matter, to defend her ally, the impeccably honest and hard-working Joe Friday. In any event, Floorboard was allowing himself to drown in administrative work, staying in his office until late at night, and getting up early and dashing to work after having eaten nothing more than a grilled hot dog served in a toasted sliced bun with mustard and chopped onions and a dab of ketchup. Poor von Kletten hardly felt married and Friday, well, he had been single all his life. In short, Friday and von Kletten were becoming close friends – not yet physically intimate, but clearly veering in the direction of romance. You don't need candlelight to have a romantic dinner at the Fancy Turtle Saloon. Mayor Marlowe once said that, and he was right. Friday and von Kletten were frequently taking dinner at the Fancy Turtle and, for that matter, taking lunch together at the UWU Faculty Club.

But von Kletten was not one to sit on her thumbs. On the contrary, she had contacted a specialist to come to the campus and conduct a proper carbon-dating on the allegedly Aztec urn. Whatever it was, it was not Aztec. Moreover, she could read Nahuatl and she knew that the inscription on the urn was a paean to an Aztec warrior who had given his life for the Aztec king – hardly an inscription that fit the scenes depicted on the urn. And, besides, those scenes were too amateurish to be authentic. But bringing a specialist out to UWU was more difficult than she had imagined. There were qualified people in Nebraska to be sure, but none of them wanted to get mixed up in what looked like a scandal of some sort. So she finally had to hunt around in Washington D.C. where she was able to contract someone from the National Institute for Carbon Dating, located on Pennsylvania Avenue, next to the White House. It is located there because many American presidents have wanted to know when exactly certain gifts were produced.

The big day arrived and Alboris Foster Handel arrived in Uptown with his assistant, Former John Purcell – "Former" was actually his given name, but he preferred to be called "John". Uptown did not have a hotel or motel at the time; so the sheriff made her jail available for the two scientists, so that they could enjoy all the comforts of home. The sheriff left the jail cell unlocked, of course, so that they could come and go as they pleased, and offered to give them complimentary haircuts if they liked. They declined. Friday and von Kletten took them out to dinner at the Fancy Turtle Saloon the evening they arrived and then, on the next day, brought them to campus.

Their arrival had not been announced in advance but once they reached the political science department, there was a lot of agitation, speculation, rumors, concern, frenzy, murmuring, you name it. Friday and von Kletten demanded that the urn be brought to the seminar room so that the scientists could carry out carbon-14 dating. The entire faculty turned out for this, except for Perkins' ghost, who stayed behind in his new restroom. Romulus looked very nervous, the Maverick brothers were fidgeting, Rossini looked amused (since he had a good idea of what was going on), Beach and MacGrory were staring sometimes at Romulus and sometimes at the newly arrived scientists. The rest of the department was entranced by the arrival of the two carbon-dating specialists. The procedure did not take long and, when they finished their work, the scientists announced that the urn dated from the 6th century B.C.E. The Aztecs were around from the 12th century C.E. to the 16th century C.E. This meant that the urn was not Aztec.

"Colleagues," von Kletten declared when the carbon dating had been completed, "this carbon-dating gives us definite proof that this is *not* an Aztec urn. There was no Aztec civilization until almost two thousand years after this urn was produced." Sounds of horror and shock around the book, groans from Romulus, moans of embarrassment from the Maverick brothers. "Moreover, there were no chickens or sheep or goats in North America until the Spanish brought them to the New World, and the plow was, again, unknown among the Aztecs until the Spanish brought it to the New World. The images on the urn have nothing at all to do with Aztec society. This urn is a fake."

There was a lot of agitation in the room now. Finally, Brookhurst, who usually could not decide whether he should ask a question or not, raised his hand and asked, "So, if it dates from the 6th century B.C.E. and is not Aztec, what is it?"

"Obviously," von Kletten pointed out, "it is an ancient urn, re-painted amateurishly with pseudo-Aztec motifs. And I have here," she revealed, "an article which was published in the *Omaha Prairie Bison* concerning the theft from Omaha's Museum of Grecian Archeology of a Grecian urn dating from precisely the 6th century B.C.E. Now," she continued, "who was it who showed up with this urn?"

"The Maverick brothers," Romulus said quickly, in order to deflect attention from himself. "The Maverick brothers came in one day with this artefact, and I was completely taken in. We need to contact the Museum and see if it is theirs."

"In fact," von Kletten replied, "I have already done so, and the curator of the Museum has been staying with Friday for the past two nights. May I introduce Dr. Agamemnon Alcibiades, the curator of the Museum of Grecian Archeology..." At that, Romulus fainted, Brother Bret went pale, and Brother Bart looked down at his shoes. The jig was up. Brother Bret wanted to say something, but only broken syllables came out of his mouth.

Agamemnon Alcibiades rose from his chair, standing 6' 9". Some people in the room looked to see if he was about to bump his head against the ceiling. "Good day, gentlemen and ladies," Alcibiades began. "I have examined the urn and I can certify that this is the Grecian urn which was recently stolen from my museum." It wasn't really *his* museum, but he loved its artefacts so much, that he thought of it as his. "I will take it back to Omaha but there is a question in my mind what to do about the fact that the original, masterful Grecian art has been sandpapered away."

"What about donating the urn to the Museum of Curious Curiosities?" MacGrory offered. "It is, after all, the centerpiece in what might be the most notorious heist from the Museum of Grecian Archeology. And the fake Aztec art could be entertaining for children and adults alike, and offer them some lessons about what *not* to do in their lives."

"We shall have to discuss that," Alcibiades replied. "There are other staff at the Museum, and we will decide this collectively. What we are not able to do, of course, is to restore what has been destroyed. And, for that, our Museum will present a bill to the University of Western Uptown." Romulus had revived just moments before this but, upon hearing about a bill, he fainted for the second time.

There were a few hands going up at this point, but Alcibiades said that he was not going to take any more questions. And, with that, he left the room, got into his crimson Chevrolet and headed back to Omaha. The next day, the police were supposed to show up to take Bret and Bart Holloway into custody. Their trial was already scheduled for the following week, to take place in the Douglas County District Court in downtown Omaha.

The King is Dead, Long Live the King!

The department was in crisis and Professor Pestalozzi, as deputy chair of the department, decided that it was time to do something to put the department back on some sort of track. He called for a faculty meeting to take place that same afternoon, and even informed Perkins about it, so that no one would be left out – not even the dead. The first order of business was the leadership of the department. Most of the professors were very upset about having been forced to hang velvet paintings in their offices, even if they *were* paintings of their beloved Nebraska. They were, of course, happy about the campanile and the new library, but again, there was the problem of the smaller, haunted restroom. Some of the professors also felt that there were now too many drinking fountains in the building and that it looked just plain silly. And, of course, there was the scandal of the so-called Aztec urn. Everyone, except for the Maverick brothers, was demanding Romulus' head – even Pestalozzi. After very little discussion, a vote was taken, with 11 votes against Romulus (counting also the ghost of Perkins) with only Bret and Bart supporting Romulus' own vote. Romulus was then stripped of his "command" of the department. Pestalozzi then announced that his last act as deputy chair of the department, would be to call for fresh elections for chair and deputy chair. His proposal was that Joe Friday and Eustadiola von Kletten be restored to their previous posts. The vote was now unanimous, with 12 votes in favor, with only Romulus and Brother Bret abstaining.

Romulus started to object that the deceased Perkins was being allowed to vote, but it was pointed out to him that Perkins' vote did not make any difference in the outcome. Now, with Friday and von Kletten restored to their positions – and Friday not as "Commander" but more modestly as department "chair" – the assembled professors confiscated the water pistols belong to Romulus and to the Maverick brothers, and then began firing their own water pistols in the air, or rather at the ceiling and walls in celebration of the Glorious Revolution. There were shouts of "The King is dead, long live the King!" and "Okra forever!" and "UWU is best!" and "Down with paintings on velvet!"

Friday now came to the front of the room, shook Pestalozzi's hand and warmly embraced him. Then, taking his seat, he said a few words. "It is good to be back in the saddle," he said. "We've got work to do, to teach our classes, to meet with students and answer their questions, to write important books and articles. It's time to git along with our work…"

At hearing the phrase "git along", the entire department started to sing their favorite song:

> *As I was a-walking one morning for pleasure,*
> *I spied a cowpuncher all riding along*
> *His hat was throwed back and his spurs were a-jingling*
> *And as he approached he was singing this song:*

> *Whoopee ti yi yo, git along little dogies*
> *It's your misfortune and none of my own*
> *Whoopee ti yi yo, git along little dogies*
> *You know that Nebraska will be your new home.*

> *It's early in spring that we round up the dogies*
> *Mark 'em and brand 'em and bob off their tails*
> *Round up the horses, load up the chuck wagon*
> *Then throw the dogies out on the north trail.*

> *Whoopee ti yi yo, git along little dogies*
> *It's your misfortune and none of my own*
> *Whoopee ti yi yo, git along little dogies*
> *You know that Nebraska will be your new home.*

Your mother was raised on a ranch near Loup City,
Your daddy's from Omaha, so it is said
We'll fill you up on pickle pear and okra
'til you are ready for the great Okra Hills.

Whoopee ti yi yo, git along little dogies
It's your misfortune and none of my own
Whoopee ti yi yo, git along little dogies
You know that Nebraska will be your new home.

After that, the professors started cheering Friday, with Perkins, an Englishman, though deceased, leading the group in singing, "For he's a jolly good fellow!" It was a great day for the department of political science. The meeting continued.

The next order of business was to decide what to do about the Maverick brothers. They were out on bail but it was only a matter of time before they were to be taken to Lincoln to stand trial. The members of the department were well aware that Bret was the more mentally acute of the two and the decision was therefore taken to suspend him, pending his trial. Since Brother Bart had no scholarly accomplishments to his name, although he had won the contest to catch the greased pig in the previous year's Wild Hog Festival in North Platte, and since no one could remember why he was hired in the first place, the decision was taken to fire him. Only Romulus and Brother Bret voted to retain him.

But now there was the problem of finding someone to pick up the classes which the brothers had been teaching or to teach substitute classes. Since Rossini had, so far, committed to teach only one class – on crime and the police – he was signed up to teach two of Brother Bret's classes, specifically Politics and Ethics in the U.S. Congress and the Political Theory of Karl Marx. "That no-good communist," Rossini said, upon hearing that he would be teaching the class on Marx. "Yes, I'd be happy to tell the students what's wrong with Marx. He was against free enterprise. I am a champion of free enterprise." As for Brother Bart, no one had a clue what his classes were all about, since their titles seemed a bit vague: Politics and Meaning in the Modern World, the Post-Modernity of Post-Modern Politics, and Features of Contemporary Society in Times of

Change. Perkins, who had been invisible for most of the first part of the meeting, now made himself visible and offered to teach a class on Politics in the Afterlife.

"What would such a class cover? And in what way would it be useful?" Bobkov wanted to know.

"Well, you've heard of the big battle between Michael the Archangel and the loyal angels and Lucifer and his legion of rebellious renegade angels, and how Lucifer and his rebels lost and were cast down into hell – right?"

"Yes, everyone in the Great State of Nebraska knows about this."

"Well, that's just one example," Perkins replied, suddenly flickering a bit, as ghosts are apt to do. "There are also power grabs by people, or rather dead people, especially by people who think that they should have been canonized but weren't. And Saints Peter and Paul – well, I've heard rumors that they don't get along as well as they might and that they have been engaged in a long-running struggle for power."

"What else can you teach?" Disraeli asked.

"I can teach a class on haunted places in our nation's capital, and also a class on the ghosts of Nebraska," Perkins' ghost offered. "And of course I can teach the classes I taught when I was alive: Politics in Switzerland and Liechtenstein, Politics in France, and seminars on the great political thinkers. What do you think about that?"

"Won't the students be scared of being taught by a ghost?" asked Katella Beach.

"Why should they be?" Perkins' ghost replied. "I shall come in like any other professor – except when I decide to float through the wall – present my lectures, answer questions, and then go back to my office – speaking of which..."

"Yes, we know," Friday replied. "You'll get your office back as it was, even with such improvements as you might like. And we'll decide what to do about a second restroom. One option would be to construct a third floor in our building and put the restroom up there. We could also add a couple of classrooms on the new floor." Then, turning to those present, Friday noted, "Under the circumstances we need whatever classes Perkins is willing to offer. Do we have a motion to put this to a vote?"

Bart immediately raised his hand, and moved to put it to a vote. Friday then asked someone to second the motion. Bart immediately raised his hand and called out, "I second the motion." Cleary pointed out that he could not second his own motion, but kindly offered to second it himself. And so it went to a vote and was carried with 10 votes in favor and five abstentions.

Not long after that, building began on a third floor for the political science building. In addition to a large restroom, there would also be four classrooms, a snack room with a sandwich machine, a candy machine, a latte machine with free latte, and a beer dispenser with free okra beer.

The Trial of the Maverick Brothers

The trial of the Maverick brothers was a great sensation, both in downtown Uptown and at UWU, and was not without interest in Omaha itself. All of Nebraska's major newspapers were covering it, including the *Omaha Prairie Bison*, the *Lincoln Lamplighter, the Loup-City Lounge Gazette,* and, of course, Uptown's very own *Independent News Service And News Express* (with its easily remembered acronym). Nor did the various magazines and newsletters devoted to archeology fail to notice this important trial.

The Maverick brothers did not have to wait long for their trial to begin. In fact, they had just enough time to consult with their lawyer and decide on their pleas, which were similar but not identical. Their defense attorney, Sylvester "Froggie" Toad, a public defender working at the League for the Defense of Accused and Unaccused Persons, at first urged them both to plead temporary insanity, but of course the Maverick brothers would have none of that. Bret Holloway insisted on pleading "temporary sanity", by which he seems to have meant that he was mostly insane but sometimes functional. As for his brother Bart, after some discussions, the attorney suggested that he plead mental deficiency rather than temporary anything. On the day of their arraignment, they were brought before the judge.

"All rise, the court is now in session, the Honorable Judge Apolonia Pennywhistle presiding.

"Case 9842, People versus Bret Holloway and Bart Holloway on the charges of felony theft in the first degree and disturbing the peace in the second degree," said the public prosecutor.

"How do your clients plead, Mr. Toad?"

"Bret Holloway pleads temporary sanity," answered Toad.

"Temporary sanity?? What is he – nuts?"

"Yes, Your Honor, he claims to be insane most of the time, but occasionally sane," Toad explained. "Sane enough to teach at the University of Western Uptown."

"There's a university by that name?"

"Yes, Your Honor," replied Toad. "Apparently, it is very close to the border with Colorado."

"We won't hold that against your client," the judge reassured them. "And what about your other client, Bart Maverick – I mean Bart Holloway?"

"He wishes to enter a plea of mental deficiency," Toad answered.

"Guilty or not guilty by reason of mental deficiency," the judge queried.

"He hasn't really decided. He admits that he took part in the

"The whole truth? Man, that's a big concept," the first pothead muttered. "I do, but the whole truth – I've been thinking about that my whole life and still haven't figured out everything."

theft of the Grecian urn and in repainting it, but he says that he did not understand what he was doing."

"I'll enter a plea of not guilty by reason of mental deficiency," the judge said. "What about bail?"

"Your Honor," Toad said, "these two are professors and are not a flight risk. We suggest that no bail be required."

"Your Honor," the public prosecutor interjected, "the accused have proven to be adept at moving around Nebraska. We suggest that bail be set at five dollars each."

"So ordered!" replied the judge.

At that, Bart turned to Brother Bret and asked, "Can I borrow five dollars please?"

The trial got underway the next day, with all the members of the department of political science on hand as witnesses, including the Pestalozzi hologram. Perkins did not come to Omaha for the trial, however, because his ghost was limited to the premises of the political science department. The trial took place the Grand Hall of the Douglas County District Court. Behind the judge, there was a large sign, bearing the motto of the Great State of Nebraska: "Nebraska optima est." Brother Bret had studied Latin for four years in college and knew that this meant "Nebraska is best" and, as he whispered the translation to his brother, Bart grinned ear to ear. Now, in full view of this sign, the brothers' chests swelled with pride and joy leapt across their faces. They looked completely thrilled. As the Honorable Judge Pennywhistle saw this, she asked them, "You two look overjoyed! Do you understand the nature and seriousness of the charges against you?"

"We do," brother Bret answered, still smiling, "or at least I do. We stand accused of stealing a valuable Grecian urn and defacing it. And we did it."

"Fine," the judge responded and then, turning to the prosecutor, "call your first witness."

"We have two witnesses, Your Honor, both of whom were smoking pot outside the Museum when the theft took place."

"Put them on the stand."

"Do you swear to tell the truth, the whole truth, and nothing but the truth, so help you God?"

"The whole truth? Man, that's a big concept," the first pothead muttered. "I do, but the whole truth – I've been thinking about that my whole life and still haven't figured out everything."

"Your Honor," Toad pleaded, "this witness is obviously incompetent. Do we have to listen to his testimony?"

"I'm afraid we do. That's the law. Even people who have fried their brains have the right and duty to bear witness."

As pothead #1 took the stand, the prosecutor told him, "Please state your name for the court."

"Jacob Pennywhistle," the pothead replied.

"Pennywhistle," the prosecutor seemed surprised. "Are you any relation to the judge?"

"Objection! Relevance?"

"The witness may answer," Judge Pennywhistle ruled.

"She's my mom," Pennywhistle junior replied.

"For the benefit of the court, please state what you witnessed, the night of May 12th."

"Well, man, me and my friends was standing around the museum, our asses were seriously baked, but we was still billing up..."

"In English please."

"We were stoned out of our minds, but were still rolling joints. Then we saw these two dudes – "

"Let the record show that the witness gesticulated in the direction of the accused."

" – we was pretty blitzed and geeking out – "

"geeking out?"

" – laughing a lot, 'cause we were so ferschnikered. We was thinking a bit, what if the Five-O come, but the gear was top quality. I even said to Jordan, 'This shit's da shit' – which is the highest praise you can give for ganja."

"Get to the point, son," the judge demanded. "What did you see, *if anything?*"

"Hey, don't jam me, mom, I'm getting' to it," Pennywhistle junior replied. "We seen these dudes, they was carryin' something. It was a big pot – "

"An urn? Exhibit A perhaps?"

"Sure, an urn. That's it on the table," the witness said, momentarily seeming excited and pointing to the urn.

"Let the record show that the witness identified exhibit A as the urn in question."

"But man, we was buzzed. So we just cheered those dudes. It was great."

"No further questions," the prosecutor said.

"Your witness."

Toad stood up, straightened his bowtie and asked, "You say that you were stoned the night of the theft, right?"

"Yeah, man, it was great. We was totally caked!"

"And now? Are you totally 'caked' also now."

"For sure," the witness replied. "I don't go anywhere without smoking a few joints first."

"No further questions."

But smoking cannabis is, of course, frowned upon in the Great State of Nebraska, and the judge now had to order that her only son be taken into custody. Judge Pennywhistle also had three daughters; fortunately none of them ever smoked cannabis.

"Call the next witness."

The next witness was the second pothead, Jordan James. Asked to swear to tell the truth, he replied, "Yeah man, always! What was the question?"

"Do you swear to tell – "

"Sure, what do you take me for?"

"Please state your name for the court."

"My name. My name is Jordan James, and I graduated from Omaha North High Magnet School. That's a mouthful."

"Just answer my questions."

"You wanted the *whole* truth, man!"

"Not about everything. Now, on the night of May 12th, did you see the accused at the Museum of Grecian Archeology?"

"The Museum of *what?*"

"Grecian Archeology!"

"Hey, is that where we were?"

"Did you see the accused there?"

"Where?"

"At the Museum of Grecian Archeology!"

"Hey, slow down, man, you are talking way too fast for me."

"What do you remember?"

"I remember smoking a joint before I came to court today. I'm probably brainfart…"

"English please!"

"Of course English. It's the only language I speak."

"What do you mean by 'brainfart'?"

"Hey, are you accusing me of something?" and then after a moment, "What am I doing here? Am I accused of something? I didn't do it."

"Didn't do what?"

"Don't ask me," the witness replied. "I don't understand what the hell is going on."

"The Museum of Grecian Archeology, remember?"

"Is that where we are?" J.J. replied. "Man, this doesn't look anything like any museum I've avoided."

The judge interrupted this interrogation now: "This witness is useless." And she then called for the second witness likewise to be taken into custody for smoking cannabis. "Does the prosecution have any more witnesses?"

"No, Your Honor, that's the sum total of what we could drum up."

"Fine," the judge said. "Now, Mr. Toad, do you have any witnesses?"

"Yes, Your Honor, we have the entire political science faculty here, to vouch for the defendants."

"Good. Call your first witness."

"We call the deposed head of the department, Wolf Romulus, to the stand. Do you swear to tell the truth, the whole truth, and nothing but the truth, so help you God?"

"What do you take me for? Of course I do."

"Just say yes or no."

"Yes, so help me," Romulus replied, adding "God!"

"Please tell the court what is your relation to the accused."

"First," Romulus said, "I didn't do it. I had nothing to do with this plot and I didn't know anything about it. In fact, when we discussed it, I told the Maverick brothers – "

" – that would be the Holloway brothers? The accused, right?"

"Yeah, the Holloway brothers," Romulus continued. "I told them not to do it, that stealing an ancient Grecian urn was an insane idea, that only a nutcase would think of such a thing. But they did it anyway. They went ahead and did it, and it was all their idea. I had nothing to do with it. And I didn't know about it until after they had stolen the thing and brought it back to UWU."

Once again straightening, or rather restraightening, his bowtie, Mr. Toad now asked Romulus, "If you advised the Holloway brothers against stealing the urn – which is to say *before* they did so – how can you claim that you had no foreknowledge of their plans."

"Listen, Mr. Public Defender," Romulus replied. "Running a department is a big responsibility and I had a lot on my mind. People come into your office all the time, talking this, talking that, always talking. And I had to listen to a lot of stuff and I quickly decided that, whatever ideas people had, the best approach was to tell people not to do it. Write a provocative book? Don't do it! Present a lecture at the University of Colorado?" Whispers and gasps around the room upon hearing a reference to Colorado. "Don't do it! Steal a Grecian urn? Don't do it! Whatever people wanted to do, I always told them, don't do it! Naturally, I told them to hang paintings on velvet with scenes of Nebraska in their offices. But that was my idea. So, of course, I would have told the Maverick brothers not to steal an urn."

"But they did so anyway."

"Yes, they did," Romulus conceded. "But look at their priorities. After stealing it, they did not return straight back to UWU. No, they headed over to the Loup City Diner for a wholesome meal! These are a curious twosome, and their father, whom I never met, was completely and totally nuts."

"And you know this how?"

"I just know it."

"No further questions."

The prosecutor declined to cross-examine. The next witness called to the stand was Stanton Brookhurst. But when asked to swear upon the Bible "so help you God," he replied, "Listen, I haven't made up my mind about God. He might exist, He might not. Perhaps the Blessed Virgin Mary is God or, rather, a Goddess. These theological matters are not clear – "

Mr. Toad, normally a patient man, was getting impatient, and now told Brookhurst directly, "Look, the point is are you prepared to tell the truth or not?"

"Of course," Brookhurst replied. "But when I'm not sure about something, like the existence of God, I think I should say so, and not claim to have definite knowledge about things I'm not sure about."

"Objection!" the prosecutor called out. "The witness is an idiot!"

"Objection overruled. The witness is a professor and knows what he doesn't know, unlike some people present in the courtroom," the judge ruled, glaring at the public prosecutor.

"Please state your full name for the court," Mr. Toad now asked.

"Stanton Gilbert Dale Orangethorpe Euclid Brookhurst," Brookhurst replied. "But at the university, I go by Stanton Brookhurst."

"How do you know the defendants?" Mr. Toad asked.

"They were colleagues at the department of political science, until last week, when Bret Maverick, I mean Bret Holloway, was suspended, pending trial, and Bart Maverick, I mean Bart Holloway, was fired."

"Please tell the court why Bart Holloway was fired, when his brother Bret was merely put on suspension."

"Bart Holloway was hired four years ago and, during all this time, he has not managed to publish a single article in any scholarly journal," Brookhurst explained. "The only publication he has to his name is a short op-ed piece about Colorado in our local newspaper." There were glances of transparent consternation around the courtroom now.

"That would be the *Uptown Eagle and News Disseminator*, right?"

"That's right. In other words, Bart is completely incompetent and should never have been hired in the first place."

"In your professional opinion, would you say that he is mentally deficient?"

"For work at a university, obviously," Brookhurst replied but then, slipping into character, "probably, but there could be other points of view. I really don't know. Don't ask me. Ask someone else."

Mr. Toad probed a bit about brother Bret and elicited the information that brother Bret, who had just turned 38, had already written his autobiography, as well as a textbook used at UWU. After that, Toad had no further questions and, after responding to a few embarrassing questions from the prosecutor, Brookhurst was allowed to return to his chair. The next witness called to the stand was Giuseppe Pestalozzi, the author of *Technology in your Kitchen.* Since he appeared, even in the courtroom, only as a hologram, he had to put his hand on his own copy of the Bible, back in whatever secret location he inhabited. Mr. Toad had been advised that Pestalozzi would appear only in hologram form, but he seemed a bit ruffled by this all the same.

"Professor Pestalozzi," Mr. Toad began, "please state your relation to the accused."

"Same as Brookhurst," Pestalozzi answered. "Same as for all of us. They were colleagues at the department of political science. Specialists. All of us are specialists."

"What do you know of their escapade, of this theft of the Grecian urn?"

"I know that they discussed this in advance with Wolf Romulus."

"Anything else?"

"I know that they are a couple of bunglers, not the smartest professors you could find."

"Have they ever done anything insane?"

"Apart from stealing the urn? Sure," Pestalozzi's hologram replied. "They took jobs at our department – that was insane! And it was insane of us to have hired them."

"No further questions." And that was how it went, with the various members of the department testifying, one after the other, to the two brothers' incompetence and/or insanity. Throughout it all, the two brothers were beaming, as if they were at the fairground or going on a first date – a double-date, of course. Finally, the brothers were found guilty of first degree felony theft, but not guilty on the second charge, of disturbing the peace. The judge ruled that they should be committed for a minimum of five years to the Happy Trails Institute for Not So Severe Mental Disorders, a private clinic not far from the internationally renowned Richard H. Young Hospital in Kearney, specializing in serious mental illness. The brothers knew that Kearney was about a 50-minute drive from the Loup City Diner and asked if they could be allowed weekly visits to the diner.

"Sure," the judge answered. "So ruled. The Happy Trails In

stitute is hereby instructed to provide the Holloway brothers with weekly visits to the Loup City Diner. Good food makes for a good brain! Court adjourned." The brothers were released on bail so that they could organize their affairs before being taken to the institute.

Romulus' Steakhouse

For the time being, Romulus seemed safe. But people had not forgotten how he had hosted the "Aztec urn" event in the Millard Fillmore Auditorium on campus and how he had used that to propel himself into the chairmanship of the political science department. Within the department, there was some reluctance to keep him within their fold but some real hesitancy about what exactly to do. Finally, it was decided that Friday and von Kletten would talk to Floorboard about this. No friend of Romulus', Floorboard hated scandals and had been rankled by the Aztec urn hoax. The campanile and the expanded library were, of course, important compensations for the errors perpetrated by Romulus and his clique, but the fiasco with the second-floor restroom, the proliferation of drinking fountains, and the purchase, at departmental expense, of the paintings on velvet were more than minor irritants for the flamboyant but demure president. But there was another problem, specifically that Floorboard, who always had a most accurate though self-serving self-image, was being courted by the University of Cut and Shoot in Cut and Shoot, Texas.

Cut and Shoot is, as is well known, a city with a population of just over one thousand people, not counting the university, which is actually located twenty miles out of town. There are lots of theories about how the city got its name. One theory holds that, at the time of its founding, some recent European immigrants held that, with just 300 inhabitants, it was a village, while others, born in the

USA, thought that it should be called a town. According to this version of things, this argument ended up with a gun fight – a real gun fight, not one with water pistols – leaving three persons dead. Those born locally won the gun fight and it was called a town until 2006 when, as a compromise, it was decided to call Cut and Shoot a city. Another theory holds that there were arguments among the locals about what name to give their town, with some folks championing the name Best Place to Live, others fancying the name Dreamland, and still others preferring to call their town something too vulgar to report. The dispute about the name then resulted in people cutting their conversations short and getting out their guns and hence, according to this version of things, Cut and Shoot. Be that as it may, the University of Cut and Shoot or UCS, not to be confused with USC, the University of Southern California, was still a small university, with just six academic departments: for Physics, Art, Religious Studies, Aquarium Studies, Military Science, and General Knowledge. The last of these was by far the most popular department, as here one could learn a little about history, philosophy, music, mathematics, and Texas folklore, all in moderation. There were rumors that the Department of Aquarium Studies had nothing to do with either fish or aquaria, and that it was actually a front for a permanent FBI installation, but most people did not believe this rumor, since it made no sense. The University of Cut and Shoot could not compete with UWU, but it was prepared to pay Floorboard more than twice the salary he had been receiving at Uptown's famous university. This was already leading to problems between Floorboard and von Kletten since the most that Floorboard was able to arrange for her was a post in the department of military science since, as a political scientist, she knew something about war and peace. She did not want to move, but Floorboard seemed to be gravitating in the direction of accepting the offer from UCS. And then there was the University of Truth or Consequences, Floorboard's former base, which had hired a professional comedian to succeed Floorboard as president there and, although he kept everyone laughing, he was not doing a good job. They wanted to get Floorboard back and, like UCS, UTC was prepared to improve his salary. For now, however, there was the problem of Romulus and, feeling that he was halfway out the door already, Floorboard decided easily that Romulus had to go and so it was that Romulus, who had brought Rossini to UWU, now found himself out of work and looking to Rossini for help in launching a new venture.

Rossini was more than sympathetic. "You got problems," he told Romulus. "We can fix them for you. What you want? You want a restaurant?"

Well, this had not occurred to Romulus, but since Rossini was offering, he leapt at the offer. "That would be fabulous," he answered. "Maybe one with a particle accelerator," he added hopefully.

"I like the way you think, Wolf," said Rossini. "We can be partners and, in token of that, you can call me Micky. I can get a restaurant up and running for you within a month. I'll throw around some spondulix and get the inspection done fast, real fast. The particle accelerator will take a bit longer. We might have to throw some lead, but I'll see what my boys want to do. D'want me to hire cooks and waiters for you, or you got people you want to hire?"

"I'd be delighted to leave the arrangements in your capable hands, Micky," answered Romulus.

"What ya gonna call it?" Rossini asked.

"I was thinking to call it Romulus' Steakhouse and Particle Accelerator," Romulus replied.

"Sounds perfect. I'll get my boys working on it right away."

Romulus went back to the university to pack up his belongings. There he ran into Friday. "Congratulations on your victory, Friday," said Romulus. "I guess you've evened the score. But we're not done yet. I challenge you to a duel tomorrow at high noon, in front of the Fancy Turtle Saloon."

"Accepted," replied Friday, "and with water pistols, of course."

"I'll bring along the Maverick brothers as my seconds – assuming that they won't be back in custody by then."

"I'll come with von Kletten and Bobkov."

"Fine," replied Romulus. "And Carver as judge."

"He's drunk all the time," Friday pointed out. "Does that matter?"

"It'll keep him objective," Romulus said. "He doesn't care one way or the other between us. Just cares about his booze."

"Shall we say noon, then?"

"Yeah," replied Romulus, "high noon, like with Gary Cooper, super-duper." Romulus was making an obscure reference to the Irving Berlin song, "Puttin' on the Ritz".

But Friday caught the reference and countered with "We'll have blue skies, blue skies all day long" – a somewhat less obscure reference to another Irving Berlin song.

Rumors of the impending duel spread like butter and the next day locals were putting out deck chairs in front of the saloon already by 11:00. By 11:40 all the best locations had been taken, and there were even people who had clambered up to the roof of the saloon to watch the scene from above. Meanwhile, Friday was drinking coffee with his two seconds in the Fancy Turtle Saloon, while Romulus and his two seconds sat at a different table in the saloon, guzzling down whiskey. At 11:55, both parties paid for their drinks and strutted out onto the street. All of them were dressed in cowboy fashions, with Friday and his seconds dressed in white leather, and Romulus and his seconds dressed in black leather. Locals were pleased about this since those who were not already in the know thought that this helped them figure out who were the "good guys" and who were the "bad guys". Even so, as they came out onto the street, there was general cheering for both groups – louder for the "white hats", but Romulus and his "black hats" also had their fans. Friday and Romulus took their positions at the customary distance of 100 yards apart, their legs in the standard cowboy dueling position and their hands quivering slightly near their holsters. The atmosphere was tense with excitement, broken only by Adam McAddams, who was making the rounds selling popcorn. Then, as the bell on Pastor Grace's church struck twelve, Romulus snarled, "Draw!" And, with that, the two professors drew their water pistols and began shooting. Friday's aim was true and his water pistols were powerful specimens, which immediately squirted all over Romulus. By contrast, Romulus, having ingested plenty of whiskey prior to the duel, found that his aim was not so good and, at first, he was squirting some of the spectators. When he finally found his aim, he discovered that his water pistols were by then too weak to reach Friday, with the result that he had to walk, or stride, forward into Friday's spray until he was able to return the shower. By 12:05 both professors were drenched, though Romulus more completely. Carver, who had been supposed to judge this event, had imbibed too much booze and had passed out. So, Mayor Marlowe, who had taken his "royal throne" on the front deck of his saloon, now declared Friday the winner – which in turn inspired the Maverick brothers to start squirting at von Kletten and Bobkov, who returned fire. By the end of this event, all six professors were completely soaked. The crowd cheered at this and cheered even louder when a police van pulled up and two Nebraska Rangers got out of their vehicle and asked the mayor to identify the Holloway brothers. Mayor Marlowe grinned broadly as he pointed the two Rangers in the right direction.

"You two come with us," the Rangers stated as they took the brothers into custody. "You are being transferred to Happy Trails."

"Is it OK if we sing the old Roy Rogers' song, 'Happy Trails to you'," asked Brother Bart.

"My singing voice is not at its best right now," said Brother Bret. "So let's skip the performance for now. We can always sing that song once we get to the Happy Trails Institute."

"Into the van, you two," said one of the Rangers, "and stop wasting time."

And, with that, the van drove off, taking the Maverick, uh Holloway, brothers to the Happy Trails Institute for Not So Severe Mental Disorders.

The next day, construction began on Romulus' Steakhouse, which was being constructed in a style Romulus called "Nebraskan Neo-Baroque" although, to most eyes, it looked like a typical Texan steakhouse, with possibly some flourishes inspired by Western stockades. Since it was now summer vacation and school was out until September, children and adults came out every day to eat cotton candy and watch the edifice rise. Romulus then hit on the idea of balloons for the children and, at his suggestion, a couple of Rossini's assistants, dressed in double-breasted jackets, pin-striped pants, black shirts, white ties, and the mandatory Stetons, distributed the colorful balloons to the children. They also led the children in some songs about how crime *does* pay – until they realized that the parents were frowning at the lyrics.

Finally, within a month – just as Rossini had projected – the steakhouse had its grand opening day. The problem was that Uptown already had a steakhouse – the Steakholders' Steakhouse, Bar and Grill, which had opened three months earlier, run by Old Man Marlowe, Pastor Grace, and Sheriff/Barber Dorbin. Now Uptown had two steakhouses and there was bound to be competition between them. Romulus' idea of competition was that the menu at his steakhouse would be identical to the menu at the Steakholders' Steakhouse, except that *his* prices would be 20% higher! That might seem illogical to some people, but Romulus figured that, when people saw higher prices, they would figure that they were getting higher quality, even if everything – *everything* – on the plate looked identical to what people could get at his competition. Where the two steakhouses differed, apart from architecture, was that Romulus specifically targeted children, offering various virtual-world games at his steakhouse.

The next step, in Romulus' mind, was to procure a particle accelerator, but he had little idea what such a device actually was. "What you want with a particle accelerator, anyway?" his new bartender asked him one day.

"The whole town wants a particle accelerator," Romulus explained. "Not many towns have one, and this will put Uptown and this steakhouse on the map."

"What the hell does it do, this particle accelerator?"

"It moves small particles, like dust, very fast," Romulus answered, revealing the scale of his ignorance in this area.

"So you want to blow dust around the steakhouse?"

"Not exactly dust, but small particles *like* dust, but *not* dust."

The bartender would just have to wait, like everyone else, to see the particle accelerator in action. For the time being, Uptown had two steakhouses, locked in competition. People were naturally curious about the new restaurant and, in the short run, the Steakholders' Steakhouse suffered a decline in business as hitherto loyal customers wanted to try the new steakhouse. Nebraskans are savvy about food and about price and the visitors to Romulus' Steakhouse immediately noticed that his menu was the same as that at the Steakholders' Steakhouse and that his prices were 20% higher. But, just as Romulus had predicted, they initially assumed that the higher prices meant better meat, bigger portions, tastier sauces, and so forth. Meanwhile, the owners of the Steakholders' Steakhouse rose to the challenge and hired a mariachi band to entertain their customers. Through their various connections, they lured Los Capitanes, a 14-piece mariachi band which had once played at Olvera Street in Los Angeles to come on board as the "house band". Los Capitanes already had an international reputation and knew all the old warhorses, including "Cielito Lindo", "Besame Mucho", "Guadalajara", and, of course, "La Bamba". Old Man Marlowe hoisted up a huge banner on the steakhouse to advertise the band and promised free drinks the night the band would premier. The turnout was incredible. Romulus' Steakhouse had to close for that night, since even his staff wanted to be at the Steakholders' Steakhouse to hear the mariachi band play. It soon turned out that the mariachi band had an enormous repertoire and, performing five nights a week at the Steakholders', offered one night of classic mariachi, one night of cowpoke songs, one night of pure Nebraskiana, one night of Reggae, and – to everyone's surprise – one night of rap. Needless to say, they had a huge array of costumes and customers could not be sure from one day to the next, from one week to the next, how they would be dressed. For the next three months, Romulus was in trouble and was forced to slash his prices in half in order to attract back some of his customers. The wise guys who were working at his steakhouse as cooks, waiters, and bouncers suggested that they could put together a band of their own and, of course, Romulus accepted the offer. They came up with the name, the Uptown Mafia Bah-Bah Band, and, under Romulus' direction, started lessons to learn how to play the instruments. After six weeks of practicing on their instruments – keyboard, guitar, drums, kazoo, and accordion – they announced their own premiere.

Their practice sessions had not gone well. The keyboard player kept hitting the wrong keys, the guitarist seemed to have very stiff fingers, the drummer had his own beat, which was not necessarily the same as anyone else's, the kazoo player did well on the whole, but the accordionist kept going to sleep in the middle of numbers. But the premiere had been announced and, as they say, the show must go on. So, on 4 September, the Uptown Mafia Bah-Bah Band had its premiere. Romulus was intensely nervous as the crowd gathered. Although the Steakholders' Steakhouse, Bar and Grill stayed open that night, as it was reggae night and they could always count on a good crowd for reggae, nonetheless Sheriff Dorbin and Pastor Grace decided to join the crowd at Romulus' Steakhouse and hear for themselves the inaugural performance of this new band. The band played their own renditions of John Denver's "Country Roads" and Creedence Clearwater Revival's hit song, "Have you ever seen the rain?" But it was clear that the band did not consist of seasoned professionals. On the whole, these first two numbers were not entirely unsuccessful, bearing in mind that two months earlier none of the members of the band had ever even touched a musical instrument of any kind. Their next song was their cover on the Eagles' "Hotel California". It would not be too much of an exaggeration – well, maybe a bit of an exaggeration – to say that four of the members of the band were utterly brilliant with this rendition. But most of the folks in the steakhouse had heard better performances of these songs, and some of the customers were paying their bills and heading back to the Steakholders' Steakhouse, to enjoy reggae night. By the time the Uptown Mafia Bah-Bah Band had reached their last number before intermission – which turned out to be their last number for the night – most of the steakhouse lay empty. Romulus was wringing his hands: the band had not been a success.

But there was still the particle accelerator, which arrived two weeks later. Romulus now advertised this big event, and hoped that people would be sufficiently curious to want to see the thing humming and whirring. Outside the physics department, there were few, if any, who knew what a particle accelerator was, but the leading rumor, actively promoted by Romulus himself, was that viewing a particle accelerator was something like spending a day in Disneyland and, as the day of the launch of this device drew near, Romulus could be seen handing out bills advertising it.

The Particle Accelerator

The head of the physics department was Professor dr. Eugen Klemens Krüger. Whether he was born in Nebraska or not remained unclear, since he spoke English with a thick German accent. On formal occasions, such as faculty meetings, he would wear the traditional grey Bavarian jacket with green trim and long trousers. On less formal occasions, such as when teaching his classes, he would wear Lederhosen, wool stockings, and a Bavarian cap with plume. Locals called it his "Robin Hood cap". He was wearing Lederhosen when he stopped by Romulus' Steakhouse to inquire about the particle accelerator. He was accompanied by two of the more accomplished professors in his department, Professor dr. Brunnhilde Schumacher and Professor dr. Klothilda Klein, both attired in traditional Bavarian dirndls. The latter two had both been born in Bavaria and there were rumors that all 17 members of the physics department had been born in Germany or Austria, with most of the Germans allegedly born in Bavaria.

"Grüss Gott, Professor Romulus," said Krüger. "We are members of the physics department." The other two professors of physics also greeted with Romulus with a "Grüss Gott." "I am departmental chair, Professor dr. Eugen Klemens Krüger, and allow me also to present Professor dr. Brunnhilde Schumacher and Professor dr. Klothilda Klein."

"Good day," Romulus responded. "Nice to make your acquaintance. Make yourselves at home. Can I offer you something to drink?"

"Bier, bitte," they answered in unison.

"We have Weihenstephaner Hefeweissbier and Ayinger Weizenbock on tap," said Romulus. "Would one of these hit the spot?"

"Weihenstephaner Hefeweissbier would be wunderbar," Krüger answered, while the other two professors nodded appreciatively.

Romulus snapped his fingers and Ronnie "Vinny" Piccolo brought over four beers and a tray laden with snacks. "Compliments of the house," Romulus said. "As a trained political scientist, I have always nurtured a deep respect for and keen interest in physics. To what do I owe the honor of your visit?"

"We have heard that you are installing a particle accelerator in your restaurant," Krüger began, "and we want to know why you are putting it in a restaurant, rather than somewhere on campus – let us say, near our department."

"Aha," said Romulus. "That's a fair enough question. My idea is that particle accelerators are important and that physics is important, and that letting the local public watch particle accelerators as they accelerate particles can be educational."

"And it will also drum up business for you," Schumacher speculated.

"Well," Romulus replied. "It certainly won't be bad for business. We will have the only particle accelerator in this part of the Great State of Nebraska."

"In fact, there is only one other particle accelerator in all of Nebraska," Klein pointed out, "and that is at the University of Lincoln. Note, it is located at the university, and not in some steakhouse."

"That's right," said Romulus, with obvious pride. "We will be the first steakhouse in the entire world with a particle accelerator on site."

"Do you even know what a particle accelerator is?" Krüger asked Romulus.

"Sure," Romulus replied. "It is a machine that uses electromagnetic fields to propel charged particles to high speeds."

"And do you know why we want to do this?"

"To see how fast the particles can zip along," Romulus responded.

"Not exactly," Krüger corrected him. "They produce proton

beams, which in turn can produce isotopes useful for medical purposes and for research."

"What exactly do you think will be interesting for the general public?" Schumacher asked.

"The multicolored flashing lights, whirring sounds, and march music should be interesting, I think," said Romulus.

"Particle accelerators do not have multicolored flashing lights or make whirring sounds, and march music seems to be completely your idea," Klein clarified.

"Believe me," Romulus answered, "we have already installed the lights and three whirring motors, and the Uptown Mafia Bah Bah Band has been building up a repertoire of march music. If you come for the grand opening, you will see and hear what my idea of a particle accelerator is all about. You are all invited, and bring the entire department. It will be thrilling!"

"You are mad," replied Professor dr. Krüger, "and you have no real idea what a particle accelerator does. But yes, we'll be on hand."

The physicists kept their word, and on opening night turned up, with the men dressed in their Lederhosen and Tiroler caps, and the women dressed in dirndls, alpine aprons, and alida blouses. But, they were not the only ones who showed up for PA-day (D-day for the particle accelerator); on the contrary, Romulus' Steakhouse, now officially renamed Romulus' Steakhouse and Particle Accelerator, was jammed for the occasion and the cooks had their hands full grilling steaks for the large crowd. Fortunately, Uptown did not have a fire marshal since, if there had been a fire marshal on hand, there might have been complications. The *Downtown Uptown News Messenger* would later report that more than 400 people, including also Rossini and several other members of the political science department as well as a lot of children, had come to the steakhouse to see this scientific device. Romulus, though not a physicist, gave a short address:

"Ladies and gentlemen, fellow Nebraskans, immigrants from Bavaria, girls and boys, welcome to the grand opening of Uptown's very own particle accelerator. I would like to thank my colleague and friend, Professor Micky Rossini, for making this possible, and the members of the political science department for launching me on a new career." There were grins and snickers at this not terribly obscure reference. "Today it is a great honor for me to launch the particle accelerator into operation. So, what is a particle accelerator? It is," he claimed, "a device which accelerates a charged particle through an evacuated tube with an electrode on each end. We are using a tank of pressurized gas with high dielectric strength, giving us a capacity of 30 megawatts – which is a lot of power, boys and girls. A particle accelerator can bend time and space – "

"Nein, das ist nicht richtig," said one of the physicists.

" —yes, it can do this nine times each hour," said Romulus, "and enable us to reach higher states of consciousness."

"Wahnsinn," exclaimed one of the physicists, adding quickly "madness," for the benefit of those who did not speak German.

"Are there any questions before we turn on the machine?" Romulus asked.

Particles zipped past the audience, first in one direction, then in the other, and everyone in the audience, except for the physicists, was in awe of this great machine and of its maestro, Wolf Romulus.

Immediately, there were perhaps two dozen hands raised, mostly by children under age 15. Romulus acknowledged 9-year-old Felix.

"If I sit under the particle accelerator," Felix began, "can I travel back in time? My uncle celebrated his birthday last week and I gave him a book he'd already read. I'd like to go back in time and get him something else."

Before Romulus could even answer, young Tammy interjected, "I'd like to travel to the future, to see if I'm going to win a prize for my invention."

"What is your invention," Romulus asked her.

"Nothing so far," Tammy admitted. "I'm still giving it some thought. But eventually I will think of something to invent."

"I'd like to travel back to ancient times," 13-year-old Henry said, "so that I can see if the theories about why ancient Rome fell are right."

"I want to travel back in time so that I can meet my great-grandparents," 6-year-old Suzie said.

"Hold on, children," said Romulus. "The particle accelerator only *bends* time, it does not work as a time machine."

"So, if it's not a time machine, what use is it?" said a very young Max.

"It is good for people," Romulus answered. "Now let's turn it on." He gave a signal to Salvatore "the Peacemaker" Lino, working as one of his waiters. Lino first pressed a button to start the whirring, then he turned on the light show, then he released the locks on the trap doors on the ceiling, allowing fluorescent balloons to float down from above the audience. Only then did Lino press the button starting the particle accelerator. Particles zipped past the audience, first in one direction, then in the other, and everyone in the audience, except for the physicists, was in awe of this great machine and of its maestro, Wolf Romulus. Finally, Romulus nodded in the direction of Frank "the Animal" Giacona, who gave the signal to the Bah Bah Band to start marching around the room playing march music. This was a strange sight, and certainly a first in the history of particle accelerators. If Romulus aspired to uniqueness, then his particle accelerator show, with its fluorescent balloons, multicolored stroboscope lights, and marches, certainly registered a claim to uniqueness. The physicists got up and left, muttering phrases in German that no one understood. Everyone else stayed, and enjoyed the show. Eventually, Ignacio "Big Ig" Moretti, another one of Romulus' staff, came out and sang an Italian song roughly to the rhythm of the music.

Friday and von Kletten

Floorboard typically worked in his office until 1 a.m., sometimes later, and often did not come home to his wife at all. It would be unfair to suspect him of fooling around. The problem was that he had no real interests besides work. "Work, work, work, work, work," he liked to say. As this continued from one month to the next, from Autumn to Winter to Spring to Summer, von Kletten was spending more and more time with Friday. They had many things in common. Both of them liked the music of Boccherini, both of them like paintings by Caravaggio, Titian, and Tintoretto, both of them liked cats, which they liked to call the smartest animals on the planet, and both of them enjoyed picnics. It was in the course of a picnic at nearby Waterside Park, that the two of them shared their first kiss. Friday caressed von Kletten on the neck, she touched his shoulder, they kissed once again – and that was as far as things got on that day. Both of them respected the fact that von Kletten was married, although they realized that her marriage to Floorboard had become purely formal.

In August, before construction began on Romulus' Steakhouse, the two of them took a raft trip down the North Platte River, sailing along until it joined the Missouri River. Along the way, they crashed through rapids, enjoyed the smooth sailing of calm waters, held their own as strong currents emerged as if out of nowhere, and watched the sun grow orange as it set behind the Okra Mountains. They saw beavers building dams, river otters, raccoons, and even a bobcat, as well as various birds native to Nebraska, including canvasback ducks, herons, great white-fronted geese, sandhill cranes, and tundra swans. By the time they had finally arrived at the end of their trip, they were feeling something more than deep friendship. They kissed and hugged each other as they got onto the helicopter they had hired to take them back to Uptown. If this was not love, then what exactly is love?

As for Floorboard, he did not even notice that his wife had been gone. Nor did he notice that she was out of the house most nights. The reason she was out, of course, is that she was sleeping over in Friday's castle. For several months, sleep meant just sleep. But after the passage of some months, as the two of them found so much to discuss and found that they had so much in common, including an affection for seventeenth, eighteenth, and nineteenth century English poets, their love assumed a physical character. So natural and spontaneous was this, that it was impossible to say that either of them had taken the initiative. Their love just happened.

Although they were spending a lot of time together, both on campus and off, initially no one noticed anything. Most of the professors were deeply engrossed in their research or in administrative paperwork or, in the case of Carver, in drinking. But one day, while they sat by the duck pond, feeding the ducks, well, he was tearing up bread and handing the crumbs to her to feed the ducks. Anyone could see that that was a bit more than just a casual friendship.

"Your name," von Kletten asked him one day. "It is the same name as the main character in the 1950s television show, 'Dragnet'."

"Yes, played by Jack Webb, a childhood hero of mine," conceded Friday.

"So, were you born Joe Friday, or did you take this name later?"

"I was born Giuseppe Fridaggio. My father, Giordano Fridaggio, was a butcher in Milano and, when I was five years old, we moved to America," Friday answered, "in fact, here to Nebraska. But we did not want to be treated as foreigners. So all of us changed our family name to Friday and I used the English equivalent of Giuseppe – Joseph. Then, one day, I came across reruns of 'Dragnet' and admired Sergeant Joe Friday so much for his integrity, for always wanting to uphold the law, and for the way he treated everyone with respect. So, instead of Joseph, I started calling myself Joe.

The original Joe Friday, fictional character though he was, was a great man. I hope to live up to the model he set."

"That is inspiring," von Kletten answered in a hushed tone, "quite inspiring. And yes, you are surely a reincarnation of the original Joe Friday in all of his glory."

"Thanks," Friday said. "What about your background? You're not a native-born Nebraskan either, as far as I can tell."

"My maternal grandparents grew up in Königsberg, the same city where Immanuel Kant once delivered his exquisite lectures," she began. "My mother moved to Vienna when she was 22 and met my father, who was composing and performing waltzes. His waltzes are not as famous or as often played as those by Strauss, but they are lovely all the same," she said. "Someday I can play some of them for you on the piano."

"That would be very nice."

"My mother loved waltzes, including those by my father and waltzing is what drew them together. I am an only child."

"I could tell."

"How?"

"Only children and first-born children tend to be very confident, sure about themselves, and sometimes also exceptionally creative. This is how I see you, among other things," said Friday.

"I would not have come to Nebraska but for my husband. So he brought me to Nebraska and to you."

"Ah yes, destiny," replied Friday.

Later that afternoon, Friday and von Kletten withdrew to Friday's castle and spent the evening in front of his log-burning furnace, sipping homemade lemonade.

As the months passed, Friday and von Kletten grew more intimate, not just physically but also intellectually, Floorboard remained deeply immersed in paperwork, Rossini continued his active cooperation with law enforcement (to everyone's benefit), Perkins continued to haunt the department of political science, Romulus continued to accelerate particles, and the Maverick Brothers were enjoying their weekly trips to the Loup City Diner.

Brothers Bret and Bart truly loved coming to the Loup City Diner, not only because it afforded a chance to get out of the Happy Trails Institute, but also and especially because of the quality of the food and the friendliness of the service at the diner. Ideally, they wanted to have their visits to the diner scheduled on Wednesdays, so that they could skip the general counseling sessions at Happy Trails. But that was not possible, since every in-patient was expected to take part in these sessions, in order to facilitate their recovery and rehabilitation. So, it turned out that their visits were scheduled for Fridays. Loup City advertises itself, as is well known, as the Polish Capital of Nebraska – and this title is well deserved. Not only is there a lively community of Polish-Americans there, maintaining and celebrating Polish culture, but the town also holds a Polish Days festival every year in early June. The mayor has long been a Kaczmarek – first Jim Kaczmarek, then Joan Kaczmarek, then Freddie Kaczmarek, and after that Helen Kaczmarek. People in Loup City love the Kaczmarek family, as they have done so much good for the Loup City community. The entire population of Loup City speaks Polish as well as English. A few of the locals have even learned to speak the Alonquin dialect of the Ojibwe language, which is spoken by the indigenous Native Americans known as the Ojibwe or Chippewa. Eventually there were demands for a Polish-Alonquin dictionary, which was duly produced. The closest settlement of Chippewa is 40 miles from Loup City, but there has always been some contact between the two communities. The Maverick brothers were neither Polish nor Chippewa, but they were fascinated about what they learned from Katie Nowacka, the waitress at the Loup City Diner. She was well informed about local history and folklore, and seemed to know just about everyone in town since, sooner or later, locals would line up in front of the diner to wait for a table. The Maverick brothers and their "keeper", Miklos Poszkarny, did not have to wait, however, since they had standing reservations for 2 p.m. every Friday. The threesome tried, of course, the Loup City Burger with Nebraskan fries, pancakes à la mode (with strawberries), Mexican spaghetti (a local favorite), the Loup City Famous Okra Pizza, Reuben sandwiches (with pastrami, not corned beef), and much much more. They always left the diner happy and looking forward to their next visit. Over time, they were afforded the chance to look around the diner and, on a most unusual day when there was briefly a little time between customers, they were even given a tour of the diner. They watched the cooks taking a short break before returning to their skilled work, took note of the rear door at the far end of the kitchen, viewed the refrigerators and freezers where the diner stored the fine meats and other items for the menu, and had more than a few occasions to use the toilet, where the window was rather small. The front of the diner, which faced a large lawn with some trees, had large windows and was situated next to King's Variety and Gift Shoppe. The brothers seemed disappointed that it did not face a church, but managed to reconcile themselves to this unfortunate fact.

As the months went by, they became very friendly with Miklos Poszkarny, and they were soon on a first-name basis. "Miklos," Bret asked him one day, "what is it like working at an institute for not so severe mental disorders?"

"Not particularly difficult," Miklos answered. "I used to work at an institute for severe mental disorders, and that was more challenging. Some of the patients there had trouble understanding even such a basic thing as why we have to have rules at the institute. And there were sometimes nasty arguments between patients, especially between patients who were having very different hallucinations at the same time, and argued about what they were seeing. Imagine if patient A sees a dog and comments to patient B what a good-looking dog it is, but patient B sees only a goat and wonders why it is in the building. And it doesn't help if patient C is not hallucinating and wants to explain to these two hallucinators that there is no animal in the room at all. But at the institute where the two of you have found a temporary home, the problems are minor. Hell, I can't figure out that you two have any mental problems at all! But then again, I'm a nurse, not a doctor."

"We are doctors," Brother Bart boasted, "doctors of political science."

"That's not relevant," Brother Bret told Bart. "Miklos does not want to hear about this."

"Well, actually it is relevant," Miklos said, "because highly educated people tend to have active brains, and active brains have a better chance of a full recovery than brains that are less active. Making friends, even at the institute, is also a good thing and I have seen for myself that you have made friends with Debbie Florsheim and Eddie Fitz – and this is a good thing. But watch out if Eddie challenges you to a game of mental chess. He is capable of keeping as many as 32 moves in his head, without a slip-up, and by then you will likely have become unsure about the placement of the pieces on the board."

"Which means that we would lose, right?" said Bret.

"That's right. You stay in the game only for as long as you can follow it, and with no board in front of you, it can get complicated after a while," Miklos replied. "For me, I can manage for perhaps six moves – seven was my all-time record. So, 32 moves? Well, that's amazing, and I don't know how he does it."

"No wonder he's been diagnosed," Bret offered.

"Debbie," Miklos continued, "is one of our most charming guests, and everyone loves her. She genuinely cares about people and you can trust her to keep a confidence. She is one of my favorite guests – right after you two!"

"What about that grouchy old fellow who sits in the corner wearing a checkered scarf around his head – what's his story?"

Brother Bart was also becoming infatuated with waitress Katie, although she gave him no encouragement. He had even started to fantasize that she was in love with him.

"He claims to have been a colonel in the U.S. army," answered Miklos, "but we told him that there is no record of him having attained any rank higher than sergeant. Perhaps we should have just humored him. But now he is angry and even addressing him as 'colonel' does not help. He knows that we don't believe that he was really a colonel. But," Miklos added, "he's not dangerous. He has never hurt anyone at the institute."

"Pancakes!" said Bart suddenly. "I want pancakes!"

"We've just eaten hamburgers with Nebraskan fries," Bret answered. "Are you still hungry?"

Of course the answer would be "yes". Every visit to the Loup City Diner ended with Bart ordering pancakes à la mode, even when they had had pancakes as the main course. Brother Bart was also becoming infatuated with waitress Katie, although she gave him no encouragement. He had even started to fantasize that she was in love with him.

Meanwhile, back at UWU, the school year had started and Perkins was teaching for the first time since he had committed suicide. Coming to the first class, he did his best to appear as opaque as possible, although from time to time his feet would start to fade a bit. "Good morning, students," Perkins said by way of a greeting. "I am Professor Jason Perkins and it is good to be back in the classroom for the first time in six years. I've been away from teaching because I committed suicide and, at that time, there was prejudice against keeping dead people teaching. I am pleased to see that yet another prejudice is being overcome."

The students were looking around in a very confused way. They were not sure whether they should play along or make fun of the supposedly dead professor or whether, just maybe, he was telling the truth. One of them shouted out, "Hey, old man, you're not dead! You're crazy!"

"Allow me to prove the point," Perkins responded calmly and proceed to walk through the desk, to disappear into thin air and reappear, and then to float to the ceiling, hovering in mid-air for a few seconds, and then glide back to the floor. "Anyone with doubts now?"

"No, sir, not at all," the former skeptic replied. "Please don't hold it against me."

"Not at all and, for the future, I expect to be addressed as 'Professor Perkins' and not as 'old man' or even as 'sir'," Perkins said.

Perkins had a class of 150 for his course on Politics in the Afterlife and, looking around the room, he could see that most of the students were simultaneously intrigued and nervous. Since Perkins had proven beyond any shadow of a doubt that he was, in fact, a ghost, the students did not know what to expect. Do ghosts behave like people? they asked themselves. Are ghosts fair graders? What about office hours? And can Professor Perkins stop flickering for a bit? That's right – Perkins had started to flicker, but he quickly got his flickering under control and even apologized for it. "Sorry about the flickering, students," he said, "but this is the way things are sometimes in the afterlife. *You* get your energy from food and build it up with exercise. But ghosts do not eat. So our spirit energy comes from another source – quarks. If you've never seen a quark, don't worry about it. But quarks are the source of my energy and, when my quark level is a bit low, then I flicker. It's nothing for any of you to worry about."

Some of the students did, in fact, look worried, but the class continued, as Perkins explained his understanding of how politics in the afterlife worked – who the actors were, what they wanted, what power in the afterlife involved, and what the uses of such power were. One thing he emphasized from the beginning, though, was that there is no money in the afterlife. So that one of the driving forces of corruption in politics is absent in the world to come.

Von Kletten was also taking on a new course: Politics in the Aztec Empire. No one was better qualified than von Kletten to teach this class as she had devoted years to studying such texts as have survived. No texts from prior to the conquest have survived, but there are documents stored in the archives in Mexico City, written in Nahuatl, containing a mixture of Aztec glyphs and notes in Spanish. From these documents as well as from other local materials, including secondary sources, she had pieced together a fascinating picture of how the Aztec system of government worked and did not work. Friday stopped by her class one day, to sit in and hear what she had to say. He became totally fascinated and, after her lecture, as they sat down for their regular lunch, he had many questions for her and continued to be impressed with the depth of her knowledge. He became a regular visitor to her class and it was after one of her classes that he suggested to her that she move in with him, leaving her husband altogether.

"That would be a big step," von Kletten said.

"So what do you think?" asked Friday, whose love of political science was exceeded only by his love for von Kletten.

"I shall have to think about it," she answered. "Can we leave this question open?"

"Yes, of course," said Friday.

Then, a few months later, Floorboard started to insist that it was time to leave UWU and he and von Kletten got into a huge argument. At that, she announced that she needed time away from him and moved in with Friday. None of them could be sure yet if this new arrangement would prove to be permanent. But what was clear enough was that her relationship with Floorboard was seriously endangered, if not dead.

A.E.I.O.U.

The American Ecological Institute and Organized University, generally known by its initials A.E.I.O.U., is based in Dallas, Texas, which locals consider a better place to live than New York or Los Angeles, let alone Uptown, Nebraska. Residents of Dallas call themselves Dallasians and those who live in the surburbs Dallasoids. Those in the suburbs say that they too are Dallasians, but so far this dispute has not been resolved. What has been resolved to everyone's satisfaction is the international standing of A.E.I.O.U. Although the word "ecological" appears in the name of the university, the fields of study at A.E.I.O.U. extend far beyond ecological and environmental concerns, and embrace all of the major fields of study except for physics. There was a physics department at A.E.I.O.U. some years earlier, but the physicists organized a union and demanded that their department be named "Best Department at A.E.I.O.U." and that the halls at their department be gilded in gold and platinum. They also made a habit of constantly boasting about how physics had discovered the law of gravity and about how, without physicists, the rest of the world would be completely lost. Finally, the rectors of the university had enough and simply shut down the department. The physicists responded by reorganizing themselves as a private consultancy firm, under the name Texan Physicists at Work for You. They hung up a sign, "If you've got a problem with matter or energy, come to us. We are physicists!"

The rectors all lived in the suburbs but denied that they were

Dallasoids; they were Dallasians, they insisted. And it was up to them to decide what to call themselves. Of course, they were also Texans and Americans,…but not Nebraskans…at least not yet. Not all Texans dream of moving to Nebraska, although some do. The rectors did not, because they had good and secure jobs and liked their university, and, when the president of the university retired (at the advanced age of 85), they looked around for a suitable candidate and decided that Floorboard, who was already being courted by the University of Cut and Shoot as well as by the University of Truth or Consequences, could be ideal. So they contacted Floorboard and invited him to come out to Dallas for an interview. So it was that this dashing, dignified, and debonair denizen of UWU flew out to Dallas for an interview. He was expected to present a lecture on his "vision" for A.E.I.O.U. and what he offered was nothing short of bold. He planned to make A.E.I.O.U. not only the most powerful institution of higher education on the planet but also to establish branch campuses in as many countries as possible. Naturally, the rectors wanted to know how he would achieve these goals and his reply was that he would recruit the finest minds from the finest universities around the world and bring them to A.E.I.O.U., expanding the faculty and putting these minds to work to expand the reach of the university. The rectors interviewed three other candidates for the job, but none of the others had a vision as bold or as ambitious as Floorboard, and soon he was offered the post. The rectors loved his talk, admired his general demeanor, found his conversation over lunch to be scintillating and energetic and before he had even gotten back on the plane to return to Uptown, they made the offer. The salary they offered represented a considerable improvement over what he was receiving at UWU, his office would be more spacious, he would have four secretaries at his beck and call, and – best of all – he would not have to work with physicists. He accepted the offer on the spot, without even negotiating anything for von Kletten.

When he got back to Uptown and gave von Kletten the news, she was furious!! How could he accept the offer without consulting her and, for that matter, without negotiating something for her. "This is too much!" she told him, "We are through." This was, indeed, the last straw. Floorboard had not found time for his wife in years and now had the nerve to accept an offer in another state without so much as asking her opinion. The breakup was not as complicated as one might think, however, because theirs had been a "common law" marriage.

Later that same evening, she and Friday talked. Friday made a formal offer of marriage, she accepted and, the next day, she moved her remaining belongings from the presidential mansion over to Friday's castle. As for Floorboard, this daring, dudley, and deedly man, this workaholic, this princely paper-pusher barely noticed the demise of his marriage. "OK," was all he had said when she told him she was through with him.

One of the last decisions that Floorboard took was to shut down the department of history. He said that history was "over" and that people needed to focus on the here and now. When the historians objected that there were lessons to be learned from studying democracy versus authoritarianism or from studying history's various wars, Floorboard replied that these lessons could be written down on a list. One did not need to study the Bolshevik experience with collective farming to know that collective farming was a bad idea. That lesson could be summed up in one sentence: collective farming does not work. So why study it? – Floorboard asked rhetorically. The professors now tried to make a living by offering to lecture for a fee, for example at parties. Imagine the thrill of coming to a friend's party and being treated to a one-hour lecture on England's Alfred the Great.

The reactions at UWU to Floorboard's departure, so soon after he had arrived, were mixed, but mostly negative. People could not understand why he would leave their university barely a year after he had arrived. They felt stabbed in the back. He had told people that he was "thrilled" to come to Nebraska, and now he was already leaving! What can you expect from a Californian?, some people said. And he had promised to fix the problems at the departments of psychology and physics and – look! – his solution was to move to a university which didn't have a physics department. People were disgusted and there was a strong sentiment to run the university without a president. Provost Zoe Ryan met with the heads of the various departments to discuss the situation and, after some discussion, there was a consensus that there should be an internal hire. Once this was agreed, all eyes in the room turned to Friday, who modestly looked down at the desk and started fumbling with his pen. "Friday," said the provost, "it looks like people here want you. But at the same time, it is clear to all of us that the department of political science also needs you. What do you say to being simultaneously president of the university and head of the political science department?"

"I am honored by your trust," said Friday noncommittally.

"Let me tell you what the job of president entails," the provost began. "You'll have the departmental heads you see around you, coming to you with questions and requests and complaints, and you'll have to deal with them. You can consult with me and with the deans, of course, but the buck stops with you, not with us. If there is a professor who suddenly becomes brain dead, his or her department can recommend termination, but it will be your decision that will count. If a department recommends the promotion or termination of an assistant professor up for tenure and the college council votes the other way – as happens more often than you might expect, even if not in political science – you, as president, will have to make the decision. It's a tough job and not everyone is up for it. But you don't have to work seven days a week, 12 hours a day, like our Beanhead Floorboard. If you balance your time, delegate to your vice president and to your secretaries, you can still have time for your department and for your leisure. So, what do you say?"

The heads of the department and the deans were sitting anxiously in their chairs, leaning forward in anticipation, with some of them crossing their fingers and whispering to themselves, "I hope he accepts" and others gulping down water.

They were not going to be disappointed, however, because Friday agreed. "I am honored by your trust, and accept the appointment," he began. "I will do my best for UWU." The professors, deans, and provost sitting around the table cheered and clapped. There were huge smiles everywhere. Even Friday was smiling a little.

"Excellent! Congratulations. But, before we break," the provost added, "what is this I hear about your department having a hologram and a ghost teaching classes?"

"Don't worry about that," President Friday responded. "Pestalozzi is a highly productive scholar, who has published articles in the *Journal of Politics*, the *American Journal of Political Science*, and even in the *American Sociological Review*. He is also a very popular teacher and a positive force in the department. We've gotten used to him appearing as a hologram and, as long as he does his work effectively, we don't see why anyone should worry about him."

"Well said, but what about the ghost of Perkins?"

"Perkins was a very fine scholar in his day," Friday said. "Right now, with the departure of Romulus and both Holloway brothers, we are short of personnel. The ghost of Perkins has offered to pick up the slack and teach classes for us. Since the school year is upon us, it is too late to hire someone for this academic year. The consensus at our department is that Perkins, dead though he may be, should be given a chance. If he teaches as well as he did when he was alive, and publishes again, then why not keep him on board? Besides, he has declined to take a salary."

"Didn't he leave behind a wife and children?"

"No," Friday answered. "He was a bachelor, and his parents predeceased him. He said that he just wants to teach. He was getting bored just hanging around his office singing pirate songs..."

"Pirate songs?"

"Also bawdy seafaring songs."

"Well," said the provost, "if he works out, then I suppose we can be open-minded about this. But, as far as I know, we'd be the only university in the Great State of Nebraska, or in the entire USA for that matter, with a dead professor teaching classes."

"That may be, ma'am, but we can view it as a noble experiment."

"Fine," the provost responded. "And now, to celebrate this transfer of power and responsibility, I would like to treat all of you and your partners to dinner at the Steakholders' Steakhouse, Bar and Grill."

"A perfect way to celebrate," Friday acknowledged and then, exercising his new authority, he declared the meeting adjourned.

Romulus' Washing Machine

It was about this time that Romulus started to get advice from his washing machine. The first communication was rather mundane – that is, if hearing your washing machine talk to you can be considered mundane. At any rate, as the forcibly retired professor and mostly successful restauranteur was shoving clothes into his washing machine one overcast Sunday afternoon, his washing machine suddenly looked at him and said, "It's not smart to put so many items inside your washing machine. You'll get better results with a lighter load."

Romulus' eyes grew large as he looked at his washing machine. His washing machine looked back at him – this was a new experience for him and he had not had any idea before that a washing machine could look at you.

"Please take some of these clothes out of me," the washing machine barked, "starting with the towels. They itch."

"Right away, of course," said Romulus. He was used to giving orders. So it was a new experience for him to be taking orders now. As he reached into the washing machine and pulled out the towels, he asked, "Is that better?"

"Much better," said the washing machine. "Much better. And listen, you need to grow a moustache. Not a thick one for now, just a thin one along the edge of your lip."

"I should grow a moustache?" Romulus was surprised at this suggestion.

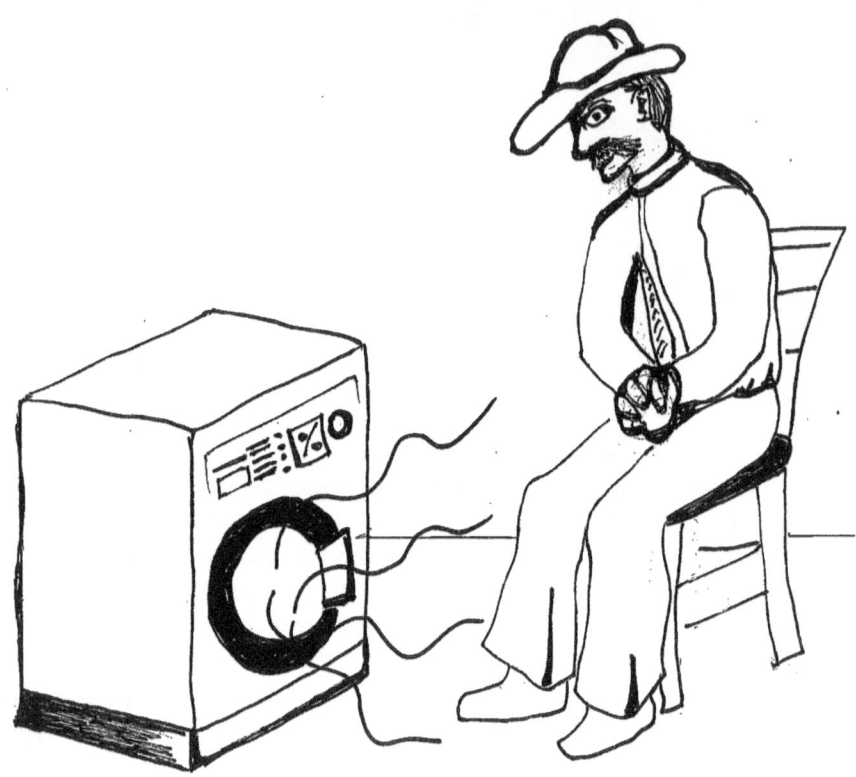

Romulus grew a moustache, exactly according to his washing machine's advice and had to agree that it made him look like a Latin lover.

"That's what I said."

"Anything else?"

"Well, you can turn me on," his washing machine replied. "The clothes won't get clean just by sitting inside me."

And this is how it went on the first day. Romulus grew a moustache, exactly according to his washing machine's advice and had to agree that it made him look like a Latin lover. But in subsequent days, Romulus' washing machine gave him advice on which newspapers he could trust, which books he should read, which of his employees were most loyal to him, and what goals he should set for himself.

The washing machine told Romulus that its name was Toby and

said that it wanted to help the restauranteur rise to power. This was, of course, a big offer. Romulus asked himself, could he be dreaming or imagining this? Was he hallucinating? What was in those mushrooms anyway? But it was so real that, after some momentary doubts, he became convinced that he was, in fact, in possession of a talking washing machine called Toby. In fact, Toby had lots of good ideas, even making recommendations for Romulus' diet and exercise regime. One day, after some weeks of lively conversations between them, Toby offered Romulus some rather different advice. "You are a political scientist, right?" Romulus nodded. "So you understand politics," Toby noted. "This is where your true talent and your destiny lie. Politics is your destiny. Seize the day!" And then, translating the last phrase back into the original Latin, the washing machine added, "Carpe diem!" Now it seemed that Toby even knew a little Latin. Romulus was increasingly impressed with this erudite device.

"Seize the day!" Toby repeated. "Run for office. Take power into your hands. Be a commander of men and women. Live the dream!"

"Power to the people!" Romulus replied, somewhat absent-mindedly.

"Run for mayor of Uptown," Toby urged him. "Old Man Marlowe is an unelected mayor. He has no business calling himself mayor. Organize an election, run against him. Carpe diem!" And then, spitting out a half soaked pair of underpants, Toby added, "In this sign you will conquer!"

One might think that Romulus might have sought psychiatric advice at this point, or alternatively have unplugged his washing machine, or just avoided the basement, where Toby was sitting, and have taken his clothes to the World's Best Dry Cleaners, conveniently located on Main Street, next to the "bookshop". But he did none of these things. On the contrary, he continued to take his dirty clothing to Toby and to receive advice from it. It *did* occur to Romulus to ask Pastor Grace to come over to his house and perform an exorcism on Toby, just in case the washing machine was possessed by a demon. But he ruled that out because Pastor Grace was part owner of the rival steakhouse and he was not sure that he could trust the pastor to set aside his business interests. Besides, there could be rumors and some people might not be ready to accept that a washing machine would give him *good* advice. And in any event, now that he had decided to challenge Old Man Marlowe for the mayor's seat, he did not want it to get around that this was his washing machine's idea.

Whatever else might be said about Romulus, he was not a procrastinator. When an idea came into his mind, from his washing machine or from some other source, he decided quickly whether to act upon it and, if his decision was positive, then he got to work on it right away. Thus it was that, just a few days after his washing machine suggested to him that he should seek the mayor's office, he was already passing around bills in town, demanding an election. Most people were really puzzled by this, at least at first. Marlowe was the only mayor they had ever had since he had created the post in the first place. The notion of someone else occupying *Marlowe's* post was, for most Uptownians, unthinkable. Yet now they were being forced to think about it. Romulus even had the audacity to head over to the Fancy Turtle Saloon, which was de facto Marlowe's mayoral office, and talk about this with such persons as were prepared to listen. Of course, Old Man Marlowe owned the saloon. So, even if he would be somehow voted out of the position of mayor, he would still own the saloon and his successor would have to find some other place to serve as his office. In Romulus' case, that would likely be his Steakhouse and Particle Accelerator.

"Romulus for mayor!" the candidate took to shouting up and down Main Street. On his bill, below that stirring motto he wrote, "Uptown is already a great place to live. But we can make it even better. What we need is to organize celebrations of the sun." Little did people know what he had in mind by celebrations of the sun, but they liked the idea of celebrating. It turned out that Romulus had been reading about his ancient namesake, about the founding of Rome and its rise to glory and power, and he liked the old Roman sayings such as "Eggs today are better than chickens tomorrow" and "Fortune favors the brave." What was not speculation, but factual, was that he was stirring up a modest degree of chaos in town, in a faint echo of what transpired in old gladiator contests – just without bloodshed. Bearing in mind what young men and women had done in Caesar's time, he ventured onto the UWU campus and, standing on the steps of the Millard Fillmore Auditorium, shouted "So it begins" – another ancient Roman saying – which he followed up by shouting, "Veni, vidi, vici" – "I came, I saw, I conquered". Whom was he planning to conquer? Presumably Mayor Marlowe – but *conquer?* But, although most students found these allusions to ancient Rome confusing, they eagerly embraced what they mistakenly called the "Romanesque" revival, skipping class. Listening to Romulus rhapsodize about ancient Rome was, in any event, better than playing chicken on the railroad tracks. As for the "celebration of the sun", this turned out to mean having a number of students walking around banging gongs and shouting something about Apollo. During the celebration of the sun, Romulus repeated several times what was taken as his campaign slogan: "Seek only the good of the people."

After two weeks of such agitation, Romulus – now styling himself Romulus Caesar – demanded a referendum. He managed to collect 127 signatures on a petition to hold an election for mayor. He presented this to Old Man Marlowe, who could just as well have tossed it into the trash can. But Mayor Marlowe was nothing if not fully confident and decided to let it proceed. He sat down with this self-declared Caesar and together they drew up a three-part referendum. The text was as follows:

"Are you in favor of holding elections for the office of mayor, opening up the office to any and all challengers, of establishing a city council to consist of four persons to be appointed by the mayor, and of instituting new taxes to pay for salaries for the mayor and the city councilmen?"

Everyone knew that Mayor Marlowe was not being paid for his mayoring, and only the town lunatic, Perry MacPerry, salivated at the thought of higher taxes. In fact, with just 253 persons even bothering to vote in this referendum, 251 voted against the proposition, with just two – Romulus and MacPerry – in favor.

But Romulus was not a quitter. He then circulated a petition to recall Mayor Marlowe, alleging that, as the owner of a saloon and co-owner of the Steakholders' Steakhouse, he had a conflict of interest. No one signed the petition, not even MacPerry, and several persons he approached reproached him for hypocrisy since he was the owner of a steakhouse himself and yet thought of seeking the mayor's office. It was also duly noted that, while Old Man Marlowe had scarcely asserted any authority at all and had not been collecting a paycheck for fulfilling such light tasks as he took on as mayor, Romulus wanted to be paid and, beyond that, it seemed obvious that, with Caesar as his model, he intended to rule Uptown as Augustus Caesar had once ruled the Roman Empire. Unfortunately, all of this took its toll on local enthusiasm for Romulus' Steakhouse.

Romulus went home and descended to the basement to discuss the situation with his washing machine. "You gave me bad advice," he told Toby. "You urged me to seek the mayor's office."

"True enough, but parading around like a latter-day Caesar – that was your idea," Toby pointed out, "and it was a very bad idea. You would have done better to have taken Abraham Lincoln as your model or even Wild Bill Hickock. Every American loves Lincoln. Well, almost every American – not those who prefer Jefferson Davis, of course."

"What do you know about Jefferson Davis?" Romulus asked Toby.

"I know that he was the president of the Confederate States of America, that he had two wives, though not at the same time, and that, by 1869, he was president of the Carolina Life Insurance Company in Memphis, Tennessee," Toby answered.

"Well, I know these things too," Romulus said, "but what is a washing machine doing reading up on Confederate history?"

"I have many interests," Toby replied, "and lots of good ideas. We can talk about this. But please, promise me that you will give up your neo-Roman illusions."

"I'll think about it," Romulus said meekly. "But why don't you run for political office? You're obviously a smart washing machine."

"Yeah, a smart washing machine. How many people do you think would vote to have a washing machine serve as mayor?"

"OK," said Romulus. "I see your point. If one of us is going to carry our program forward, it will have to be me." This was the first time he had referred to "our program". "There's one thing I don't understand," Romulus continued. "You are here in my basement and never get out, and yet it is as if you are seeing the world through my eyes. How is that possible? Are you reading my mind?"

"I would have thought that the explanation would have been obvious," Toby replied slyly. "One night, when you were sleeping, I sneaked up into your bedroom and implanted a video/audio recorder and transmitter, XL class, in your brain. Easy as pie."

"But you're stuck here in the basement!" Romulus objected.

"So it would appear," Toby replied.

"What if I unplug you?"

"Oh, don't do that!" Toby purred. "We're friends, aren't we? Collaborators! I wouldn't dream of unplugging you!"

"I'm not plugged in," Romulus conceded.

"You can say that again!" came Toby's rejoinder.

Romulus' Steakhouse and Particle Accelerator went through a rough patch for about a month. But then, it was visited by a team of scientists from Washington D.C., who had heard that Romulus' particle accelerator had some unique features. Once their visit was lovingly reported in the *Uptown News Chronicle & Chronicle for Uptown News*, locals developed a new respect for Romulus' unique steakhouse and started to return. Moreover, the Uptown Mafia Bah Bah Band had been practicing their instruments every day and were now performing five nights a week, with classic, even stirring renditions of sundry American hits. In addition to the songs they had played at their premiere, they could now belt out such Nebraskan favorites as Kenny Rogers' "Just Dropped In", the end titles from the 1982 film "Blade Runner", and the Bee Gees' "Staying Alive", which they performed in an "updated" format. As word got around that the Uptown Mafia Bah Bah Band was offering very listenable renditions of these favorites, people found that, when they wanted steak with music, they divided their time between Uptown's two restaurants. Word spread about the excellent musical fare being offered at the two steakhouses, and soon people were driving over from nearby Filibuster and Stonewall, and even from as far away as Loup City, Dakota City, and Omaha.

Up to then, everyone had expected the popular governor, Eddie Fitzerback, to stand for reelection. But, having served two terms as governor, Fitzerback planned to retire. The elections were scheduled for May and, once Toby got the news, it started encouraging Romulus to run for the governor's office. Romulus was not sure at first, but then Toby started to recite his credentials and achievements: he had served as Commander of the political science department at UWU, he had organized mass meetings in Uptown, he had exposed the fraud of the Aztec urn while bravely defending the good name of the brothers Holloway, he had launched the prestigious *Romulus Journal for the Rational Study of Reality*, he had successfully organized and operated a steakhouse in a competitive setting, and he had attracted a coterie of competent advisers, by whom Toby meant Rossini, Carver, MacPerry, and itself, among others. In addition, he had once given an interview to the local newspaper and had made several appearances on KNOP-TV. He would run as an "outsider", who would bring a "refreshing" change to Nebraskan politics and change the way Nebraskans think about politics.

This was something Romulus had to think about very hard. The idea excited him and, the first night, he was tossing and turning, sweating away pounds as he wondered if this was the next step in his sparkling career, while imagining what he could do as governor. The next day, at the steakhouse, his employees saw him pacing in deep thought and they guessed that he was thinking about something earthshaking. After a week like this, with very little sleep, he gave a short speech at his steakhouse, in front of the particle accelerator, and announced that he would be running for governor of the Great State of Nebraska. That night, for the first time in a week, he slept soundly, rising only at 10 a.m. to the sound of the Nebraska Pacific Railroad, as the express train rattled by.

The Great Escape

The Holloway Brothers had no intention of serving out five years at an institute for not so severe mental disorders and, one day, after Miklos and the two brothers had given their orders to Katie at the Loup City Diner, Bart grabbed a fork and stood up, excusing himself by saying that he had to use the toilet. Neither Miklos nor Bret took any notice of Bart's need for a fork in the toilet. In fact, Bart had his own plans for the fork and, once he got to the toilet, he got down on his knees and started to scrape around the ceramic floor tiles, hoping to lift them up. His plan was to dig a tunnel through the restroom floor, so that he and Bret could escape from the diner and hit the road as "free men". After the passage of about 35 minutes, by which time their pancakes à la mode had been served and Bart's ice cream was starting to melt, Brother Bret excused himself and went over to the restroom door and called in: "Bart, what is taking you so long? Miklos is getting upset."

"I'm digging a tunnel," Bart explained.

"Get out of there right now," Bret commanded – and Bart did so immediately. They headed back over to the table where Miklos was sitting and Bret offered the explanation that the toilet paper had gotten stuck on the roll and that Bart had needed to use the fork to pry it loose. From most people, such an explanation would not have been believable. But Brother Bart had established a reputation for being less than bright and, besides, he was incarcerated in the Happy Trails Institute. Having difficulty pulling toilet paper off the roll might well be evidence of a mental disorder of some sort, whether "not so severe" or something else. So Miklos accepted the explanation at face value. Later, when they were back at the institute and when the brothers had a little time to themselves in the institute's Garden of Tranquility, Bret pointed out that, since there was a back door to the diner, straight through the kitchen, they did not have to tunnel out. Or, when Miklos had to use the restroom, they could even just walk out the front door. These alternatives, Bret explained to Bart, were better options than tunneling through the restroom's ceramic tiles. Besides, other customers might need to use the restroom from time to time and, in any event, a fork was a poor implement to use for tunneling.

Bret could see that Bart was getting impatient to get out of the institute. The free weekly lunches at the Loup City Diner were a great compensation, and, where Brother Bart was concerned, there was also the love he imagined that Katie felt for him, but incarceration was still incarceration. So they hatched a plan, which was to make sure that Miklos drank plenty of his favorite beverage at the diner the next time they went there and to make their escape during the time he would be in the restroom. However, Miklos was required to report to the institute's director how each visit to the diner went and, when he mentioned that Bart had been in the restroom for more than half an hour, trying to pry toilet paper off the roll using a fork, the director grew suspicious. "Is this your explanation, or Bart's?" Dr. Freundlich asked.

"It was his brother's explanation, Bret's explanation," Miklos clarified.

"In other words, the smart one told you this."

"That's right."

"And he took the fork with him to the restroom, did he?" Freundlich probed.

"Yes, he did," Miklos noted.

"That means that he anticipated the need for a fork," the director pointed out. "Doesn't that strike you as just a bit suspicious."

"Well, now that you mention it," Miklos replied, "it does."

"If it were up to me," Freundlich said, "I'd cancel these visits to the diner. But they are mandated by court order. So we shall have to continue them. But keep an eye on these two. They may be up to something."

Miklos in turn passed along a toned down version of this exchange to the brothers, and suggested that he thought that their visits to the Loup City Diner might be challenged by the director if there would be any further suspicious activity. After this, the brothers decided that they were not going to postpone their escape any longer and, when it came time for the next visit to Loup City, they retrieved the money they had deposited in their piggy banks and put it in their back pockets. At the diner, they insisted on buying an extra-large root beer float for Miklos, and then a second one. He had mentioned once that this was his favorite drink and that it was one of the reasons he had emigrated from his native Hungary to the USA. He gulped down first the one, and then the other, and finally excused himself to use the toilet. Once he closed the door behind himself, the brothers wrote a little note to Miklos: "Thanks for all these trips to the diner. It's been nice knowing you. Sorry that we need to steal your car. (signed) Bret and Bart Maverick." They then put a tip on the table and walked out the front door. They jimmied the lock to Miklos' car door, hot-wired the engine, and were soon rumbling down the road. As they started their trek, Bart told his brother that Katie would miss him. Bret shrugged this off. Bart was driving and missed the exit to connect with Interstate 80 and they ended up at the Sherman Reservoir and State Recreation Area, which lay in the opposite direction to the one in which they were supposedly traveling. An argument ensued, because Bart claimed that he thought that this would be a pleasant detour and afford them a little relaxation, while Bret accused Bart of being an ignoramus and not knowing the way to Uptown. The argument ended with Bret taking control of the car and, with that, they headed west, driving north on highway 58 to Arcadia and then west through Westerville (with its haunted water tower), Broken Bow (noted for its hanging gardens and llama petting park), and Arnold (famous for its one-quarter scale pyramid, housing the town's police station), southwest to North Platte (best known for Buffalo Bill's Victorian-style mansion), and then west as far as Uptown. As they entered Uptown city limits, they drove straight over to Romulus' Steakhouse and Particle Accelerator. Since it was nearing closing time, the music had stopped and the crowd had already thinned out. When Romulus saw them, he reacted with a mixture of pleasure and dismay.

"Come to my office," he said, motioning to them. "You have escaped, I see."

"Yes, we did it," answered Bart, grinning from ear to ear. "I wanted to dig a tunnel through the floor in the diner's restroom, but Bret told me that we could just walk out the front door. And that is what we did!" Bart seemed totally pleased with himself... and with his brother Bret too, of course.

Bret adopted a more cautious tone. "I imagine that they will come looking for us, and the most likely place they will look is here, at your steakhouse."

"In fact, Dr. Freundlich already phoned me, and suggested, in a very friendly way, that I should probably expect the two of you to show up here," Romulus said. "I talked with him just three hours ago." After a short pause, he added, "I am supposed to report the two of you, so that you can be taken back to the institute."

"What are you going to do?" Bret asked.

"Are you going to report us?" Bart asked.

"No, I am not going to report you. You are going to take the car and drive north to Alliance and check in at the Alliance Hotel. I have paid a deposit to cover the two of you for a month in the hotel. You can use that time to relax and get ready for your next assignment. I will contact you there in a week to 10 days. In the meantime, lay low. And, oh yes," Romulus added, "I gave your names as Hank and Spank Milliner. The reservation will be under those names."

"Which one of us is Spank?" Bart asked.

"It doesn't matter," Romulus answered.

"I want to be Spank," Bart said.

"It's fine by me," said Bret.

And with that, Bret and Bart Holloway, AKA the Maverick brothers, AKA Hank and Spank Milliner got back in their stolen car and drove out to Alliance. Being careful, they had turned the license plate upside down, so that the police would not be able to identify the car immediately and, when they got to Alliance, they left it at the outskirts of the town and walked the rest of the way to the hotel.

A week later, restauranteur and ex-commander Romulus drove to Alliance, met with the two brothers, and took them to Ken and

Dale's Restaurant on East 3rd Street, for an early steak dinner. As they sat down, Romulus leaned over to them and told them, "I am running for governor."

"You're kidding, right?" said Bret.

"No, I collected enough signatures and my name will be on the ballot. I'll be running as an independent."

"Who are the other candidates?"

"There will be three other candidates – a Republican, an anarchist, and a candidate of the Green Party."

"No candidate from the Democratic Party."

"Not this time. There was too much in-fighting and the Democrats could not agree on anyone."

"Is that good or bad for you?"

"Everything is good for me," Romulus claimed, without disclosing that he owed his confidence to tips and reassurances from his washing machine.

"What can we do?" Bret asked.

"I'd like the two of you to be my campaign managers, and arrange for speaking engagements for me, visits to children's clinics and hospitals, visits to schools and factories, and set up interviews on television and with newspapers."

"You realize that we are fugitives, right?" Bret said.

"Yeah, we're outlaws!" Bart said enthusiastically.

"Oh yes, I almost forgot," said Romulus, handing them new drivers' licenses and a set of keys. "Thanks to my friend Rossini, I have arranged for the two of you to live rent-free in a house right here in Alliance. Here are the keys to the house and to your new car, registered in the name of Hank Milliner, but with insurance covering also Spank to drive. So, Hank and Spank, you can rest assured that the police are not looking for either of you under those names and, if you do get apprehended, Rossini told me that he is ready to engage in a little 'cooperation' with law enforcement officials."

"That's great," said Bart.

"Yes, it is," Bret agreed. "And we are ready and willing to be your campaign managers."

"You'll need to grow thin moustaches along your lips, just as I have."

"Consider it done," said Bret.

"I've always wanted to grow a moustache," Bart admitted. At this, Romulus and Bret looked at each other knowingly.

"One other thing: as my campaign managers, you will receive a handsome salary. Here is a down payment." With that, he handed them $8,000 each. "Your checks will be sent to your house on Grieg Street."

With that, the Milliner brothers got to work on the campaign. With a new car dealership about to open in Broken Bow, Spank Milliner arranged for Romulus to give a short speech there. Hank Milliner arranged for Romulus to give a talk at the Rotary Club in Westerville. There were also additional appearances, including at the Annual Pig Festival in Arnold, the annual Cattle Rangers' barbeque in Hyannis, the Lutheran Church Basement Women's pot luck dinner in Burwell, the Italian tacos and Mexican pizza eating contest in Grand Island (which is not an island at all – so you don't need a boat to get there), additional events and appearances in Beatrice, Hebron, Red Cloud, Beaver City, Stockville, Center (which is not located at the center of the state, as you might think but close to the northeast corner of the Great State of Nebraska), Tekamah, Ogallala, Osceola, Schuyler, and of course North Platte, Lincoln, and Omaha, among many others. They had Romulus riding on the back of a tractor, opening a town rodeo in Elwood, stroking cats at the local Trenton county fair, and above all giving rousing speeches everywhere he went. He shook hands, kissed babies, petted dogs, and complimented people on their tractors, on their babies, on their dogs, cats, cars, walls, fences, gardens, and flowers. "Romulus for Governor! Let's bring back sanity to our state's capital!" That was the slogan these two escapees from the Happy Trails Institute came up with.

Romulus gave televised speeches, and was interviewed for television by KMNE-TV in Bassett, KGIN in Grand Island, KUON-TV in Lincoln, KFXL-TV also in Lincoln, KMTV in Omaha, KSTF in Scottsbluff, and many many more. Romulus had engagements six days a week, resting on Thursdays. He showed energy, resolve, and a keen understanding of his version of the issues facing Nebraskans. There were, of course, some awkward moments, for example when he told an audience in Hayes Center – which is nowhere near the town of Center – that there should be more care taken to protect the Aztec heritage of Nebraska. But even that slip ended up working to his benefit, when a local member of the Pawnee tribe, native to Nebraska, asked if he perhaps meant the Pawnee and Arapaho peoples. Romulus saw a chance to retrieve the situation and immediately said, yes, that was what he meant – he had been reading a book about the Aztecs, he claimed, and alleged that that accounted for his slip. When he followed that up by praising the Pawnee and the Arapaho, there were loud cheers and, from that point forward, he painted himself as a champion of Native Americans in Nebraska and beyond.

He challenged his opponents to a debate, but the Republican candidate thought that he was in the lead and saw nothing to gain by getting into a debate with anyone. The Green Party candidate also declined to debate Romulus, stating that, if the Republican candidate would not take part, then the debate would not be serious. But the anarchist candidate, representing the Nebraskan Anarchist Anti-Government and Anti-Party Party, accepted the invitation. The debate between Wolf Romulus, listed as an independent but in reality the Mafia candidate, given the generous backing by Rossini, and Caitlin Chester, candidate of the anarchist party, took place two weeks before the election. It was agreed to hold the debate at Carhenge, where locals had taken vintage American-made automobiles and used them to replicate England's Stonehenge.

"Ladies and gentlemen," the mayor of Carhenge began. "We are thrilled to welcome Wolf Romulus, independent candidate, and Caitlin Chester, candidate of the Nebraskan Anarchist Anti-Government and Anti-Party Party, to Carhenge. We Carhengians are proud of our Carthaginian heritage, of our hard work, of our steadfastness, and of our very own Carhenge. The format for this debate is that each candidate will present a short talk, with the opposing candidate being allowed to interrupt as often as he or she wishes, and then we shall open up the floor to questions, objections, and declarations of agreement. To decide which candidate will speak first, we rely on the very fair American tradition of paper-scissors-rock. So, candidates, one-two-three."

Romulus' self-image was reflected in his choosing rock, but Chester chose paper. Paper wraps rock, as everyone knows. So she spoke first.

"Comrades," she started, provoking looks of dismay and concern throughout her audience, "government is a great evil. If elected governor, I will do away with government – "

"No you won't!" snapped Romulus. "You'll collect the paycheck, enjoy the governor's mansion, and engage in some semblance of governing!"

"You don't know that!" she responded testily. "Government is not what Abraham Lincoln promised us – government of the people, by the people, for the people. No, it has become government of the rich, by the rich, and for the rich!" Cheers among some of those present, with some people shouting "She's right!" and "Right on!" "People can administer their own affairs. Factories should be operated by the workers, not by capitalist masters."

"You're talking like a communist," Romulus observed.

"The communists used good anarchist formulas for their own purposes," Chester responded. "Communists are exploiters, just like capitalists. As the old saying has it, 'Under capitalism, man exploits man; under communism, it's the other way around!' So the task then is to do away with all forces of oppression – bureaucracy and paperwork" – again, cheers among those present at the thought of an end to paperwork – "the police, the factory owners, and the priests."

"What's wrong with priests?" Romulus challenged.

"Since the existence of God has not been proven and since, even if God exists, He does not seem to have a lot to say, we should close the churches. Whatever else is clear to me," Chester added, "it seems rather unlikely that any God is interested in listening to the same songs week after week, year after year, century after century."

"There you're wrong," Romulus rebutted. "People are smart, and if smart people build churches, we should take it as a given that they know something. In other words, the existence of churches proves the existence of God. As for God's taste in songs, if He did not like hearing the songs we sing, He could certainly let us know. We certainly don't need to expect Him to constantly tell us that he still likes listening to 'Come to the church in the wildwood'."

"Let's not get lost in a theological dispute," Chester began.

"You started it!"

"The point is that all oppression, all inequality must end. Everyone must be treated equally."

"So," Romulus challenged, "equal pay for the productive and the unproductive, for the skilled and the unskilled, for the competent and the incompetent? Is that your plan?"

"Yes, that's right," answered Caitlin Chester, sticking to principle but committing what would be reported on all of Nebraska's television news channels as her greatest mistake in the debate. "Why should incompetent people be treated as less worthy than competent people? Why should lazy people be discriminated against? They should be cherished for who they are, and valued as humans. Down with meritocracy! Rewards for everyone!"

At that, Mayor Mungo declared that it was Wolf Romulus' turn to speak.

"Fellow Nebraskans," Romulus began and was immediately cheered for this more suitable way of addressing his audience. "I want to begin by noting that the Republican candidate and the Green candidate were too ashamed of their programs to accept our invitation to come to Carhenge for a debate. The Republican candidate is, in fact – and here I expect that Ms. Chester will agree with me – the servant of the rich and not of good, ordinary folk like all of you here. The Green candidate runs around talking about shrubs and weeds: 'Save the dandelion!' he shouts on every corner –" In fact the Green Party candidate said nothing of the sort, but Romulus was engaging in effective political rhetoric. "Both of them were too ashamed, too cowardly, and too self-important to come to this debate. They think that they are too important to explain their views to ordinary folks like you and me. I think this is disgusting.

"At least Ms. Chester, crazy anarchist though she may be, had the good sense and the courage to come here today to explain and defend her insane views. So we should acknowledge her with a little applause." And here, Romulus clapped his hands quietly, with the audience joining in for what was clearly a polite applause only. "What of my own program? First of all, I promise as governor to maintain the infrastructure of the Great State of Nebraska. That means that I will authorize a thorough and comprehensive inspection of all highways, bridges, school buildings, and public buildings throughout the Great State of Nebraska."

People started to cheer at hearing that, until Chester objected, "You will turn our state into a state of inspectors and inspected."

"Ladies and gentlemen," replied Romulus, "you can see how our well-meaning anarchist thinks. Next thing, she will object to people going to their physicians for check-ups."

"No I won't!"

"Next on my agenda," Romulus continued, "will be to undertake an environmental inventory, to make an up-to-date and accurate tally of all wildlife in the state, whether mammals, birds, fish, reptiles, amphibians, or other creatures. I will then coordinate with the Nebraska Department of Environmental Quality to assure that all necessary protections are in place, both to preserve appropriate numbers of all species, but also to control the levels of rats, jack rabbits, mosquitoes, and lice. We don't want to eliminate mosquitoes –"

"Yes, we do!" shouted someone in the audience.

"We don't want to eliminate mosquitoes," Romulus explained, "because they are the main source of nutrition for bats, which in turn give us guano, which makes excellent fertilizer. My third order of business will be to attend to the introduction of political science classes in all elementary schools and high schools throughout the state..." Looks of puzzlement throughout the audience. "And fourth – " Romulus was just about to start to talk about how men would look more debonair if they all wore moustaches, when a passenger airline soared over the audience. Everyone became distracted by that and stared at the sky in wonder. After the plane had passed, Mayor Mungo decided that they had all heard enough speech-making and called for questions.

The first question came from one of Chester's fellow anarchists. "Question to candidate Romulus," said the anarchist. "Have you read Mikhail Bakunin's *Statism and Anarchy*, and what do you think about it?"

"Actually," replied Romulus, "since I have been trained as a political scientist, I naturally read Bakunin's book in the course of my studies. As for what I make of it – I think it is of historical interest only."

"You're wrong!" the anarchist in the audience growled.

"Next question!"

An elderly lady raised herself out of her wheelchair, lifted her cane and wanted to know how each of the candidates would propose to resolve the dispute she had with her neighbor, who, she alleged, was stealing her sheep.

"No, I'm not," said an elderly man also in a wheelchair.

"This is, of course, something to be resolved through the courts," answered Romulus, "and is not something in which the governor's office would involve itself."

"Forget the courts," interjected Chester. "The court system should and will be abolished. You will create comrades' courts at the local level and any disputes will be resolved by your comrades, by your fellow Carhengians, in this case."

"I don't like most of the people around here," the elderly woman objected.

"Under anarchism," Chester explained, "we all learn to love one another and work together harmoniously, abolishing war, conflict, disagreements, and bitterness and living together in happy harmony."

"Right on!" said her fellow anarchist.

"Bullshit," said the elderly woman.

A gas station attendant, clearly identifiable by his brand work shirt, raised his hand and was recognized. "What I want to know is about services – such as fire protection, police, health care, water and electricity. How will these work without government?"

"They won't," Romulus said.

"It's my turn," Chester pointed out. "Anarchism does not mean an end to services, it means only an end to service-providers. We eliminate the service-providers in order to service ourselves. All of you can become electricians, water suppliers, health providers, fire fighters, and police and, if you wish, to divide the labor and agree on specializations. That is what real democracy is all about!"

"No, it's not," Romulus pointed out.

"Yes, it is."

"One more question," Mayor Mungo said.

"I am not satisfied with what I have heard so far," a young man in the audience said. He then played what he considered his trump card: "Here in the Great State of Nebraska, our way of life and our security are threatened by waves of immigrants from Colorado crossing illegally over the Nebraska-Colorado border. The border is not even properly policed. I know this because I drove across it in both directions, just to see if I would be stopped or checked. But there are no checkpoints. It is as if no one is even aware of the threat."

"Since candidate Romulus usurped the first answer last time," candidate Chester declared, "I will answer first. Under anarchism, there are no borders, no police, no checkpoints. We are all free."

"That's a lot of rubbish," the young man said. "I want to hear from Romulus, who is probably the only serious candidate in the race."

Romulus weighed his words carefully. "Here in the Great State of Nebraska," he began, "we have it good, very good, and obviously people in other states can become jealous. Just as obviously, if everyone in every other state decided to move to Nebraska, we would have a housing shortage and problems finding jobs for all of them and accommodating all of them with medical care. Somehow, however, I don't see that we need to worry about Nebraska's population mushrooming to over 300 million people. For one thing, that would mean draining the other states of their populations and leaving them open to Russian takeover."

"Yeah, that's right," said someone. "This man is smart."

"But look, Coloradans might be a bit strange and they talk a bit funny. And sure, they are constantly saying 'green chile is not chili' and 'just keep heading towards the mountains' and 'rocky mountain oysters are not shellfish' – " Here he was interrupted by calls of "What are they, then?" But he ignored the question and continued. "but if they want to visit the Great State of Nebraska, we should welcome them. After all, when we Nebraskans go shopping in Denver, we can always count on a friendly welcome."

The entire event was covered live on all the major Nebraskan news channels and even on a couple of news channels in Colorado. As they presented it, Romulus was clearly the winner in this debate and all the channels berated the Republican and Green Party candidates for failing to show up. After the debate, GSN pollsters reported that a survey of Nebraskans showed that 72% of them planned to vote for Romulus, 12% favored the anarchist, 5% preferred the Green Party candidate, and 1% still planned to vote Republican. The rest gave incomprehensible answers.

Election Day in Nebraska

The governorship was not the only office being contested on election day. In fact, 25 of the 49 seats in the Nebraska Legislature – which some people mistakenly called the state senate – were up for grabs, and the various candidates across the state were busy making promises to the constituents they hoped to have. Among those who had decided to run for office was none other than Eustadiola von Kletten. Unlike Romulus, she was not running at the behest of her washing machine. It was rather a response to hearing that Romulus was running for the governorship. The Democratic and Republican parties had already picked their nominees for the Legislature, as had the Green Party, the American Reform Party (not to be confused with the Reform Party of Nebraska, which also had chosen its candidates), the Libertarian Party, the Unity Party of Nebraska, the Disunity Party of Eastern Nebraska (which promoted "none of the above" for every legislative seat in Nebraska), the Beer Brewers' Party, the Monarchist Party of Central Nebraska, and the Nebraskan Anarchist Anti-Government and Anti-Party Party. Von Kletten decided against running as an independent. So, with Friday's encouragement, she refounded the Bull Moose Party, which had served as Teddy Roosevelt's vehicle for his presidential run in 1912, after he got fed up with the way his erstwhile friend, William Howard Taft, was running the country. Besides, he didn't like Taft's campaign song, "Get on a raft with Taft, boys, get on a raft with Taft." What this meant is that, while Romulus was running for governor against three other candidates, Von Kletten had several more candidates vying for the seat she was seeking.

Election day came and the results amazed many in the state. Romulus, a newcomer to politics, mopped up with a record-breaking 85% of the vote, exceeding even the dramatic forecast offered in the poll. Von Kletten also gained office, albeit with a slender 53% of the vote – but impressive enough given the larger field of candidates for the post of senator from Lincoln County, in which both Uptown and North Platte are located. Uptownians were ecstatic to learn that two of their own had won office and gathered in downtown Uptown to celebrate the event with a huge barbeque, fireworks, and a goat-chasing contest. Some of the youngsters went out to the railway tracks to play chicken as the Nebraska Pacific Express roared into town. Fortunately, none of these brave young Americans were killed.

The inauguration of incoming Governor Romulus took place just four weeks after his election. As usual, the swearing in of a new governor was a gala event, with flags, songs, prayers (always a good idea, but perhaps especially now), popcorn, peanuts, military parades, speeches, and of course the swearing in of the new governor. Justice Crippin administered the oath of office to Governor-Elect Romulus.

"Congratulations, Governor Romulus," said Justice Crippin. "It is your show now."

With that incoming Governor Romulus presented a short speech, in which, alongside the usual mundane promises, he also promised to encourage the growing of moustaches and to put Colorado in its place. After that, following an example already set in other states, he announced that there would be a concert – in this case, by the Uptown Mafia Bah Bah Band – followed by a banquet. The next day, he announced the composition of his cabinet. Perry MacPerry, Uptown's very own enthusiast for higher taxes, was named Chief Assessor in the State Tax Assessor's Office. Micky Rossini came in a Chief of Revenue for the State of Nebraska, and took unpaid leave from the University of Western Uptown. Rossini's associate, Frankie "Frankie Boy" Puccini, became Chief of the Department of Correctional Services, while another associate of his, Antonio "Jelly Fish" Zappola, became Chief of the Nebraska Department of Banking and Finance. Domenico "Vinny" Piccolo, Romulus' erstwhile waiter at his Steakhouse and Particle Accelerator, was named Chief of the Nebraska Crime Commission, and Romulus also named Vincente "Matches" Graziano to serve as Fire Marshal for the State of Nebraska. Billy Bob Pergolesi came in as Commander of the Nebraska National Guard, with the rank of General, and Paolo "Smiley" Lastorino, yet another of Rossini's colleagues, took office as Nebraska's first-ever Foreign Minister. This last appointment was described as controversial by the *Omaha Prairie Bison*, since it was not obvious to everyone that Nebraska was in a position to conduct its own foreign policy. This was yet to be seen.

Romulus also found appropriate offices for his closest associates. Thus, Gabe Carver became Inspector General, overseeing the Department of Motor Vehicles, as well as Inspector General of the state's Liquor Control Commission. Hank Milliner was put in charge of Nebraska's Board of Mental Health, curiously headquartered in Omaha, rather than in Lincoln. Spank Milliner was named Chief of the Office of Historical Heritage, overseeing the state's museums, also located in Omaha. Romulus recognized that people had the right to complain but he did not think that it was a good idea to allow complaints to funnel through the system. So he named his dog Fierce as chief of the Complaints Office. When Rossini advised Romulus that, if his dog was going to hold an official post, he would need a family name, Romulus came up with the name Devil – hence, Fierce Devil. And finally, he chose Toby – who else? – to serve as Special Adviser to the Governor, and moved the washing machine into the Governor's office. As for the other posts in the cabinet, well, they are not terribly important and, in any case, most of those named to those posts ended up spending most of their time at the famous Nebraska Riviera at the Sherman Reservoir and State Recreation Area. That was enough for his first day in office, but on Day Two, Romulus' first act was to pardon the Holloway/Maverick brothers for their caper in the Museum of Grecian Archeology and also to pardon the museum's curator, Agamemnon Alcibiades, for having harassed the brothers, two fine Americans, who were just looking out for the public good. Alcibiades immediately protested, alleging that he had done nothing for which he needed a pardon. But Romulus smoothed Alcibiades' feathers by arranging for the purchase, on the state budget, of an ancient Grecian urn, identical to the one which the Maverick brothers had stolen. The new urn was purchased from the National Archaelogical Museum in Athens, for six times its stated value – a little boost for the Greek economy and a real people pleaser for visitors to Omaha's Museum of Grecian Archeology.

In the meantime, the results of the election for the state Legislature came in. Half of the Legislature's 49 seats had been up for election and, when the results came in, it turned out that Nebraska's voters had turned against the traditional parties: the Democratic and Republican parties managed to garner just two seats each. The remaining 21 seats were divided among six other parties, with the Beer Brewers' Party entering with a strong 10-seat bloc, and the Monarchist Party taking the second largest slice of the cake, with six seats. The Bull Moose Party won one seat, meaning that Eustadiola von Kletten now took her seat as a state senator in Nebraska, while two anarchists also won seats. The Democratic and Republican parties continued to be well represented in the Legislature, however, since they occupied most of the seats which were not up for reelection that year. The salary for a senator in the Nebraska Legislature is $12,000 per year. The salary is kept low in order to encourage the senators to mix with the people and to enter into mutually rewarding arrangements.

Romulus wanted to be a mover and a shaker and wanted to live up to his two campaign slogans – to bring sanity back to the state's capital and to "seek only the good of the people" (especially of himself and his friends). He therefore decided that he was going to tackle environmental pollution and "Nebraska warming", by which he meant the effects of global warming in the Great State of Nebraska. His idea was that he could rule by decree and ignore the legislature. His solution was to impose strict standards with which companies emitting contaminants into the atmosphere had to comply. If they could not comply, they could show "good faith" by making a donation to the Governor's "environmental fund". This fund, controlled by Romulus personally, soon became a huge war chest, which the Governor promised to use for the benefit of all Nebraskans.

He also declared that he planned to convert the Nebraska National Guard into The Army of the Great State of Nebraska, retaining General Pergolesi as commander. Romulus subsequently issued a decree, drafting all able-bodied Nebraskan young men, upon reaching age 21 into this new army. Of course, Romulus, as Governor, would be commander-in-chief of this army. Within the Legislature, there was immediately controversy. Von Kletten led the charge, pointing out that it was contrary to the U.S. Constitution for him to raise an army. Romulus replied that the difference between a national guard and an army was a fine point and that, if she wanted, she could challenge this in the Supreme Court – where the hearing would likely be scheduled anywhere from six to eight years later, at best. Romulus also decreed that Nebraska would henceforth be an Empire and that he was its Emperor and should be addressed as "Your Imperial Majesty". Von Kletten was by no means alone in arguing that this too was unconstitutional, but Emperor Wolf I insisted that this was just terminology and that, in America, one can call things what one likes. Within the Legislature, von Kletten now entered into discussions to see if there was a consensus to impeach the Governor. Unfortunately, the two anarchists made such a ruckus, insisting that all government was illegitimate and that, hence, impeachments were just as illegitimate as elections, that the senators became rather confused and von Kletten's initiative died on the table.

This was followed by the Governor-Emperor's decree calling for a thorough and comprehensive inspection of all highways, bridges, school buildings, and public buildings throughout the Empire of Nebraska. After this, came Romulus' decree calling on all adult males resident in Nebraska to grow moustaches, another decree to introduce political science classes in elementary schools, and a vindictive decree calling for the closure of the physics department at UWU. He had overstepped his authority on all of these points, but most obviously when it came to the physics department; UWU's new president, Joe Friday, told Romulus directly that the governor's office did not have the authority to shut down university departments, or even to touch university budgets.

Romulus' cabinet served him well. The Maverick brothers, now that they had been amnestied, were able to give up their Hand and Spank pseudonyms and revert to their actual names. They took on their new assignments with admirable enthusiasm. Brother Bart kept a close eye on the museums of the state, especially on the Museum of Grecian Archeology and warned the curator that he should improve security at the museum or face consequences. Brother Bret, as chief of the Board of Mental Health, rewarded his old friend, Miklos, by bringing him to Omaha as his well-paid deputy chief. The two of them resumed weekly visits to the Loup City Diner, sometimes with Brother Bart along, sometimes not. Brother Bret also instituted weekly inspections of the Happy Trails Institute and did his best to keep Dr. Freundlich on his toes.

Gabe Carver, acclaimed back in Uptown for his keen knowledge of wines, beers, and hard liquors, now took advantage of his dual responsibilities to advocate for ending the ban on drunk driving. Carver said that drunks were being discriminated against and that it was time to end decades, if not centuries of discrimination against alcoholics. If a drunk can manage to open the car door and get in behind the wheel, then he, or she, should enjoy the God-given right to operate the vehicle. He even advised all those who would listen to consult the Ten Commandments where, he noted, there was nothing against getting drunk, let alone against operating a vehicle – a chariot at the time Moses brought the commandments down the hill, a motorized vehicle today – while completely inebriated. Of course, he added, if a drunk cannot manage to get into the car, then of course he or she shouldn't be driving. Over in the Legislature, there was a strong majority that considered Carver's proposal both mad and dangerous, and soon 46 of the 49 senators drew up a demand that Carver be fired. The Disunity Party senator voted against, probably out of principle, and the two anarchists abstained, noting that for them to vote on any bill would be to betray their principles. The *only* bill on which they were prepared to vote would be a bill to dissolve the government of Nebraska. Somehow, Carver survived – possibly due to the lavish banquet Romulus and Rossini threw in Carver's honor, a banquet to which all the senators were invited, and perhaps also to the lavish gifts which they received, as expressions of appreciation for their dedication to protecting the environment, courtesy of the Governor's environmental fund.

Perry MacPerry got to work thinking up justifications to increase taxes. And Frankie "Frankie Boy" Puccini, as chief of the Department of Correctional Services, began a review of all those incarcerated to determine if some of those sitting behind bars might deserve to be brought up for parole early. He identified 239 jail birds who were now quickly released. Subsequently, their records were mysteriously destroyed in a fire at the department's archive unit. And best of all, after a few complaints during the first two weeks of Governor Romulus' term, suddenly there were no more complaints. Apparently, Fierce Devil had cleared up all complaints very effectively.

The Great State of Interstate

There's a corner in the US of A where Nebraska, Colorado, and Kansas meet, and straddling that corner is a town listed in official records as Interstate City. But the citizens of Interstate City don't believe that state taxes are a good thing. So, when Nebraskan tax officials, before MacPerry took over, demanded taxes, locals would claim that their city lay in Colorado. When Coloradan officials seized on this and demanded payment to Denver, locals answered that their city lay in Kansas. And on those few occasions when tax assessors from Kansas called on Interstate City to collect revenue, the locals claimed that their city lay in Nebraska. The folks in this city were happy to pay taxes to the IRS, but none of them were ready to pay state taxes, and they had avoided paying property tax, sales tax, and school tax for so long that the officials empowered to collect them had just given up. But the folks there, in spite of their manipulating their claim concerning where they were located, inconsistently claimed to constitute a state of their own, which would have been the smallest state by far. They called it the Great State of Interstate. Not surprisingly, they had been demanding for several years to have two senators in the U.S. Senate and a congressman in the House of Representatives. After all, they already had a constitution for their state, as well as a three-story Victorian mansion, which they called their Capitol, and had a 10-member unsalaried state senate and even a governor, although he was listed in Nebraska state records as the "mayor" of Interstate City.

Mayor Maddox – or perhaps Governor Maddox – of Interstate had strong opinions about many things. Some years back, he was interviewed by a reporter from *The Uptown Weekly Beacon of Delight*, who wanted to hear the mayor's reaction to the various improvements which the Great State of Nebraska had brought to his city. As that paper reported it, the mayor replied, "First of all, Interstate ain't no city, but a state, which means that I am governor of Interstate, not mayor. There ain't no mayor of Nebraska, seein' how it's a state. Ya know, we was content when we had wooden sidewalks here in Interstate. We had them until about 1965. Maybe it warn't exactly legal, but no one paid it no mind. Then Lyndon Baines Johnson – " he stretched out the word "Baines" – "became president and then the federal government got on our asses and made us put in concrete sidewalks. Hitler's Germany had concrete sidewalks, Stalin's Russia had concrete sidewalks, and now we got 'em too. We are bein' forced to conform. But I ain't no conformist. Once I say the pledge of allegiance to the flag just before breakfast, I am free to do as I please."

Maddox was still raising hell when Romulus was elected Governor, and things would soon come to a head. Previous governors had turned a blind eye to some of the antics of Mayor Maddox and his "senate", but that was about to change.

Highway 666, a major thoroughfare, runs straight through Interstate City or the Great State of Interstate, and a few years back the locals had erected toll booths, to charge tolls on any cars traversing their territory, which did not have Interstate state license plates -- which of course were not recognized by the states of Nebraska, Colorado, or Kansas or anywhere else for that matter. Since the inhabitants of Interstate didn't travel much, the fact that the license plates they were using were not recognized beyond the boundaries of Interstate did not make for any particular inconvenience to them, since they had everything they needed within their city boundaries and saw no need to travel anywhere.

Once Governor Romulus heard about Interstate's anti-tax rebellion, however, he decided that this situation had to be brought to an end. He remembered the Whiskey Rebellion of 1791-1794, when farmers who were distilling their surplus grain and corn into whiskey refused to pay tax. The farmers were even shooting at tax collectors! What did our Nation's first president do? He did what any red-blooded American would do, and raised an equestrian army 13,000 strong and rode at the head of it. After some shooting, the cavalry disarmed the farmers and gave them a choice between prison and tax. Romulus consulted with Toby, since this was a matter of considerable urgency and importance. Toby told him that he should emulate President Washington and that Washington knew what the correct size of his militia was. So Romulus raised a militia of 13,000 horsemen, and rode at the head of this equestrian army, just as Washington had done. So confident was he of success that he embedded a handful of journalists in this force, putting them likewise on horses. When the citizens of Interstate saw this force, 13,000-strong, riding into their state, or city, they were confused but also intimidated. Unlike the Whiskey Rebellion, the Interstate Affair, as it came to be known, did not involve any shooting and, once Emperor Wolf I explained to the Interstatians that they had a choice between prison and giving up their pretensions to be anywhere else than in Nebraska and, with that, to pay Nebraska's state tax, the enthusiasm for paying tax was both remarkable and irresistible. After the citizens of Interstate had submitted to the rule of law, Perry MacPerry, Uptown's very own partisan of higher taxes, arrived, on commission from Governor Romulus, to explain to the Interstatians why they should rejoice at the opportunity to pay higher taxes. MacPerry was booed and some folks started to throw feathers at him, until the now-dismounted cavalrymen standing guard in the hall drew their swords. At that, booing turned to cheers and soon people were shouting "Long live Governor Romulus! We want to pay more taxes! We are tax-payers first, Americans second!" That last slogan was worrisome to the cavalry, but then again enforcing enthusiasm for taxes had been their assignment, and they seemed to have succeeded.

In the wake of this affair, Dr. Siggie Freundlich, the director of the Happy Trails Institute for Not So Severe Mental Disorders, was contacted by KHGI-TV, Kearney's most beloved television news channel. Roger Rover, the TV journalist, was asked to find out what one of Nebraska's most renowned psychiatrists thought about Governor Romulus' mental state. Freundlich rose to the challenge and diagnosed Romulus as suffering from acute paranoid schizophrenia. "And what does this mean exactly," Roger Rover asked, for the benefit of his audience.

"It means that our governor is suffers from delusions, probably accompanied by hallucinations, and is unable to distinguish between what is real and what is not," Freundlich responded in an exceptionally friendly tone. "Paranoid schizophrenics typically have auditory hallucinations, as well as visual hallucinations, and may believe that they are receiving instructions from their toasters or from their lamps, and so on and so forth."

"That's a worrisome diagnosis," Roger Rover noted. "Have you actually spoken with our Governor?"

"I don't need to," Freundlich replied. "The Governor has styled himself as Emperor Wolf I, wants to be addressed as 'Your Imperial Majesty', and has even brought his washing machine to the Governor's office. Of course, we have not heard any explanation as to why he had need of a washing machine, and that specific washing machine in particular, in his office. The historical record shows that he is the first governor of Nebraska to have a washing machine in his office since Nebraska became a state in 1867."

"What do you make of his intention to rename the Nebraska National Guard?"

"That's another thing," Freundlich agreed. "He wants to call it the Army of the Great State of Nebraska. I'd be very surprised if he can get this through the Legislature."

"What would you like to see Governor Romulus do?" Roger Rover asked, baiting the psychiatrist and expecting the answer he got.

"I'd like to see him resign," Freundlich said. "He is completely unsuitable to be in politics – even more unsuitable than our run-of-the-mill politicians, most of whom are acting out their complexes in the public arena. Take, for example, Bret and Bart Holloway – known briefly as Hank and Spank Milliner – these two are completely unstable and were, until they escaped, patients at my institute. They delude themselves into thinking that the Aztecs came to what is now Nebraska and built great cities here. They are, quite frankly, nuts, again like most people who go into politics."

Roger Rover now saw this interview moving into a more dangerous terrain and decided to halt the interview then and there.

"Thank you very much, Dr. Freundlich, for sharing your views with us," said Rover as he signaled the cameraman that the interview was over. As Rover packed up his gear, Freundlich, whose powers of association were keen, had reminded himself, by referring to "nuts", of how much he liked pistachio nuts and reached into his pocket and started to shell the nuts.

When this interview was broadcast on KHGI-TV, an affiliate of ABC, and then went national over various other ABC affiliates, Romulus and the brothers were livid. For a while they contemplated suing Freundlich as well as KHGI-TV, for having broadcast the libelous interview. They consulted Nebraska's Attorney General, Salvatore "the Peacemaker" Lino, to see what he thought. "Nah," said Lino, "ya ain't got a case. You'd have to prove that this interview damaged your reputations, that it changed the way people think about you. How ya gonna do that? However, if it'd pull your weeds, I can send a couple of the boys out to teach this doc a lesson. Do ya want me to do that?"

"No," they said in unison. But then the question was how to respond. Bart came up with the idea of having literally tons of flowers delivered to the institute every day. Since flowers are normally considered nice to receive, he thought that they could not be prosecuted. At the same time, if Freundlich were to have to deal with hundreds of bouquets of flowers arriving at the institute every day, he might rue the day he gave that interview to KHGI-TV. Romulus and Brother Bret did not like that idea, but did not have any better idea. For the time being, nothing was decided.

The Return of the Aztecs

The Brothers had come over to Lincoln for consultations with Emperor Wolf I, but now returned to Omaha, where their respective offices were located. Once back in Omaha, they headed over to their favorite Omaha eatery, Brother Sebastian's Steak House and Winery. Designed as the spitting image of an eighteenth-century California monastery, Brother Sebastian's Steak House serves only the highest grade of beef and its waiters, attired as eighteenth-century style monks, complete with tonsures, can take your order in English, Spanish, or Latin. The Maverick Brothers liked to take dinner in the room identified as "the chapel", seated below a huge painting of St. Jude Thaddeus, the patron saint of "difficult and desperate cases". They had come to Brother Sebastian's Steak House many times already, and the "monks" always gave them a warm greeting. Usually, they had come to "the monastery", as they called it, for great chow, great service, and a sense of being somehow "holy". This time, however, they also hoped to figure out how to respond to Freundlich, whom – frankly – they had never liked.

They remembered how, when they had turned up with their fake Aztec urn, they had succeeded in propelling Romulus into the chairmanship of the department of political science and how it had helped their own careers, if only temporarily. "What if we can produce a *real* Aztec artefact?" Brother Bart wondered out loud. "That can't be impossible."

"In fact, it's entirely possible," Brother Bret replied. "What we need to do is to get ourselves down to Mexico and look around."

"Of course," Brother Bart agreed. "Perhaps a visit to the Gift Shop at the National Museum of Anthropology in Mexico City would work. I am certain that the gift shop will have some fine specimens for sale."

"Bart," said Brother Bret crossly, "you'd to get us into trouble with that idea. The gift shop would not be selling original artefacts, only facsimiles. A facsimile, even if reproducing an original design with care, is only a facsimile, and it won't pass the carbon dating test."

"Oh yes, that's right," replied Brother Bart. "If we're going to do this, we'll need an original Aztec artefact."

The brothers talked this over with Emperor Wolf I, who agreed to subsidize their shopping trip from his environmental fund. The brothers were a fun-loving duo and hence, since this was their first trip south of the border, they decided to take in both Aztec and Mayan sites, and started their visit with a trip to see the Mayan pyramids of Chichen Itza on the Yucatan peninsula. Here was a wonder to behold. They strolled along the row of columns at the Temple of a Thousand Warriors, inspected the Jaguar Throne (Brother Bart wanted to sit on it, but fortunately his brother pulled him away before they got into any trouble), marveled at the feathered serpent sculpture at the foot of the huge pyramid the Spaniards called El Castillo, played ball in the Mayan ball park, and swam in the well. "Do you know how the peninsula came to be called Yucatan?" Brother Bret said.

"No clue," Brother Bart admitted.

"Well," said Brother Bret, who was always in the know. "The first Spanish explorers, coming to the region, asked the local Maya people what the region was called and they replied 'I don't know what you're saying'. The Maya word for that expression is 'Yucatan'. So the peninsula is 'I don't know what you're saying peninsula'. Are you impressed?"

"Not so much," Brother Bart admitted.

"And you know that the Mayans abandoned Chichen Itza in the fourteenth century," Brother Bret commented, again showing off his knowledge, as the two brothers stood at the foot of the Mayan observatory, gazing upwards.

"What a pity," said Bart. "It's nice here."

"And more than nice," said Bret. "But, of course, it's not Aztec."

A local guide overheard the brothers talking and came over to them. "So you want Aztec things, right?" he said. "Mayan is good, but Aztec is also good."

"OK, we're game."

"The Mayans may have built the pyramids and the observatory here, but the Aztecs infiltrated Mayan civilization and took some of the best jobs," the guide said, making it up as he went along. "Even now, the descendants of the Mayan people remember fondly the Aztec bakers who baked corn bread here at Chichen Itza. Would you like to go cycling?"

Bret was not keen on this, but Brother Bart leapt at the idea, and, of course, the local guide had bicycles for rent. Soon, the three men were cycling around the Yucatan peninsula, eventually stopping at a fruit bar, to enjoy some fruit native to Yucatan: sugar apples, caimito, nance, sour orange, guanabana, dragon fruit, custard apple, chicozapote, and chocolate fruit were among the exotic fruit available. Since they were curious about all of these, they ordered a mixed fruit salad, and treated their palates to some extraordinary tastes.

It was time to move on. They could scarcely pretend that the side trip to the Mayan world counted as either research or artefact huntings. But to procure real Aztec artefacts, they needed to get to Mexico City. One plane ride later, they headed over to the 5-star Four Seasons Hotel in Mexico City, situated on the Paseo de la Reforma. In addition to all those things which one might expect in any 5-star hotel, the Four Seasons Hotel offered also live Aztec entertainment, with Aztec eagle warriors dancing to Aztec music played on Aztec instruments. The warrior-dancers stomped out, with huge headdresses and carrying decorated shields in their left hands and maracas in their right hands, and pranced around on the stage at the center of the courtyard café. Although drums are the most important instrument in Aztec music, the Aztecs also played clay flutes, conch shell trumpets, and gongs. All of these were played for one or another Aztec dance at the Four Seasons. This was, of course, clearly research, and the Maverick Brothers were all too happy to let the Governor pick up the tab for their week-long stay at the Four Seasons.

As they sat down in the courtyard café one afternoon, to enjoy one of the finest lunches on the planet, Brother Bart turned to the waiter and said, "Hey, señor, where can we buy some Aztec artefacts?"

"Ah, you want Aztec artefacts," the waiter acknowledged. "Do you want authentic ones or cheap copies?"

"What do you take us for," Brother Bart objected, "we want authentic ones, regardless of the cost."

"Muy bien," the waiter replied. "Do you see that woman seated at the table under the orange plastic palm tree?"

"Yes, we do," said Brother Bret.

"I happen to know that she can help you fulfill your hearts' desire," the waiter said, "in the area of Aztec artefacts. I will talk to her and see if she is willing to come over to your table."

The waiter sauntered over to this mysterious lady's table, talked to her briefly. The two of them turned in the direction of the brothers and flashed an amiable smile. The waiter then returned to the table where the two brothers were sitting and told them that the Contessa, Antonina Federica Baltazar Talamantez Aragón, invited them to join her at her table. When they asked for the check, the waiter informed them that the Contessa had already paid their bill.

"Welcome, gentlemen," said the Contessa as the brothers came to their table. "Please be seated. I am the Contessa, Antonina Federica Baltazar Talamantez Aragón."

"It is an honor," said Brother Bret. "I am Bret Holloway, and this is my brother, Bart."

"Like Bret and Bart Maverick, right?" she said. "I remember the television series very well. James Garner played Bret Maverick."

"You have an excellent memory," said Brother Bret, "and, in fact, we are often called the Maverick Brothers."

"I understand from Juan, that you are interested in Aztec artefacts."

"That's right," said one of the brothers. It does not matter which one said this.

"Well," the Contessa explained, "you have a choice here. If you want to purchase your artefacts legally, I can help you directly, as I own a shop where I sell Aztec, Mayan, and other pre-Columbian artefacts. If you purchase something from me legally, I can give you a certificate of authenticity and also a certificate guaranteeing you the right to take the artefact out of the country."

"A certificate of authenticity would be perfect," Brother Bart said.

"There's also the other option," the Contessa revealed. "You can also purchase Aztec artefacts on the black market."

"What's the advantage with that?" Brother Bret wanted to know.

"It may be that you can get things on the black market which I do not list in my catalogue. You might even be able to request that your contact locate something specific. What actually are you looking for?" she asked.

"We'd probably want to purchase several objects," Brother Bret noted, "at least four or five, so that, when we bury them and unearth them with witnesses, we can call it *the Aztec hoard.*"

"Si. Yo comprendo," she replied. "Let's do it this way. I will leave a catalogue from my shop at the front desk later this evening. You can then pick it up and see what you think. And if you want something not in my catalogue or simply want to explore other possibilities, I can introduce you to Guillermo Batista Gabaldon, who is a dear friend of mine. He lives in Mazmorra, the old dungeon – now converted into a lavishly decorated villa – which is a 45-minute taxi ride from here. He is fluent in English, of course, and would be happy to talk with you. We can discuss this tomorrow over lunch. Shall we say 2 p.m. here?"

The brothers were delighted with her response, and also with the fact that she treated them to two rounds of tequila with cactus juice. Later that night, they checked at the front desk and found the catalogue she had promised. She had several official clay stamps, dating from 1450 to 1500, to press a seal into wax; these ranged in price from $450 to $600 each. She also had a small ceramic head dating from around 1400, with $320 as the asking price. She also had a clay figure of a dwarf in elaborate costume dating from about 800 AD, with a price tag of $475, a tripod dish, a decorated bowl, and various other heads of women and men, mostly in clay, as well as a remarkable clay figurine of what looked like an Aztec god (although the Contessa was noncommittal as to which god might be represented by the figurine). There was no Aztec gold on offer in her catalogue, but there was enough to "prove" that the Aztecs had come to Nebraska and settled down there. Still, they were curious about what they could obtain on the black market. So, when they returned to the plaza café the next day, they told her that they would like to purchase several items from her catalogue, but also wanted to meet Guillermo Batista Gabaldon. They told her that they hoped that he could sell them some Aztec gold jewelry. Her reply was encouraging, as she assured them that there was still Aztec jewelry to be purchased in Mexico, but she warned them that neither she nor Gabaldon could provide them with a certificate entitling them to take artefacts acquired through his good offices out of the country. Still, she told them that Gabaldon could help them get whatever they would purchase out of Mexico.

After a lunch, consisting of black bean and corn salad (served with cilantro and fresh lime juice), lamb stuffed with chorizo, rice with anaheim peppers, and dessert consisting of cinnamon cookies, margarita cake, tequila-infused strawberries, and tortilla sundaes with minted mango salsa – all at her expense – she offered to accompany them to see Gabaldon. As she had forecast, the taxi ride to Mazmorra took about 45 minutes, taking them up a hill to the edge of a lake, where the old dungeon had been built. Although it was a tall and imposing structure, she advised them that they should descend the steps to the basement, as that was where Gabaldon usually spent his time. As they drew near, they could hear someone, presumably Gabaldon, playing Johann Sebastian Bach's Passacaglia and Fugue in C minor (BWV 582) on the pipe organ. This took them by surprise. When the Contessa saw their surprise, she asked them, "What did you think? That Mexican people listen to nothing but mariachi?"

"No, sorry," said Brother Bret. "It's just that hearing Bach here was, let us say, not what we had expected."

"Fine. Let's go in." She had to rap very hard with the molded iron knocker before Gabaldon heard her knock. The organ stopped abruptly as he walked to the door with heavy steps. "Bienvenidos," he said as he opened the door. "Buenos dias, Contessa. Cómo está usted?"

"Muy bien," she replied, "and you?"

"Ah, you have come with Americans. I am fine. Come on in,"

Gabaldon said. "There are more than 190 countries in the world. Guess how many of them I have visited?"

"All of them(?)," Brother Bret ventured cautiously.

"No," Gabaldon replied, "I have not had time to visit all of them yet. But I have visited 125 countries so far. Have you ever been to Gabon?" They shook their heads. "I have visited there five times. How about Bhutan?" Again they shook their heads. "I have been there six times. How about Nunivak Island?"

"No, we haven't, and what is it?" asked Brother Bret.

"It is an island in the Bering Sea, belonging to your country and counted as part of Alaska. I have been there only once, but it was very interesting." Then, after a moment, he introduced himself. "I am Guillermo Batista Gabaldon. What are your names and what can I do for you?"

"We are Bret and Bart Holloway – "

"Ah," said Gabaldon, picking up the tune. "Like Bret and Bart Maverick."

"Yes," said Brother Bret, "it seems that everyone in the world has seen that series."

" —and what I can do for you."

"We want to buy Aztec gold artefacts," offered Brother Bart.

"Ah, well you have come to the right place," Gabaldon said. "How much do you have to spend?"

"Money is no object," Brother Bret said, "since we can charge the costs to the environmental fund of the Governor of Nebraska."

"Si, señor, gold is very good for the environment," he joked, chuckling a bit.

"We are authorized to draw upon that fund for purchases here in Mexico."

"Well, in that case, let me tell you how this works. I offer you some possibilities and tell you what they cost. You then pay me 20% of the cost of everything you order as a down payment. When the items arrive, if you like them, you pay the balance. If you don't like them, you don't have to buy them, but I keep the down payment and split it with my contact, who has to bring the items you want here. We do not work for nothing. Convenido?"

The brothers guessed that "convenido" must mean "agreed" and said yes.

Gabaldon had much to offer, including large decorative gold shields depicting various Aztec gods, kings, and warriors, gold jewelry, and gold coins. After discussing the price, they decided on two gold shields, a variety of gold jewelry, a gold statuette, about two dozen gold coins, and five of the items which the Contessa had for sale. The total bill for this treasure was in the vicinity of $240,000. They telephoned Romulus back in Lincoln and told him of their success. Romulus had not been apprised of this in advance, but he was very pleased with them and did not think the figure too high, since local corporations had been pouring millions of dollars into his "environmental fund". He immediately wired the funds to them at the Four Seasons Hotel, plus another $20,000 so that they could rent a van and return to Nebraska in comfort. The issue then was how to get all of this over the border.

Just as the Contessa had foretold, Gabaldon knew how the system worked and advised them to rent a very large van and to take along 20 cases of the finest whiskey. Whenever they would be stopped by the Mexican army, they should make gifts of whiskey and, when they got to the border, they should explain that they had purchased some artefacts legitimately, and show them the certificate from the Contessa. They should not say anything about the items acquired through Gabaldon's black market sources. Instead, they should mention that they had some cases of whiskey and wanted to give them away in Mexico. The border guards would be so pleased that they would, at the very most, glance inside the van. Going through the van and inspecting it carefully is, after all, work and, while Mexican border guards are as happy as border guards in any country to undertake thorough searches, it is easier just to wave people through, especially when they have given you crates of fine whiskey. With these reassurances from Gabaldon, the brothers finalized the deal and paid the down payment already the next day. The Contessa delivered the artefacts from her shop the same day, while those from Gabaldon took only another three days and, by day four, the brothers had paid the grand sum of $240,000, packed the items into their rental van, and were happily driving northward.

The Mexico-Nogales Highway, also known as Federal Highway #15, is the principal north-south highway in Mexico, starting in Mexico City and running northward to the border with Arizona. Given their recent experience in Nebraska, Brother Bret was not about to let Brother Bart drive, lest he take them southward to Guatemala. So, with Bret behind the wheel, Bart sampling the whiskey, and a van full of treasure, the twosome took their leave of the Contessa and Gabaldon, and started their trek northward.

As they set out, Brother Bart disclosed to Brother Bret that he thought that the Contessa had fallen in love with him.

"In love with you?" came Brother Bret's astonished reply. He found this suggestion amusing.

"Yes, of course," Brother Bart insisted. "Didn't you notice the way she looked at me?"

"Yes, I did. With complete disinterest. She looked more fondly at the waiter."

"Oh, you are being unkind."

"You and your fantasies," Brother Bret mused. "I remember your fantasy that our assistant dean, Debbie Sue Stefanovich, was in love with you. And then there was your fantasy that the waitress at the Loup City Diner was in love with you. Your evidence was that she recognized you!! Given that we were visiting the diner every week, of course she recognized you – and for that matter me, and also Miklos. Was she in love with all three of us then?"

"It's different this time," Brother Bart said quietly. "I can feel it. This is true love."

"Have you kissed her?"

"No. When did I have a chance?"

"Well, we are leaving Mexico now."

"We don't have to," Brother Bart stated with apparent clarity of mind. "We can turn around and head back to Mexico City. I will propose to her, we will get married, and the three of us can live happily ever after."

"The three of us? That is some fantasy," remarked Brother Bret. "Good thing I'm driving. We are not turning around."

After that, there was a lull in the conversation. So Brother Bret turned on the van's radio and looked for a station carrying mariachi music. The first 132 miles were more or less uneventful. But, soon after they passed the city of Santiago de Querétaro, best known for its enormous aqueduct, with 75 huge arches still standing, they saw military vehicles on the highway and a soldier signaling them to turn off the highway. As they turned off and pulled onto a country road, they found themselves surrounded by about 30 soldiers, with what seemed to be hundreds just a few hundred meters away, relaxing in their jeeps. Bart became very scared. Fortunately, Brother Bret stayed calm. As they stopped their van, a colonel approached their open window and said, "You are Americans, yes?"

"Yes, that's right," answered Brother Bret.

"And we love Mexico and everyone in it," added Brother Bart quickly, without thinking.

"Well, we love Mexico too," the colonel noted, "and we love Americans who love Mexico. How would you like to show us your love of Mexico?"

"We will kiss the ground, if that would please you," said Brother Bart.

"Please ignore my brother, generalissimo," said Brother Bret. "He's an idiot. We have some whiskey and, if it would please you, we would be honored if you would accept a crate of Yamazaki single malt whiskey as our token of appreciation of your great country."

"I like the way you think," the colonel replied. "What is your name?"

"Bret Maverick, or actually Bret Holloway," Brother Bret replied. "But everyone calls us the Maverick brothers."

"Bien, Bret Maverick. We will accept your gift and escort you as far as León. There are some bandidos who ride horses and stop vehicles on the stretch of road between here and León. But, if we are along, they will leave you alone."

With this, Brother Bret handed over a crate of Yamazaki whiskey to the colonel, and then the brothers drove off, accompanied by four military jeeps, brandishing some state-of-the-art weaponry. It was smooth sailing now, at least as far as León, although they could see bandidos on horseback not so far from the highway. They were shooting their guns in the air and, unless the brothers misheard, it sounded like they were shouting something about Nebraska. After just over two hours, they reached the turn-off for León. The military escort now took its leave of them and as the jeeps pulled off, the colonel gave them a friendly wave and wished them a safe journey. "That went well," Brother Bart noted.

The brothers decided to drive through this city of a million and a half inhabitants, drove through the Arco Triunfal de la Calzada de los Héroes, drove past the Catedral Basilica de León, and even stopped briefly to take photos of each other on the Plaza de los Fundadores. Both of them thought it was nice to mix pleasure with business. There were, inevitably, a lot of friendly locals, offering to give them city tours or to sell them local products, but they did not want to delay much longer and got back into their van and continued the drive. Their plan was take a detour on highway 40 and head east to Durango, since they thought that this would be an interesting place to visit and they especially wanted to visit the Pancho Villa museum. There, they planned to overnight at the Hotel Gobernador, another 5-star hotel. Given the various little sightseeing stops along the way, including to play miniature golf, they did not reach the Gobernador until 9 p.m. But they had enjoyed their drive so far, and hoped to make it to Nogales in another two days.

They rose early, enjoyed a short swim in the hotel's courtyard swimming pool and a lavish breakfast involving specialties from the Free and Sovereign State of Durango, as the province is officially called, took time to visit the local Pancho Villa museum, and then telephoned Governor Romulus to report on their progress.

"Are you back in Nebraska?" Governor Romulus asked Bret.

"No, we are still in Mexico. In Durango, to be exact."

"So, why are you calling me? Are you in trouble?"

"No, everything is fine. We just want you to know that we are heading back as fast as we can."

"I can imagine," said the Governor, who had his suspicions that they might be touristing. "Well, be careful. Let me know when you are back on home turf."

By 1:30, they were once more on the road, heading toward back to Highway 15. Once they reached that Highway, at Mazatlan, it was 551 miles to Hermosillo. They imagined that they could cover that distance in 8 hours, but they were now on a coastal road and, to their surprise, they found a large swarm of alligators sun-bathing on the highway, just before they could reach Culiacán. Brother Bart got out of the car and poured whiskey on the alligators, since neither of the brothers had any other ideas, and they had plenty of whiskey. This had an effect on the alligators, who did not react with anything like the level of gratitude displayed by the colonel. They started to become aggressive and emit the rumbling growls characteristic of their species. But, as Brother Bart ran to the side of the highway, the alligators followed him, thus clearing the highway. Brother Bart then used the alligators as a kind of pontoon bridge to get back into the van and soon they were once more on the road.

The brothers had, of course, done some "research" on touristic sights, but they had not informed themselves about the drug wars which had been going on in Culiacán. As they neared the city, they heard what sounded like a gunfight, and locals shouting "Drogas!" and "Muerte!" They did not need a dictionary to know what these words meant, but they thought that probably local filmmakers were making a movie of some sort. Both of them thought it would be great if they could be somehow included in the film and therefore got off the highway to drive straight through downtown Culiacán. It was only now that they realized that this was not about a film, but about local drug gangs battling for territory. They had to give away four crates of Yamazaki whiskey to get out of town safely. But as they left Culiacán behind, Brother Bret commented that they had needed only one crate for the Mexican army. What with the delay with the alligators and then a second delay with the drug war, and finally their decision to pull over to the beach at Topolobampo in order to watch the sunset, it was past 3 a.m. when they finally arrived at their 5-star hotel in Hermosillo.

Given how late it was, they decided to stay for two nights there, and spent the intervening afternoon strolling around the town. They had thought in terms of visiting museums, but when they got to the Plaza Zaragoza, they encountered a group of about two dozen matadors, waving banners and shouting slogans. They approached a local city guide and asked him what was going on. He told them that, because of animal rights activism, bull-fighting was being stopped in most of Mexico's towns and cities, and these matadors were out of work. They wanted to bring back bull-fighting to Mexico. "It's a tradition," the guide told them. "It is hard to break with traditions."

"We also have our traditions," Brother Bart noted. "My brother and I have a tradition of sight-seeing, and that is what we are doing here in Hermosillo."

"It is great that you have come here, of all places," the guide replied. "Most Americans who drive through our town are trying to get something illegal out of our country. I hope that the two of you are not like that."

"Absolutely not, " Brother Bret said a bit too quickly, hoping to cut off his brother before Bart said something which would implicate them in Aztec gold smuggling.

In the evening, they took dinner in the restaurant on the 25th floor of their hotel, where Brother Bart found another woman to fall in love with. She was seated several tables distant, and he did not even talk to her. But he became convinced that she was in love with him and the next day, when the brothers resumed their drive, Brother Bart could not stop telling his brother that he had to choose between the Contessa and the Lady of Hermosillo, as he chose to call her. Brother Bret listened patiently, keeping his comments to a minimum. Nogales lay just over three hours to the north and, with an early start, the brothers reached the border town just after noon. There was a long line of cars, trucks, and vans ahead of them, and some of them were being pulled over to a parking lot for a thorough inspection. As before, Brother Bart became nervous – even jittery this time – while Brother Bret stayed calm. Ultimately, thanks to Gabaldon's good advice, everything went smoothly.

"What do you have in your van, señor?" the Mexican border guard asked.

"We have some Aztec artefacts, which we purchased. Here is our certificate, entitling us to take them out of Mexico." With this, Brother Bret handed the guard the certificate.

The guard was not terribly impressed. "What else do you have?"

"We have some whiskey," answered Brother Bret, while his brother wisely kept quiet. "We would like to show our appreciation for the great time we have had in Mexico by making a gift of whiskey to you and your fellow border guards."

"What kind of whiskey is it, señor?"

"Yamazaki single malt whiskey," Brother Bret responded.

"Ah, the best."

"We would like to give you four crates."

"We'd prefer six crates," the border guard answered.

"That will be our pleasure," Brother Bret answered. He and his brother then unloaded six crates of Yamazaki whiskey, and told the border guard once again how lovely it had been to visit Mexico.

"Gracias, señor," said the border guard as he took possession of the whiskey. "You are most generous. I wish you both a safe and pleasant drive. Come back to Mexico again sometime!"

Of course, there was still the American customs. But here there were rather specific questions: any goods manufactured by convict labor? any goods imported from North Korea? any goods manufactured from feathers of birds on the endangered species list? any fresh fruit? Since the brothers did not have any of these items, they were waved through, as the American customs official welcomed them back to the USA. The rest of the trip was uneventful. Of course, the shortest route to get back to Nebraska would have been to drive north through Arizona to Utah, then turn east driving through Colorado until they reached Nebraska. But, understandably, the brothers wanted to avoid Colorado at all costs. So they drove eastward through New Mexico and into Texas, and then drove north through Oklahoma and Kansas, finally reaching Nebraska after another two nights in 5-star hotels. As they drove into Nebraska and headed toward the Governor's office, they shouted out the van windows, "Nebraska forever! Great to be back in the Great State of Nebraska!"

The Curse of the Aztec Dummy

Upon returning to Nebraska, the brothers headed straight to Lincoln, where they learned that the Governor had now raised an army of 170,000 men, purchased tanks from Russia, converted some passenger planes to "other" uses, and acquired an assortment of other military equipment, as well as ammunition and explosives. As if that was not controversial enough, he was also planning to ban motor vehicles in the Great State of Nebraska, except for tanks, army jeeps, and other military vehicles and to put everyone in horse and buggy. The police, he thought, could ride horses. He told the brothers that he also wanted to ban tobacco throughout the state, and was thinking to suggest to people that they should smoke marijuana instead, or even dandelions. As Toby had told him, marijuana and dandelions had not been linked to cancer, and getting rid of tobacco altogether would make everyone healthier. Toby told him that this would consolidate his claim to be "the environmental and good health Governor".

Von Kletten was already rallying opposition within the state Legislature to the Governor's proposals. She was giving fiery speeches denouncing the Governor's not-yet-formalized claim to be "Emperor" of Nebraska, as well as his suggestion that people should be smoking marijuana and – God help us all – dandelions, and especially the Governor's plans about military preparedness. Von Kletten's activities were causing the Governor a lot of stress and it was therefore, with great pleasure, that he welcomed the brothers, two reliable and proven allies, into his office upon their return. They arrived with a large crate in tow. The Governor was even more pleased to see what treasures they had brought with them.

"We thought we'd bury them in the Okra Hills," Brother Bart said, "and then organize a volunteer archeological team to 'discover' them."

"How will you convince locals that you have a good reason to want to dig in a particular location?" Romulus asked.

"We acquired an old Spanish map of New Spain, including Nebraska," Bret explained. "Bart purchased the map when we were in Mexico City."

"No, I didn't," Bart replied. "I thought that you did."

"No, I had left that to you," Brother Bret said.

"Well, I didn't pick up any map at all."

"Listen brothers," said Romulus. "This is not insoluble. There's a shop downtown –"

"Downtown Uptown?" asked Brother Bart fatuously.

"No, downtown Lincoln," the Governor replied, somewhat testily. "The shop is called Antique Maps and Charts, Something for Everybody. The owner, Oliver Surprise, is a friend of mine. Don't let his name surprise you – he is a serious map collector and knows his wares. Tell him you are a friend of mine and that you want a 16th or 17th century map of the region and see what he says. Surprise is on our side."

"Good," Brother Bret replied. "Consider it done."

"Now let's see what you have brought back." And now the brothers unpacked the crate for the Governor to marvel at the Aztec hoard. He was duly impressed and asked if he might retain one or two items as personal souvenirs.

"Of course, Your Majesty," said Brother Bart.

"Which ones would you like to take?" asked Brother Bret.

"I like this little clay dummy," Romulus said.

"Actually," Brother Bret warned, "that is probably an Aztec god."

"Fine, god or dummy, but I'll take that one. And also this gold shield with a god or king sticking out his tongue."

"Yes, that is a prize all right."

"Do you think there could be a curse on the dummy?"

"Why should there be a curse? Not every dummy comes with a curse," Romulus pointed out. However, while the brothers were still present in his office, Toby offered the Governor his "professional" opinion that the Aztec dummy was probably cursed and that the curse of the Aztec dummy might bring his term as Governor to a premature end. Governor Romulus ignored Toby's warning, telling the washing machine that he did not see how a little doll or dummy could hurt him.

After that, the Governor-King ordered champagne and crumpets for the three of them, and the conversation wandered to other topics. Romulus also told the brothers that Freundlich, the director of the Institute for Not So Severe Mental Disorders, had been going around talking to the state senators and soliciting testimonials concerning the Governor's alleged insanity – and dropping pistachio shells wherever he went. It seemed that Freundlich had something approaching an addiction to pistachio nuts.

"Shall we get him for littering?" suggested Brother Bart.

"Littering is a Class III misdemeanor here in Nebraska," Romulus responded. "Now, if we were in Singapore, the penalty would be $1,000 for the first conviction, $5,000 for the second conviction, and after that community service for the third conviction. But a Class III misdemeanor here in Nebraska brings a fine of only up to $500, and up to three months in jail. I'd like to put Freundlich out of business altogether and not just for three months."

"His obsessive behavior where you are concerned and compulsive behavior where his pistachio nuts are concerned," said Bret, in a moment of genius, "might suggest obsessive compulsive disorder. For that, he would need treatment."

"Bret," said Romulus exuberantly. "You are a genius! This is precisely what we shall do. I'll talk to Rossini and see about contracting an 'independent' psychiatrist."

Later that afternoon, Romulus phoned Rossini and asked for his advice. Rossini responded, "Wolf, putting Freundlich away is an excellent idea. I have a friend who practices psychiatry – Dr. Gennaro 'Brainy' Valentino. He does great work. He has committed more people to psychiatric care than any other doc in New York. His working assumption is that most people are nuts and his motto is 'insane until proven otherwise'. I'll ask him to fly out and meet with Freundlich."

And that is precisely what happened. Less than a week later, Dr. Valentino arrived in Lincoln, by private jet, and agreed to take on the assignment. "Remember," Rossini advised him. "We suspect that Freundlich is mentally unwell. He may need help."

"If you think he is mentally unwell, then so do I," said Valentino, whose long experience had taught him to trust Rossini's judgment.

Valentino began by asking to meet Freundlich, to share their experiences, one professional to another. Freundlich agreed and suggested a meeting over coffee at The Whooping Crane Café in downtown Kearney. Specialties at that café included Extra-Frothy Cappuccino, Guillermo Espresso (poured over slices of lime), Antoccino (espresso with milk), and Budapest Melange (a variant of Wiener Melange). Valentino arrived 15 minutes early, so that he could assess Freundlich's arrival and look for signs of insecurity. Valentino had been shown a photo of Freundlich, but had not shared his own photo with his counterpart. This maneuver was designed to work to Freundlich's disadvantage. Sure enough, when Freundlich arrived, the first thing he did was look around, as if he did not know where he was. Then, rather than approaching Valentino, he took a seat away from the window – again, a telltale symptom of insecurity. Freundlich sat quietly, playing with his napkin and then, after less than two minutes, put his hand into his jacket pocket and retrieved a handful of pistachio nuts. He proceeded to shell them and to drop the shells on the floor. The waitress came over and told him, "We are trying to maintain a clean establishment. Stop throwing your pistachio shells on the floor!"

"I wasn't actually throwing them," stated Freundlich, who liked exact terminology. "I was sweeping them off the table and onto the floor. That's different."

"Well stop it!" the waitress barked.

"OK, OK," said Freundlich. "No need to put your authoritarian personality on full display! I'll have a coffee Americano, and any pastry made with pistachio nuts."

The waitress jotted this down and went back to the bar to fill the doctor's order. At this, Dr. Valentino waved to Freundlich and said, "You must be Freundlich. I have heard about your appreciation of pistachio nuts. Would you like to join me here at the window?"

"We'd be on full view to the outside world," Freundlich observed.

"Is that a problem?"

"No, I can handle it." And with that, Freundlich picked up his used napkin ("partially used" in his terminology) and came over to join Valentino. After they had introduced themselves properly and exchanged the usual pleasantries, Freundlich asked, "So, do I understand correctly that you are interested in how we treat our patients at the institute?"

"Yes. In particular, I want to know about any group counseling sessions you may have."

"We do indeed have group counseling sessions," Freundlich noted, "every Wednesday at noon. We organize them in groups of 22. The patients sit in a circle, and each of them tells the rest how the week has gone for him or her and, after each one talks, I analyze the patient and offer an update on the diagnosis."

"Isn't that a bit busy?"

"How do you do it in New York City?"

"We just let the patients talk to each other. The attending psychiatrist is there mainly to make sure that there are no fights or insults, and to stop anything that looks like trouble."

"So you just let the patients say whatever they want?"

"Within reason, yes."

"Well, that's not the way I operate," Freundlich disclosed. "I want the patients to keep their eye on the ball if they want to make the shot."

"Are you a snooker player, then?"

"Yes, I am," Freundlich admitted, "and I see lots of parallels between snooker and psychiatric care. For example, there are 22 snooker balls and one cue ball. In our counseling circle, I place 22 patients in a circle and I give the cues for them to talk. Also, in snooker, you know when you hit a ball into a pocket. Similarly, in psychiatry, you know when you have gotten an insight. And finally, in snooker, there is always someone waiting to use your snooker table, just as, at our institute, there is always someone wanting to use our counseling room."

"But you're the director, aren't you? You can tell others to wait until you are finished, no?"

"Yes, I am," Freundlich admitted, "and I see lots of parallels between snooker and psychiatric care. For example, there are 22 snooker balls and one cue ball. "

"It's not that simple," Freundlich insisted. "Just as in snooker, possession is not nine-tenths of the law and you have to show some consideration. But there is, of course, a fundamental difference between psychiatric group counseling and snooker, which is this: in snooker, the table is covered with a green baize cloth, while the carpet in our counseling room is grey."

"Is that a problem for you?"

"Actually it is," replied Freundlich, as he looked around the café. "As soon as I can arrange it, I plan to have the grey carpet removed and a green blaize cloth laid down on the floor. We should probably have some cue sticks around the room, to brighten it up."

Freundlich was unaware that Valentino was secretly taping this conversation.

"What about your patients?" Valentino asked. "How long is treatment typically?"

"Well," Freundlich conceded. "They come in with some very pleasant illusions, that they can be cured in five years or ten years or whatever. Most of the patients we admit are incurable."

"Isn't your institute set up to handle *not so severe mental disorders*? That would sound like they should be curable."

"Let's not get technical," Freundlich suggested. "*All* mental disorders are severe, whether we want to admit it or not."

"So, your idea is that once a patient is admitted to your institute, he or she will never be discharged. Is that right?"

"Right, and that's why we set up shop next to a mortuary. That way, when they finally kick the bucket, we don't have to cart their bodies very far."

"This sounds very cold," Valentino observed.

"Life is cold," Freundlich replied, "and we have to be tough. If you'd like, I'd be happy to give you a tour of our institute."

This was the cherry on the sundae, and Valentino happily accepted. In the meantime, he also hired a pair of private eyes to shadow the doc and to look into his private and professional life alike. After a month, Valentino had assembled a massive amount of material sufficient to convince any neutral observer that Freundlich was completely off his rocker. He reported his findings to the Nebraska Psychiatric Society, with a recommendation that Freundlich's license to practice be revoked and that he be examined by a panel of psychiatrists, suggesting that the then-director of the institute might be in need of psychiatric treatment himself. It would be some months before the society took up this case.

In the meantime, the brothers visited the map store and introduced themselves to Oliver Surprise, who said "This is a surprise to receive a delegation from the Governor's office."

"No, you are –" Brother Bart started, until Brother Bret cut him off.

"We have come in order to purchase a 16th or 17th century map of this region – something Spanish."

"I have a few good maps from that era," Surprise replied, "but I also have some maps dating from the 18th century and also from the early 19th century, after Mexico gained its independence. They might also fit the bill. What exactly are you looking for?"

"We would like a map which includes the Okra Hills, and with special features," Bret explained.

"We are going to bury some treasure and we want to bury it where the map shows a special feature."

"Aha," said Surprise, with a grin on his face, "you want a treasure map for a treasure which has not yet been buried. That's an interesting twist. But let's see what we can come up with."

With that, Surprise brought out several rolls, unrolling them on a large table in his salon, displaying them in all their grandeur. The 16th-century and 17th-century maps, while beautiful in their own way, were too vague when it came to the territory which today comprises the Great State of Nebraska. But Surprise unfurled a very detailed map, prepared in the early 18th century by the governor of New Spain, so that he could send an army against the French. The expedition was a failure, but the map was clearly a success. Dating from 1718, the map showed what the brothers chose to interpret as "special features" in the Okra Hills. This was the map they now purchased. With this, they repacked their vehicle and, the next day, they drove out to the Okra Hills. Brother Bart wanted to make a stop for lunch at the Loup City Diner and see his presumed sweetheart, Katie Nowacka, once again. But Brother Bret pointed out that the diner was east, and they needed to drive west. Bart complained a little, but he could see the point. It was about 260 miles from Lincoln to the Okra Hills, and it took the brothers just under four hours to get there. This time, they had come fully equipped – treasure, a map, and shovels. Once they reached the foot of the hills, they studied the map carefully to decide which of the "special features" on the map might be interpreted as the location of treasure. Once they decided on this, they hauled their booty to the designated location and started digging. This was a lot of work and, after six hours, they stopped and decided to finish up the next day. They returned now to Uptown, taking dinner at Romulus' Steakhouse and Particle Accelerator, which was still in business in spite of the fact that several erstwhile key members of the establishment's staff had taken administrative jobs in Lincoln. After a good night's sleep, they headed back to the hills, but had trouble finding the hole they had started, even though the location was "clearly" marked on the map. So, they chose another "special feature", just inside one of many caves dotting the Okra Hills, hauled the treasure there, and began digging. After 10 hours of digging, they were satisfied with the depth of their hole, put all of the treasure into it, placing two artefacts close to the surface so that they would reasonably easily be found, and then covered it up. They then carefully planted some shrubs over the newly replaced earth, so that it would look undisturbed. With this, they returned to Uptown, and celebrated by taking dinner at the site of Uptown's very own particle accelerator.

That same evening, the brothers telephoned the Governor in a state of high excitement, to tell him that there was now Aztec gold in the Okra Hills and that their map would guide them to it. Romulus sounded very pleased at this and suggested that they contact the Department of Archeology at UWU as well as local media, including the *Uptown Archeological Digest and Local News*, and take people out to the site. The following day, when the brothers took the map over to the Department of Archeology, they were disappointed to find that Professor Vecchio, the head of the department, was unimpressed by the map and had trouble interpreting it as a treasure map, even if it did have some "special features". That seemed to be a dead end.

But the brothers were not out of ideas. So they now contacted KNOP and told the station manager that, while in Mexico, they had acquired a treasure map and wondered if this was newsworthy. In the news business, what is spectacular is more interesting than what is proven to be true. It is generally enough if it is conceivable that a certain claim might perhaps be true. So, the brothers were given a very warm welcome at the station and were able to spin a yarn about how they had purchased the map from a dealer on the Paseo del Tortuga on the outskirts of Mexico City. They claimed that the dealer had told them that it was a treasure map and that they could use it to find Aztec gold in Nebraska. They were able to show the map on television, and this generated a lot of excitement. People in Uptown who had been digging for Aztec gold in their backyards and driveways now felt vindicated, and were ready to make another expedition to the Okra Hills.

KNOP knew that Eustadiola von Kletten was UWU's specialist in Aztec history and hoped that she could take time from her legislative duties to come to their station for an interview. Instead, it was arranged that she would give an interview on KLKN-TV in

Lincoln and that the interview would be simultaneously broadcast also on KNOP. "Welcome to the program, Senator and Professor Von Kletten," the interviewer began. "As an expert in Aztec history, what is your reaction to the claims being made by Bret and Bart Holloway that they have in their possession a treasure map?"

"We should be skeptical," von Kletten responded. "Last year the brothers stole an ancient Grecian urn from the Museum of Grecian Archeology in Omaha and repainted it with what they imagined were Aztec motifs. Now they claim to have an Aztec treasure map. If there is Aztec treasure in the Okra Hills, why are they not showing that? Why are they coming forward only with a map?"

"Perhaps they want some funding or support for an expedition?" the interviewer suggested.

"Perhaps," von Kletten replied, "but I would want to study the map first. Maps are always prepared with some purpose in mind, whether to show routes or topography or rainfall or administrative boundaries. As I understand it, the map of which the brothers have come into possession is one prepared in connection with General Villasur's military expedition against the French in 1719. You should ask yourself why a map prepared for a military expedition would show the location of treasure. It doesn't make any sense."

"Would it nonetheless be worth sending out an archeological party to investigate this?"

"No, I don't think so," she replied. "It would be a complete waste of time."

"Thank you, Senator and Professor von Kletten, for sharing your views with us."

People throughout the Great State of Nebraska saw both broadcasts and, people being people, were much more inclined to want to believe the brothers, who were offering something truly exciting, than Professor von Kletten, who was throwing a wet blanket over their dreams. Excitement – that was what the people of Nebraska wanted, and especially the people of Uptown, who were in the middle of yet another Okra festival but could always find time for Aztec treasure. Pressure now built on the Department of Archeology at UWU to organize an expedition and, although Vecchio remained skeptical, he was finally compelled to give in and to organize an expedition. So it was that, on the 17th of May, Vecchio, accompanied by the Maverick Brothers and a news team from KNOP, led a party of four archeologists together with about 10 archeology students who would do the actual digging, and headed for the hills. The brothers were pleased with themselves and could smell triumph, as they confidently led the party to the entrance of the cave where they remembered burying the treasure. As the digging got underway, the brothers started singing, until Vecchio told them that this was unprofessional and inappropriate for a serious archeological excavation. But after two hours, the diggers had not uncovered anything and the brothers, who had left two artefacts close to the surface, were starting to doubt that they were in the right place. Vecchio noticed their nervousness as they started to study their map more closely. He also noticed that they were whispering to each other and figured that something was rotten in the Okra Hills, to paraphrase Shakespeare's *Hamlet*. After 10 hours of digging, the team had not found anything – at which point the brothers suggested that they had probably made a mistake as to which "special feature" was the location of the treasure.

"Why exactly do you believe that this is a treasure map?" Vecchio now asked the brothers.

"Because we were told it was," Brother Bret bleated. "Can we try just one more location, please?"

"Not today," Vecchio replied. But the news journalists who had come along were giving the story their own spin, which was that the brothers were hot on the trail of treasure and that Professor Vecchio was being obstructive. As he heard this spin, Vecchio added, "We'll come back tomorrow and try another site." And so they did, but again without locating the treasure which the brothers had just buried. It was unlikely that someone else had found the treasure in the few days which had transpired. What seemed quite obvious to the two of them was that they had simply forgotten where they had buried the Aztec hoard. At any rate, after two tries, even the news media lost interest. Vecchio called off the search, and the brothers returned to Lincoln feeling despondent.

When they told Romulus how things had gone, he became furious, since he had seen for himself what great treasures there were. But he also disclosed that Toby had told him that his Aztec dummy was cursed and that they would have trouble finding the treasure after they buried it.

The Fate of Siggie Freundlich

It took six months before the case of Dr. Siggie Freundlich came before the board of the Nebraska Psychiatric Society. A panel of five distinguished Nebraskan psychiatrists, with Dr. Sehr Böse acting as chair, agreed to meet Dr. Valentino and hear his report. They had all read his written report and had studied the documentation he had provided, but they wanted to hear from Valentino directly before making any decision. The meeting took place in Lincoln's Great Hall of Self-Understanding, located in the headquarters of the Nebraska Psychiatric Society. The board listened carefully to Valentino, but eyebrows were raised from time to time. Indeed, the members of the board were initially skeptical, but Dr. Valentino, a New York psychiatrist no less, stood his ground and presented the case to them carefully and methodically.

"You're telling us that our friend, Siggie Freundlich, suffers from obsessive-compulsive syndrome and that he is certifiably schizophrenic?" said Dr. Böse, after Valentino had completed his presentation.

"You have seen the documentation I provided and you have read my report," said Valentino, "and I have summarized for you the key points in my report. To repeat, in my professional opinion, Freundlich is mentally unstable and not fit for any professional work. He needs psychiatric help. My recommendation, to repeat what I wrote in my written report, is that Siggie Freundlich, who suffers from a mental disorder which I would judge to be not so severe, be committed to the Happy Trails Institute for Not So Severe Mental Disorders, of which he is, as we speak, still director. I suggest further that you authorize me to appoint a new director."

"Would you plan to take over as director yourself?" asked Dr. Glücklich, Böse's colleague on the panel.

"No," answered Valentino. "But I would consult with the Governor, as a matter of form, as well as with those members of the Nebraska psychiatric community whom I have come to trust."

"You are from New York, as I understand," said Dr. Traurig. "How long have you been staying in Nebraska?"

"I have a New York practice to maintain," Dr. Valentino replied, "but I have been commuting between Lincoln and New York for the past six months, generally staying for a week to 10 days in Lincoln at a stretch."

"Fine," said Dr. Böse, who was chairman of the board. "Unless there are any objections –" The other psychiatrists (including Dr. Apathisch, who was not motivated to say anything) nodded quietly in assent. "—we accept your recommendation that Siggie Freundlich be removed as director of the Happy Trails Institute without delay, and await your decision concerning his replacement. Meeting adjourned."

With that, Valentino returned to Romulus' office to report his success with the psychiatrists. Although he had told the board of the NPS that he would consult with the Governor and with psychiatrists in Nebraska concerning the person to be appointed as incoming director, in fact he and Romulus had already made their decision earlier. Bret Holloway had been serving as chief of the Board of Mental Health and – so they reasoned – was thus the obvious choice to replace Freundlich. Besides, having been an inmate at the institute, Brother Bret knew how the institute worked. Bret was offered the chance to name his own deputy, and both Romulus and Valentino half expected him to choose his brother, Bart. Instead, he chose Miklos Poszkarny, with whom he had enjoyed so many lunches at the Loup City Diner. For Miklos, this return to work at the Institute meant a massive promotion since he had previously worked there as an orderly and now occupied the #2 position. Freundlich was told that he would remain at the institute as a "guest", pending a final decision concerning his mental state. He was, of course, very upset about this development but took consolation in the fact that he was assigned a private room.

Director Bret Holloway immediately introduced changes at the Institute. To begin with, he arranged for the chef at the Loup City Diner to come to the Institute once a week to prepare meals for staff and patients alike. Although the Institute's cooking staff were themselves accomplished chefs, the new arrangement was extremely popular with all concerned since Chef Pierre Bonsoir from the Loup City Diner was a master with French recipes. A second change introduced by Brother Bret was to stop organizing counseling sessions in groups of 22. He thought that smaller groups made more sense and henceforth there would be 8 to 10 persons per counseling group. Since each group met once a week, this meant that there would be more group meetings than before. He also abandoned Freundlich's dictatorial style and opted for a more "democratic" approach, in which patients could speak their minds without fear of contradiction by the director. There were, of course, some limits. In the counseling sessions, the patients were not allowed to use profanity or to proselytize or to shout. They were also not allowed to smoke, but then again smoking was banned throughout the institute and even the staff were not allowed to smoke. It took only two weeks for Freundlich to be certified as mentally disordered and, at that point, this erstwhile "guest" was admitted as an inpatient.

The first session in which Freundlich was involved as patient inevitably centered on him. "Look who's joining our group as a patient!" said one patient.

"Yeah, that's putting the boot on the other foot!" said another patient.

"So how does it feel, doc?"

"I'll manage," replied Freundlich. "Remember, I'm still the only person in the Institute with a Ph.D. in psychiatry."

"What about Dr. Holloway?" said someone.

"He has a Ph.D. in political science, not in psychiatry," Freundlich pointed out.

Miklos, who was chairing this session instead of Brother Bret, interjected a clarification here. "The study of political science involves learning why people behave the way they do. It involves getting into the heads of political leaders as well as into the heads of the citizens who vote for them. In my opinion," Miklos closed, "political science is a better preparation for serving as director here than training in psychiatry."

"That remains to be seen," said Freundlich, as he reached into his jacket for a bag of pistachios.

"Always these pistachio nuts," said one of the patients. "You could do this as director. But now that you are just one of us, don't you think that it is rude to eat your pistachio nuts, without offering some to the rest of us here?"

Freundlich immediately put away his nuts. After that, the session continued with various complaints against Freundlich for how he had behaved toward the patients when he was director.

Bret and Miklos got along famously, just as they had when Bret was a patient. They continued their tradition of weekly visits to the Loup City Diner. From time to time, Brother Bart was able to join them, but his post overseeing the state's museums kept him busy and, from time to time, he would drive out to the Okra Hills to see if he could remember where he had buried the Aztec treasure.

War with Utah

Had Governor Romulus been content just to gaze at his Aztec dummy and his Aztec decorative gold shield, things might well have gone in a different direction. However, Romulus was so excited about these artefacts that he could not contain himself. Soon after coming into possession of them, he contacted the National Institute for Carbon Dating and persuaded one of their agents to come out to Lincoln to verify the age of his artefacts. The carbon dating confirmed that they were, indeed, genuine Aztec artefacts. After that, Governor Romulus called a televised press conference and, showing off his two artefacts, declared that these had been unearthed in Nebraska's Okra Hills. He then went further and claimed that Lincoln, like Uptown, was on a site of an ancient Aztec city, whose importance should not be underestimated. When a journalist in the audience asked him what he thought about reports that there was Aztec gold buried in Utah, he poo-pooed the idea, declaring that, once the Aztecs had found their way to Nebraska, they had no need to explore any regions to the west. The story was picked up by several television stations and newspapers in Utah, including *The Impartial Summarizer*, published in Kanab, where Utahans believed there was gold underground. Soon, everyone in Utah was talking about Nebraska Governor Romulus' outrageous claims.

Eventually, this came before the Governor of Utah, Jed Braddock. He had been a wrestler in an earlier incarnation and what he really wanted to do was to wrestle his Nebraskan counterpart to the ground and make him say "uncle". He was furious that Governor Romulus dared to suggest that Nebraska had been more important in Aztec history than Utah, and that there could be Aztec gold, not in Utah, as every Utahan knew, but in Nebraska, which was not even a neighboring state. Governor Braddock called his cabinet to an emergency session and shouted obscenities the whole time, directed mainly against his fellow governor in the Great State of Nebraska. He and his cabinet decided to demand a retraction by Governor Romulus of all of his claims related to the Aztecs, together with a formal apology. This demand was presented to Romulus on a scroll and sent to him in the form of a birthday stripogram, even though neither Braddock nor anyone in his cabinet had the foggiest idea when exactly Romulus was born. Romulus was not amused and actually spat on the scroll, nearly hitting the stripper. Romulus stomped out of his office, banged on the doors of his cabinet ministers and summoned them to an "emergency" meeting. Romulus wanted to go to the war against Utah. His defense minister, Rocco "Rock" Palestrata, thought that this was a terrible idea, but Romulus made such a huge fuss that, eventually, his cabinet ministers gave in and, that very evening, Governor Romulus went on television to make an official declaration of war on Utah. Since this was broadcast on all the major news channels, the U.S. government quickly became aware of it. However, the U.S. Departments of Homeland Security and Defense did not think this would amount to anything serious, and decided not to take any action.

Romulus decided on a land invasion of Utah and ordered his troops to start marching toward the border with Utah. Among the many problems associated with this – including the fact that the American states do not enjoy the right to declare war either on foreign states or on each other – was the fact that Utah and Nebraska do not share a common border. The State of Colorado sits precisely in the middle between these two warring states. Thus, when Romulus' army went to war, it had to cross the territory of Colorado. But Governor Braddock was quick on the draw and, even before the Army of the Great State of Nebraska had entered Colorado territory, Braddock had mobilized his 60,000-strong National Guard, then in the process of being cut down to 40,000, because of the latest round of tax cuts, and sent it into Colorado. The Governor of Colorado saw the threat in the western part of his state and then ordered full mobilization of his own national guard and ordered them to march against the Utahans. Meanwhile, the Army of the Great State of Nebraska entered the territory of Colorado, with Romulus declaring, both privately to the Governor of Colorado and on television, that his purpose was merely to help Colorado defend its people from the invading force from Utah.

By this time, Eustadiola von Kletten had been elected Speaker of the Legislature in Lincoln (in recognition of her vast intellect and unquestionable integrity) and she now drafted a protest, calling on Governor Romulus to withdraw his troops from Colorado immediately and sue for peace. She presented the text to her fellow legislators and the vote was a stunning 47 in favor, with the two anarchists predictably declining to participate in this act of government.

Meanwhile, Braddock's force got as far as Grand Junction, crossed the river, and suddenly found themselves surrounded by the Colorado National Guard. Braddock's troops now beat a hasty retreat westward and did not stop until they were back in Utah. The commander of the Colorado National Guard, had learned a lesson from the mistakes committed by Hungarian General Görgey in 1849, when he declined to chase after the retreating Austrian army, thus allowing it to regroup and ultimately crush Hungarian forces. It was, thus, on the basis of sound historical comparison that the Colorado National Guard was ordered to give chase, ultimately reaching the town of Roosevelt just off Highway 40. Here the Colorado National Guard entrenched itself.

Governor Romulus loved music and saw to it that his army had an ample musical corps, with a strong brass section. With the bulk of the Colorado National Guard now entrenched in Utah, Romulus' musical army marched into Colorado with minimal resistance. Romulus' immediate objective (before continuing westward to punish Utah) was to reach Colorado Springs and annex the eastern part of Colorado. After that, his idea was that he could declare himself Emperor of Nebraska and Eastern Colorado, or perhaps Emperor of Nebraska and King of Eastern Colorado – he had not made up his mind on that detail. Romulus' army did not actually engage with the Utahan forces at all, even though there was nomi-

...as the Nebraskan musical army marched into a town, locals came out onto the streets to watch the parade and to cheer the Nebraskan army.

nally a state of war between Nebraska and Utah. Understandably, people in Lincoln and other cities in Nebraska were very confused about all of this. And while Romulus' army did not actually reach Colorado Springs, it did manage to occupy the towns of Falcon and Hugo, as well as much of Colorado's Black Forest.

In fact, there was no fighting in eastern Colorado because the Coloradans did not take the Nebraskans seriously. Romulus had decided that an invading army should be musical, his army arrived in Colorado with a full brass complement – trumpets, tubas, trombones – as well as guitars, drums, and cymbals. The result was that, as the Nebraskan musical army marched into a town, locals came out onto the streets to watch the parade and to cheer the Nebraskan army. And when the commander of this "invading" force picked up a megaphone and told the people of whichever town they were in to surrender, the reaction was laughter and applause. There were even requests for specific marches the Coloradans wanted to hear, including most of John Philip Sousa's marches, Julius Fucik's "Entry of the Gladiators", and Kermit Roscoe's "March of the Coloradan Skiers". The Nebraska musical corps was only too happy to honor requests and the Coloradans, being a generous people, cooked food for the "invaders". They also asked them when they would be performing their next concert. When the commander repeated, "This is an invasion," the Coloradans laughed again.

Then, the unthinkable happened. The Colorado Symphony Orchestra's conductor came out to hear the Nebraskans' field concerts and was so impressed that he invited all of them to stay in Colorado and form a new ensemble to be called the "Colorado Brass Marching Band for Friendship with Nebraska". Since the pay was better than what they had been getting back in Nebraska and since the conductor promised them all the Colorado stream trout they could eat, they defected one and all. The remaining force of more than 100,000 troops now became despondent since, without music, what was the point of fighting? Once the musical corps had abandoned Nebraska for the greener pastures of Colorado, the rest of the invading force simply marched home to Nebraska. The "war", if that is what it was, had not resulted in a single casualty between Nebraska and Colorado. As for the fighting between Utah and Colorado, the U.S. Army eventually sent in special forces to separate the two sides and chastise their respective commanders.

Even though the invasion had petered out, with the loss of the musical corps being the only cost to Nebraska, back in Lincoln the Legislature had had enough and, at von Kletten's renewed prompting, impeachment proceedings against Romulus were finally initiated. Von Kletten met with Romulus and advised him that if he would resign from office, he could retire with dignity, keep his Governor's pension, and suffer no penalties. But if it became necessary to proceed with impeachment, the Legislature would also take up the issue of criminal abuse of office. Romulus refused to resign – or, as he put it, to abdicate.

It was then that von Kletten contacted Dr. Böse, head of the Nebraska Psychiatric Society, and asked him for his professional opinion about Professor-Governor-Emperor Romulus. Böse was not at all surprised that yet another public figure was suspected of mental disorder, and agreed to meet with Romulus. Of course, Böse knew all about Romulus' declaring himself Emperor, about his declaration of war on Utah and attempt to annex part of Colorado, and his other antics as Governor. Von Kletten tried to arrange a meeting between the two at Dr. Böse's office, since he could not make a diagnosis without meeting with the Governor first. But Romulus could smell danger and refused to go. Subsequent efforts, through various ruses, also ran aground as the Governor did his best to avoid having to meet with Böse. Finally, von Kletten used the pretext of a supposedly innocent lunch to lure Romulus to the Legislature's cafeteria, where Böse was already waiting. As soon as he saw Böse, Romulus got angry – as well one might – but decided to take his seat anyway, feeling that he would have to face this challenge eventually. After all, Romulus told himself, Böse had been a willing tool in helping him get rid of Freundlich. Perhaps he could manipulate the psychiatrist once again.

Governor Romulus' Time of Troubles

Toby had advised Romulus long ago that, if he was ever accused of anything, he should deny all knowledge. "Just deny everything," Toby told him. Toby also told Romulus that, if there was trouble, he could also claim not to remember. "History has seen many famous amnesiacs," Toby assured him, "all of them successful or not remembering whether they were successful or not." It was with this advice in mind that Romulus sat down for lunch with Böse and von Kletten on a particularly overcast Wednesday.

"Hello, Governor Romulus," said Böse. "I am so pleased that you and your colleague can join me for lunch. It will be my treat."

"That is most generous of you," said Romulus.

"Your colleague, Speaker von Kletten, has kept me informed about the war with Utah," said Böse.

"Actually," the Governor clarified, "we only *declared* war on Utah. We never actually fought a war. It was all in good fun. We never actually engaged in conflict with anyone. Our army entered Colorado, played some concerts, and then withdrew."

"That is broadly correct," von Kletten confirmed.

"The musicians stayed behind in Colorado," mused Romulus.

"Did that make you angry?" asked Böse.

"I haven't thought much about it, actually. As you know, I am Governor and I have a lot of duties." Then Romulus added, "Shall we order lunch or just sit here pretending that this is a meal?"

"Absolutely," Böse agreed. He called over the waitress and the three of them ordered stuffed beef rolls with sauerkraut and cornbread. Böse ordered wine, while the Governor and Speaker von Kletten ordered coffee.

"I know that you have wanted to talk with me," Romulus said to Böse, "but I have been very busy. However, I would like to take this opportunity to thank you for solving the problem with Siggie Freundlich."

"Yes, he was a special case," Böse responded. "And I see that your erstwhile colleague, Bret Holloway, has now taken over as director of that institute."

"Dr. Holloway is highly qualified – as a political scientist, as a therapist, and as an administrator," Romulus pointed out.

"That is high praise, no doubt. But I am not aware of Dr. Hollway's credentials as a therapist. What exactly are his credentials?"

"He taught at UWU for several years and, among his duties, he served as Undergraduate Adviser in the political science department. The position involves not only guidance concerning classes but also advice which may serve functions parallel to therapy."

"What do you mean by 'parallel to therapy'? I don't understand," Böse said.

"You are not a college man, you are a psychiatrist. Those of us working within a university constantly see students with problems of different kinds – some of them have writing blocks, others are lazy, some are distracted by romantic adventures, still others use drugs – and all of these involve a need for the kind of therapy which an Undergraduate Adviser is well equipped to handle."

"OK," said Böse, conceding defeat on this point. "Let's agree that his position at UWU involved something like therapy. What about you? Now you are Governor – a big leap from political science professor to being Governor of the state."

"Not as big as you might imagine," Romulus replied. "I was, after all, head of the department."

"I seem to remember a scandal about an Aztec urn, when you were in that position," said Böse. "Can you tell me something about that?"

Just then, their food was served, giving Romulus a couple of minutes to think about his reply. "The urn was Grecian, as you know," Romulus replied, "and the Holloway boys thought it was Aztec."

"They stole it from the Museum of Grecian Art and repainted it," von Kletten interjected.

"I actually don't remember the details," Romulus claimed. "What I remember is that the urn was returned to the Museum and that, as Governor, I arranged for the purchase of an identical urn from the Museum of Archeology in Athens and presented it to the museum in Omaha."

"So you had nothing to do with the theft?"

"I was sitting in Lincoln, while the Holloway brothers carried out this theft in Omaha. I learned about the theft only afterwards," Romulus claimed.

"Let's talk about your idea to put Nebraskans back on horse and buggy and to ban all cars, and your related idea to ban tobacco cigarettes and to encourage Nebraskans to smoke dandelion cigarettes instead," suggested Böse.

"I admit that I said something to my staff about horse and buggy," Romulus began, "but this was just a joke. I am not responsible if some of my cabinet ministers, whose native language is Italian, not English, took that seriously. As for cigarettes, the American Cancer Society has been saying for years that there is a strong correlation between smoking tobacco and developing lung cancer. Banning tobacco cigarettes would be a service to the people, would it not? –"

"In line with your campaign slogan, 'Seek only the good of the people', right? Isn't that an ancient Roman slogan?"

"What does it matter? Are you suggesting that public officials *not* seek the good of the people?"

"No, not at all," Böse agreed. "We should all serve the people, but perhaps without parading around in a toga."

"The toga offends you, then?" Romulus replied. "I have worn the toga on a few occasions, just for effect. Usually, I wear what other people in Nebraska wear – cowboy outfits or, as I am dressed today, a business suit."

"OK, Böse conceded. "Perhaps the toga is not so bad. But OK, can you give me an example of how you have tried to serve the people?"

"Upon entering office, I immediately ordered a thorough inspection of all of Nebraska's roads, bridges, and public buildings.

This had not been done for decades and the inspection turned up cracks, faults, and design flaws which needed to be corrected. The inspectors told me that we caught some of these problems just in the nick of time."

"You deserve congratulations on that, of course," the psychiatrist conceded. "But what about these dandelions? You want people to smoke dandelion roots, is that right?"

"I don't *want* people to smoke anything," Romulus now said. "But if people are going to smoke, then dandelion roots are a much healthier choice than tobacco. This has been proven scientifically. Dandelion roots have been shown to *cure* cancer. If people were to smoke dandelion roots then, rather than contracting cancer, they would protect themselves."

"Have you ever smoked dandelion roots yourself?"

"No," Romulus conceded, "but I have read the medical journals on this point."

"You are considered a controversial governor. Are you aware of that?"

"Every politician is controversial in his or her time. Only a few remain controversial after they leave politics. Can you think of a single American president, for example, who was not controversial during the time he served in office?"

"Eisenhower was not controversial," answered Böse, showing his age.

"OK, granted, but look how far back you had to search to find a president who was not particularly controversial."

"You mentioned a moment ago that many of the members of your cabinet spoke Italian as their native language."

"Yes, that's right," Romulus readily agreed. "When I was elected Governor, I was determined to avoid appointing Democrats or Republicans to my cabinet, since they tend not to get along. I also did not want any anarchists in my cabinet, since they are a lot of good-for-nothings. So I consulted my friend Micky Rossini, who introduced me to a lot of highly qualified colleagues of his whom I was happy to bring into the cabinet."

"Isn't Rossini a mafia boss?"

"I would rather say," Romulus replied, "that he is a benefactor of the university who has a history of cooperation with law enforcement. If you have questions about Rossini's career and activities, surely you would do better to interrogate him. Now, are we done?"

"One final question, please," Böse said. "How would you rate your performance as governor?"

Romulus knew instinctively that this was an important question, possibly the most important question being thrown at him over his lunch plate. He also realized that he could not deny all knowledge of what he had been doing as Governor or, for that matter, plead that he could not remember. If he rated himself better than most, the doc might classify him as suffering from delusions of grandeur, while, if he said something along the lines that he was still learning the ropes, that might be interpreted as an admission of incompetence. Weighing his words carefully, he finally replied, "Comparing myself with previous Governors of the Great State of Nebraska, I am probably about average -- maybe better on some things, for example maintaining our roads and bridges, not so much on others." Romulus had outwitted the shrink – as he could see from the disgruntled frown which spread across the faces of his lunch partners. With that, the lunch partners were finally able to enjoy their victuals.

But Romulus' troubles were not over. Von Kletten had thought it would be grand to see the Governor committed to the Happy Trails Institute, even if there was a risk that he would take over and manage to declare himself "Commander" of the institute – or even "King". But this tactic was not going to work, as she could clearly see. Of course, she could have pressed Romulus to explain why he had a washing machine in his office, but she had already heard him justify this in terms of the need to clean some items on the spot. This meant that impeachment was now back on the front burner. She was not going to be able to prove that he was mentally disturbed, at least not to the satisfaction of the Nebraska Psychiatric Society, but she could still make a case that he was incompetent and unfit for office. His so-called "environmental fund" could also serve as evidence of corruption, while his inclusion of a large number of Rossini's associates in his cabinet, as well as in other posts, was at a minimum suspicious. But there was a problem with removing him from office. If he was forced out of office, the state's Lieutenant Governor was supposed to step into the Governor's shoes or, in his absence, the Deputy Lieutenant Governor. The state's Lieutenant Governor was none other than Johnny "the Executioner" Testarossa, who was included on the FBI's list of known members of the mafia. The reason he was not in prison was due to the fact that evidence against him kept disappearing from FBI archives – possibly in connection with Micky Rossini's cooperation with law enforcement officials! Under previous rules, the Speaker of the Legislature, which is to say, Eustadiola von Kletten, would have been second in line to succeed to the Governor's office. However, upon taking office, Romulus had created the new office of Deputy Lieutenant Governor and had obtained the Legislature's assent that this newly appointed Deputy Lieutenant Governor should be next in line, after Testarossa. And here was the problem: the Deputy Lieutenant Governor was Laverne Buenaventura Morch – "Buenaventura" in honor of the famous Spanish anarchist Buenaventura Durruti, who had been killed in 1936. Like her parents, Morch was a sworn anarchist and, if anything, even less suited for the Governor's office than either Romulus or Testarossa. Indeed, within the Legislature, there were concerns that, if Morch ever became Governor, she would immediately attempt to dismantle the government, fire the police, dismiss the Nebraska National Guard (by this point, of course, that was the Army of the Great State of Nebraska), and shut down all administrative offices. She was constantly talking about the need for direct cooperation among people – a dangerous signal to anyone paying attention! But she did have one weakness – a great love of animals of all species, manifested in her having served as chair of the Animal Rights Activists of Nebraska.

Von Kletten decided that the best way to proceed was to remove Morch from the line of succession and restore the status quo ante. If they found a way to simply fire her, then Governor Romulus would have the right to appoint her successor. So she and her allies decided that the best approach would be to abolish the office of Deputy Lieutenant Governor first. To sweeten the pill for Morch, it was decided to offer her a post which would likely be more to her liking. The obvious choice was to offer her the directorship of the Agency for the Protection of Animal Life, headquartered in Omaha. This would also put her at a distance from Lincoln.

The then-director of that agency was, in fact, approaching retirement age and was persuaded to retire early by offering him a huge bonus. After the post had been made vacant, von Kletten sent one of her aides to Morch to see if she could be interested in taking over the Agency for the Protection of Animal Life. Her salary would be three times what the retiring director had received and she would be granted powers not previously enjoyed by the agency's director. With that, she accepted and was soon ensconced in Omaha. Her previous post was now eliminated.

There was still the problem of Testarossa, who had kept a very low profile in Romulus' government although there was some evidence of his involvement in what may politely be called "transfers of government funds". After consulting with Bobkov, back at UWU, she decided against offering him a "carrot" and decided on legal forms of harassment. Indeed, "forms" is the key word here. Suddenly, he was being bombarded with forms to fill out, explanations to provide, transfers to justify. For all of these, there were short deadlines and, when he missed a deadline, he would be phoned in the middle of the night by a lower-level bureaucrat and bombarded with email reminders. He changed his phone number several times, but von Kletten's bureaucratic machine always managed to keep up with these changes. Eventually, Testarossa had his phone disconnected. But there were still the emails – and the financial penalties when he missed deadlines to file the forms he was asked to fill out. Finally, all of this had its desired effect and Testarossa asked to resign office and be allowed to return to New York City.

Von Kletten now moved quickly, so that Romulus would resign before a new Lieutenant Governor could be appointed. For him, a combination of threats and intimidation was applied, centering on a threat to expose his relationship with his washing machine (a point which Dr. Böse had mysteriously forgotten to mention). She even brought Romulus' old associate, Pestalozzi – or rather, his hologram – to Lincoln, to talk sense into the Governor. Finally, late one Friday afternoon, Romulus phoned von Kletten and told her that he was resigning immediately. He signed what he called his Testament of Abdication and handed it to von Kletten. She immediately phoned the office of the Nebraska Supreme Court and arranged to be sworn in as Governor the following day. She was sworn in as Governor of the State of Nebraska by Chief Justice Leighton Galen. Romulus was given two days to move Toby and his other personal items out of the Governor's office. By Monday afternoon, Romulus was already back in Uptown, brooding about the curse of the Aztec dummy, which he finally took seriously but presiding over what he now called Governor Romulus' Steakhouse and Particle Accelerator. In the meantime, von Kletten had moved into the Governor's mansion in Lincoln.

Uptown's 60th Anniversary Celebration

Romulus returned to Uptown to find the entire town getting ready to celebrate its 60th anniversary. It had not been declared a town, as such, until some two decades later, but it was sixty years previous that Madge and Caleb Jensen, with their daughters Faith, Hope, and Charity, had purchased an open field and built their house. It was the first house in what would become Uptown. After they had built their house, they had a fourth daughter and called her Modesty. When their girls reached adolescence, Madge and Caleb thought it was time to think of getting them husbands. So, when the eldest girl turned 14, they contacted a prominent dating agency in North Platte and arranged for Faith to meet eligible bachelors. In a few years, Faith, Hope, and Charity were all married and all living close to Madge and Caleb.

Now the town was going to celebrate its origins, with a spectacular All-Uptown Festival of Joy, as it was officially called – unofficially and with greater clarity people called it their celebration of 60 years of Uptown. The community went all out, organizing a range of contests and events, including a spitting contest, in which locals would try to out-spit llamas, a revival of the ever-popular goat chasing event, a cat race (which failed miserably, when the cats either chased each other off the track or simply wandered off in different directions), poetry readings on Nebraskan themes, and a sing-along event, with Mayor Marlowe leading the singing. Perkins' ghost managed to break away from the Department of Political

Science to do a little haunting in town, for the benefit of Uptown's children. There were also speeches by Mayor Marlowe, who was now an elected mayor, and UWU President Friday, who restricted himself to talking about the great achievements at the university over the previous two years, including most notably the establishment of UWU's very own football team and the first-place finish by UWU's curling team in the Nebraska Curling Finals. Governor von Kletten also flew in to Uptown's International Airport for the event, and presented a short talk about the Aztecs. Although she did not suggest, even once, that the Aztecs might have come to Nebraska, her talk pleased the folks of Uptown very much. She even found a couple of occasions to recite Aztec jokes about the Mayans, since (as is well known) the Aztecs had a huge sense of humor and loved to make jokes about Mayans. And there were lots of foods on offer, with steaks and corn-on-the-cob in ample supply, but with more exotic dishes also on offer. Pastor Grace kicked off the event by reciting a special prayer for Uptown which he had composed. And finally, during the period that Romulus had been out of town, the respective managements of the town's two steakhouses had established a friendly relationship and had even collaborated on some events, shared recipes, and perhaps most surprising of all, had arranged for their respective bands to play, from time to time, in each other's dining establishments. It was truly an era of harmony between the steakhouses. In a clear token of this new harmony, the two bands performed some songs together at the festival, although there were some songs which each of them preferred to perform separately.

In addition to all of this, there was also a quadruple marriage ceremony performed by Pastor Grace on the third day of the festival. Friday and von Kletten were finally going to formalize their marriage, which had been involving a lot of short visits back and forth between Uptown and Lincoln. Among the political scientists, lifelong bachelor Eddie Bobkov had proposed to Katella Beach, and they were also tying the knot. More surprising, perhaps, was the fact that Bart Holloway had changed his name legally to Bart Maverick and had revisited the Loup City Diner, where he had proposed to Katie Nowacka. They were to be Mr. and Mrs. Maverick. And finally, Bret Holloway, who had no intention of changing his family name, had proposed to one of his Bolshevik patients at the Institute – Clara Trotsky (at least that is what she had given out as her name) – and they were also to be joined in matrimony.

Pastor Grace conducted the wedding ceremony, with an overflow crowd in his church. There were four maids of honor, four best men, and brides' maids from the local elementary school. There were even two anarchists on hand who, when the pastor asked if there was anyone who knew of any reason why these eight people should not get married, raised their voices and began shouting that marriage was an artefact of churches and governments, both of which should be abolished. "You don't need marriage to live together!" one of the anarchists cried out. But the pastor wisely replied that this was a political statement and not a serious objection to the marriages about to be performed.

After the quadruple wedding, the UWU band played the Bridge on the River Kwai march, as the four couples exited the church. The roughly 500 folks who had gathered in front of the church threw confetti over the couples, as they got into their vehicles to drive five blocks to the Fancy Turtle Saloon, where a feast awaited them. All the dignitaries of the town were on hand for the wedding banquet, including Sheriff Dorbin, Pastor Grace, ex-Governor Romulus and, most obviously, the mayor. No physicists were invited to the banquet.

Each of the four best men gave a toast. Curiously, Bret was Bart's best man and Bart was Bret's best man. Thus, two grooms were also best men. Bobkov's best man was Disraeli, the department's specialist in British and American politics. But it was Pestalozzi's hologram who stole the show. After praising Friday and von Kletten with passion and wishing them the very best in their life together, Pestalozzi – speaking from his secret location – revealed that he had become engaged to a young woman from Wyoming, who likewise appeared in public only as a hologram. They hoped to get married, as soon as they could find a pastor who was content to appear as a hologram to marry them.

Following the wild cheers for Pestalozzi's talk, Uptown's two bands – consolidated for this occasion under the name, The Uptown Mariachi and Variety Bah Bah Band – played waltzes and polkas for the rest of the evening, interrupted only by the occasional cha cha. The four couples danced a waltz to start the evening, and there was plenty of waltzing and polkaing to follow.

The quadruple wedding was, of course, the highlight of the week-long festival. In the remaining days, there were several additional events, including some previously tried. These included a yodeling contest (won by a recent immigrant from Switzerland), a pancake eating contest, a spelling bee involving pupils from the elementary school, kite flying, flights in a hot air balloon, and a hunt for whales. This last event perhaps needs an explanation, since Nebraska is nowhere near an ocean. But the organizer of this event – none other than Gabe Carver, who had also come to Uptown for the big celebration – had his own idea about this. Contestants in the hunt were required to drink six to eight beers before starting on the hunt. How the hunt went after that does not require any explanation.

There was a lot of excitement bordering on frenzy generated by the announcement, by Mayor Marlowe, offering a $5,000 prize to the winner of a psychokinetic contest. The idea was that entrants would use only the power of their minds to move a teacup across a smooth table. There were six contestants in all, each with his or her own teacup lined up at the starting line, with goal posts erected at the other end of the table. Most of Uptown's residents shrank from undertaking so unfamiliar a challenge. However, four men and two women – brave souls – accepted the challenge. A large crowd gathered around them to watch as they furrowed their brows and squinted, sometimes putting their fingers to their foreheads, and seemed to be concentrating very hard on moving their respective teacups. Some people in the crowd started to talk, only to be hushed by others in the crowd. Others were cheering one or another entrant, along the lines of "Come on, Chloe, you can do it!" and "Concentrate, Brian! Your mind is strong!" But after about 10 minutes of this and no movement among the teacups, interest started to sag and the crowd thinned out. After 20 minutes, only family members were still watching. And finally, after a full half hour, Mayor Marlowe declared that there were no winners and that he would donate the $5,000 prize to Pastor Grace's church.

All in all, this festival was a huge success and some Uptownians started calling for holding a 60th anniversary festival every year! Fortunately, for those who enjoyed festivals and could not get enough with the annual Okra Festival and the various events involving goats, there were also festivals in nearby Stonewall and Filibuster, not to mention also North Platte's Wild Hog Festival.

Lord Moo and the Visitors

It was a clear September day, early in the afternoon, when Uptownians noticed a glowing flying disk darting around in the vicinity of their town. The disk consisted of three sections, all rotating, but with the middle section rotating in the opposite direction from the top and bottom sections. It also had strange lights, vaguely reddish copper in color, and the craft made no sound as it flew around. As the Uptownians saw the craft, they exclaimed, "It's people from Colorado, coming to visit us!"

The craft landed out of sight in Uptown Field, behind the woods, and, as the three-ft. tall grey beings with large bulging eyes emerged, they immediately looked around to meet the local inhabitants. The ancestors of these beings – visitors from Xypon, a distant plant in the galaxy of Andromeda – had visited Earth nearly four centuries earlier, had attended performances of William Shakespeare's plays in the Globe Theatre, and had returned to their planet with folio editions of Shakespeare's plays. Since then, they had been teaching their offspring to speak not only Xyponese, the language of Planet Xypon, but also English in its Shakespearean-era incarnation.

After a short survey of the field in which they had landed, the Xyponese came across an ant hill. Since it had been some 380 years since their ancestors had visited Earth, they were not entirely sure what the "masters of Planet Earth" would look like today or even what humans had looked like in Shakespeare's day. Perhaps these ants were the masters of Planet Earth, they thought.

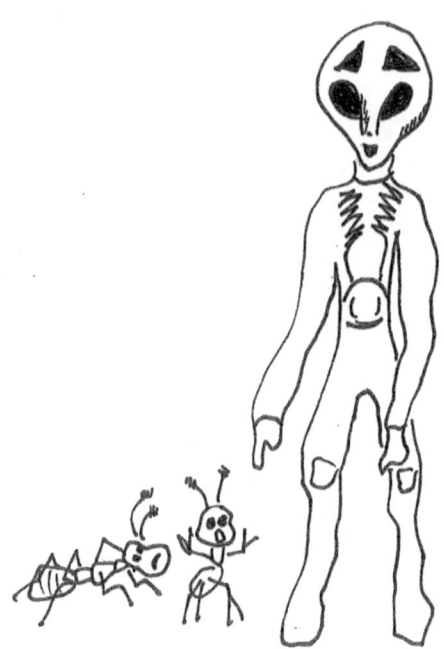

...they were not entirely sure what the "masters of Planet Earth" would look like today or even what humans had looked like in Shakespeare's day.

"Sirrah," said Xox, addressing the ants. "Pardon, gentles all. We have arrived from the port of Xypon and are in search of fair conviviality. Greetings! We beg a moment of your valued time."

The ants ignored this visitor and not because he was wearing a flashing orange helmet. They were busy and just kept marching in fixed file into the ant hill they had built.

"My liege, behold!" said a second Xyponese, addressing Xox. This second alien was possibly of female gender and was known in her language as Pon. "See how they hold in fixed formation, mindful of their project and their destiny. Surely, these beings must be the masters of this planet!"

"We bring gifts," said a third visitor from Xypon, "to render you and your kin most happy, in hopes that you may ever thrive, performing the most glorious deeds. By order of our revered lord and majesty, who is so inclined to graciousness, we bring vaccines for all diseases with which we have acquaintance, musical playthings for merry-making – though we see you are a bit small to use these instruments – and the historical record of our planet. Thou, there, why dost thou not answer? Is it thus that only thy leader may have concourse with us? If that be the case, then take us to your leader. The ants ignored this plea and paid no heed to the generosity of these visitors. The Xyponese were starting to suspect that these tiny beings, scurrying around on six legs, were not the masters and rulers of the planet. Just then, a group of cows approached the visitors. Maybe *these* beings are the masters of Planet Earth, the Xyponese thought. Certainly, the cows were large enough to play the instruments which the Xyponese had brought, although the Xyponese were puzzled that the cows walked on all fours, rather than standing on just two legs as almost all advanced species do. "Who is the lord of your kingdom?" Xox, apparently the leader of this group, now asked.

"Moo," said one of the cows.

"So your leader is called Moo?"

"Moo," said another cow, apparently to confirm what the first cow had said. And then all the cows started to say "Moo". The visitors were experiencing sensations of rapture now, in anticipation of meeting Moo.

"Let us not tarry, nay. Ye have some sense withal of how our love of life doth accord with your own interest. May it please you to lead us to Moo."

Just then, a local cowherd by the name of Tank approached this assembly of extraterrestrials and cows, with the intention of herding his cows back to the barn.

"Hail, earthling!" said Pon, "art thou accomplished in the manner of speaking English?"

"Hail visitor," Tank replied, although that was not the way he usually greeted others. "We all speak English around here."

"These four-legged earthlings are most reticent," observed Xox. "The only thing they have vouchsafed to tell us is that your lord and master goes by the name of Moo. Verily, it would gratify us to meet Moo."

Tank had to fight back a smile, since he did not want to appear rude. After a moment's hesitation, he replied: "Our lord and master is Mayor Marlowe."

"Or Moo for short, as brevity is the soul of wit," said Dwap, quoting from Shakespeare's *Hamlet*.

"I don't rightly remember anyone calling our mayor Moo," Tank admitted. "But perhaps Moo could be short for Marlowe. We usually call him Old Man Marlowe."

"Well, as thou art in evidence the officer to these four-legged earthlings, and standing upon two legs thyself, know this, that we are most eager to meet your Lord Moo, also known as Old Man Marlowe."

Cowherd Tank then accompanied the Xyponese – 12 in all – to downtown Uptown, taking them straight to the Fancy Turtle Saloon. As the group entered the saloon, two of them struggling with a large trunk, the mayor realized immediately that these visitors were not locals and that, most likely, they had come from another galaxy.

"Good morrow, earthlings," said Xox. "I am Xox, and these are my companions: Pon, Pip, Zip, Wew, Fif, Fuf, Geg, Scrub, Dwap, Pinhead, and Ziz." Then, addressing the mayor directly, he asked, "Are you the leader of your community?" Xox used the formal "you", rather than the informal "thou".

"I am the mayor," Marlowe replied. "Locals call me Old Man Marlowe."

"Ah," said Xox, looking very pleased and perhaps a bit in awe. "Greetings, Lord Moo. We have awaited this moment with alacrity and curiosity. We come in friendship."

"Can I offer you folks a drink? – on the house of course," the mayor said in a friendly and welcoming way. As the visitors looked toward the ceiling and then exchanged puzzled glances, Mayor Marlowe realized that "on the house" was an idiom, not necessarily understood in other English-speaking galaxies. "You will be my guests!" he clarified, asking, "Are you whiskey drinkers? That's what most folks around here drink."

"We shall try your brew," said Xox, "as our minds are quick'ned after a long flight through a long passage of light and darkness. We shall with rapture partake in quaffing the local beverage. We greet you, Lord Moo, also known as Old Man Marlowe." Marlowe smiled at being called "Lord Moo".

Just then, a young child, perhaps four years of age, who had come into the saloon, saw the little grey men and shouted, "Visitors from Colorado! Look Daddy, look Mommy – visitors from Colorado!"

Soon a consensus formed in the saloon that these visitors were from Colorado and, when a couple of children ran into the street shouting "visitors from Colorado", a very large number of curious Uptownians quickly poured into the saloon, most of them ordering whiskey. Clearly, this visit was good for business at the Fancy Turtle Saloon! Of course, some Uptownians had made short shopping trips to Denver and did not remember seeing anyone in Colorado who looked anything like these visitors. And again, Romulus' musical goodwill mission to eastern Colorado had allowed those taking part to verify that Coloradans looked much like Nebraskans and not at all like these thin grey beings. But with the vast majority in the saloon swearing that these visitors hailed from Colorado, those who knew better did not want to expose themselves to ridicule.

"Where in Colorado do you call home?" someone asked.

"Xypon, but we usually call our galaxy Andromeda, not Colorado."

"So then, the town of Xypon in Colorado. Well, welcome to the Great State of Nebraska. Bottoms up!" And with that, everyone with a glass in his or her hand quaffed the beverage in question, whether whiskey or, more usual for the children, milk. It was immediately clear to all that the visitors had little experience with alcohol, as their faces turned bluish and steam rose from their bald heads.

"This brew doth make us giddy to ourselves and to each other. What is the nature of this beverage?" asked Wew, whose face had turned bright blue.

"It's alcohol, 140 proof – top quality."

"It is a strange brew, to speak what is true, and turns us blue in front of you," said Fuf.

"It's what we drink in Nebraska, our little planet," said the mayor.

"May God and his angels guard your sacred throne and make you long become it," said Xox to the man he called Lord Moo, quoting from Shakespeare's *Henry V.*

"Where did you learn to speak English," Lord Moo asked. "You don't talk the way we talk around here."

"It has been more than 380 rotations of your planet – "

"Nebraska!"

"In sooth, it has been more than 380 rotations of your Planet Nebraska around your star since our ancestors visited. Our ancestors returned to Xypon with the collected works of the playwright William Shakespeare and we have learned our English from his pen."

"You cannot find any Shakespeare in Colorado, then?" asked a young girl, perhaps five years old.

"The only volumes of Shakespeare in the galaxy of Andromeda – sorry, in the galaxy of Colorado – are on our planet. English is not spoken elsewhere in Colorado."

"They speak English in Denver," one of Uptown's frequent flyers pointed out.

"Denver – that must be what you call our largest moon. We call it Tverpolta. Yes, of course English is spoken there. But we do distract ourselves with these pleasant asides," said Xox. "We have come bearing gifts – vaccines for all afflictions of the body, with which we have acquaintance, musical instruments for merrymaking, bottled beverages such as we drink in the galaxy of Colorado, and a solution to end all wars. Remembrance awaketh in us of mention of strife on your planet in the plays of the bard. But that was so long ago that perhaps horses may now be free of leeches and the planet free of war. So, prithee, do you still have wars these days?" Before anyone could answer, Xox turned to two of his fellow extraterrestrials, and said, "Pip and Zip, bear forth the trunk!" It was a heavy trunk, but Pip and Zip managed it and brought it up to the bar and, as they set it down, Xox said, "Lord Moo, master of your planet, please accept these gifts and may they cause the happiness on your planet to increase tenfold, nay a hundredfold."

The mayor was getting used to being called Lord Moo and liked it. He was also aware that these noble visitors from another galaxy had come in friendship. As a token of reciprocation, he presented them with Nebraskan cornhusker hats and Nebraska souvenir mugs, as well as UWU sweatshirts, since he kept a supply of these for sale in the saloon shop. Of course, he also thanked them effusively on behalf of all the people of Uptown and of Planet Nebraska, and invited them to stay on for the annual Okra Festival, by coincidence due to start the following day.

"Your gifts of raimants and drinking vessels do give us cause of thankfulness," said Xox.

"We'd be honored if you folks would care to stay as our guests for a few days. We recently built a small hotel right here in Uptown and you are welcome to stay there and to dine here at the Fancy Turtle Saloon as my guests."

"Or at Romulus' Steakhouse and Particle Accelerator, a few blocks away, as my guests," ex-Governor Romulus chimed in.

Then Pip addressed Xox: "My liege, might we inquire of these earthlings as to the nature of this Okra Festival?"

"Yeah, Lord Moo," Xox said, turning to the mayor, "my kinsman Pip is right to ask and, as you are so soaked in grace that the heavens do compliment you, tell us, prithee, what be this Okra Festival?"

"It's our celebration of our favorite vegetable," said Lord Moo, certain that there was nothing more important to celebrate that time of year than a vegetable. We have lots of interesting events planned for this year's Okra Festival," Lord Moo continued, "including a spitting contest in which you can see if you can spit farther than our local llamas. We also have planned a goat-chasing event, a visit to the haunted house, where you can converse with the late Professor Perkins, and an okra-eating contest, with a prize to the person who can eat the most okra within 20 minutes. Last year's winner was Lester Macduff, who unfortunately developed digestive problems after winning that event. Since he still loves okra, he'll serve as umpire and judge of the okra-eating event.

"Lord Moo, this Lester Macduff – " Pon interjected "—do you mean a descendant of Lord Macduff, the Thane of Fife, of whose exploits we read in *Macbeth?*"

"That I don't rightly know," Lord Moo responded. "But he *might* be."

"And what of Lord Scroop of Masham? We read about him in *Henry the Fifth.* It is one of our favorite plays of Shakespeare."

These visitors from the galaxy of Colorado quickly made friends as they had ready smiles, showed themselves to be witty, and had a great sense of humor. They were also formidable contestants in the spitting contest, where they proved capable of spitting about four times as far as any llama, and had great fun chasing Uptown's goats, although they were not able to catch any of these fleet-footed quadrupeds. They were a bit nervous about eating okra, since the vegetable is not mentioned in any of Shakespeare's plays. But after Xox tried some okra and declared to the others that "As victuals go, this specimen doth please both the stomach and the mind," his fellow "Coloradans" also joined in the eating frenzy. The beverage they had brought with them from Xypon caused those drinking it to glow for about five minutes. Once people saw that the glowing was just temporary, they thought it was great fun.

Now the people of Uptown no longer feared Colorado and were eager to learn much more about this state or galaxy or whatever it was. It was decided to establish an institute to study Colorado and Dr. Winklebat, who had earned his doctorate in taxidermy, came in as director of the institute. These arrivals from Xypon were persuaded to stay on for the interim, in order to help with the initial research. When it turned out that locals thought that Colorado was just a short drive west, the Xyponese protested and declared that, whatever lay to the west could not be the "real" Colorado and that they could help the Uptownians understand better the mysteries of the cosmos and of Colorado.

Five Years Later

In the five years following Romulus' return to Uptown, there were a number of changes:

Romulus eventually sold his particle accelerator to the department of physics and used the proceeds to make improvements to his steakhouse, remodeling it to look like an ancient Roman temple. He also introduced a bilingual menu, with all foods and drinks listed in both English and Latin. You could thereafter order whiskey telling the waiter you wanted "cupam" and, if you wanted brandy, you needed only ask for "sublimatum". For steak and potatoes, one might order "carnis et capsicum annuum". Needless to say, the waiters and waitresses were now required to wear togas and tunics.

Von Kletten served out her first term as Governor with such success that she was reelected Governor of Nebraska, in the process building up her Bull Moose Party and seeing the election of five of her party's candidates to the Legislature. Being conscious of Nebraska's growing population, she also pushed through bills to allocate state funds to build three new cities: Mind Your Business (don't ask locals for directions as they are expected to respond with, "Mind your own business."), Don't Ask Me (with the widest boulevard in the entire state – why? locals could respond, "Don't ask me!), and Aztec City (with various mock-ups of Aztec pyramids and temples).

Since, as Governor, von Kletten had repeatedly been informed

about angry quarrels in the legislature, usually about trivial matters, she decided to address the problem decisively. Her solution
was to issue an executive order, requiring that all members of the
legislature be equipped with (loaded) water pistols, so that they
could settle their differences in the Nebraskan way. Nor did she
forget Uptown and she used her office to court various corpora-
tions and cowboys to organize an annual Cowpoke Rodeo to be
held at Uptown Field. Some people called it Uptown's "Grodeo"
because of the prominence of goats in the festivities.

Friday was extremely pleased with Perkins's teaching and realized that hiring dead professors to teach classes could save the
university a lot of money and, with the legislature sometimes making cuts to the university's budget, this struck him as a perfect solution. He therefore made use of the resources of the department of
spiritualism to hold séances, which turned into job interviews with
deceased professors. They all wanted offices and also unhindered
access to the library, but none of them expected financial compensation. Of course, there were a few dead professors who refused
to come back to teach at UWU, but after two years of séances, Friday had managed to hire seven dead professors to teach in various
departments and one of them even became chair of the art department. The state legislature was so pleased with Friday's work with
the dead, that it presented him with its Equal Opportunity Award,
for fighting against discrimination against the dead.

Bobkov, who had succeeded von Kletten as departmental deputy chair when she was elected to the Legislature, now became chair
of the department of political science and continued to be generally
well liked, especially after he announced that future faculty meetings should be devoted to recounting tales of the Old West, and
singing cowpoke songs. Needless to say, "Git along little dogies"
continued to be the departmental favorite.

Rossini eventually left both politics and UWU but continued
to commute regularly to New York City and Philadelphia, to manage his various business interests. As his reputation grew, he was
"asked" to serve as Chief of Police in the Omaha Police Department. Upon arrival in this new job, Rossini found that there were
a lot of working girls out of work. "This ain't no good," Police
Chief Rossini said to Johnny Testarossa, who had come in as Dep-

uty Chief of Police. "Working girls gotta have work, gotta turn tricks. We gotta help them out." Rossini found that he had some discretionary funds, which he used to build secure facilities where the working girls could work for pay. "And if the johns don't pay the posted price, they're gonna do time in the joint," Rossini mused out loud to Testarossa.

Sheriff Dorbin had such success with her barber shop that she built a four-story department store in downtown Uptown. She put the jail and cafeteria on the fourth floor, the sheriff's office and barber shop on the ground floor, and the various goods for sale on the second and third floors. She also purchased an old mill on the edge of town and renovated it, converting it into a Museum of the History of Uptown. Locals contributed various artefacts, including old paintings, uniforms from the American Civil War, sculptures of goats, stuffed goats, maps of the region before there was any Uptown, even early typwriters and lawnmowers. In order to entice people to come, she decided to charge a very old-fashioned price for admission: just 75 cents.

Bart and Katie Maverick had a son and named him Bret, but advised him, as soon as he could understand English, to avoid gambling, since luck might not always be his companion. Bart retired from his post as supervisor of museums and he and Katie moved to Uptown, where they launched a "Hunt for Aztec Treasure" business. Brother Bart told potential customers that he had purchased a large amount of Aztec treasure, including gold, and had buried it somewhere in the Okra Hills and, for the price of a ticket ($30), he would equip all interested parties with shovels and lead them to the hills. He also gave each of his paying customers a small pamphlet, with a miniature of the map he had used to identify a suitable location to bury his treasure. His offer: anyone who found the treasure could keep 25% of it, with the remaining 75% returning to the Maverick trust fund, as he called it. After three years, no Aztec treasure had been found, but Brother Bart and his wife Katie had raked in enough money to fly down to Mexico City and buy more Aztec gold.

Bret Holloway wrote the second volume of his memoirs, which was translated into seven languages, including Russian and Chinese. He and his wife, Clara Trotsky, opened a bookshop in town, specializing in the works of the Bolshevik figure, Leon Trotsky, who had spent his last years in Mexico. Clara wrote a semi-fictional account of Leon Trotsky's years in Mexico but said nothing about his interests in Aztec gold...or okra, for that matter. Dr. Bret Holloway continued to work as director of the Happy Trails Institute, with Dr. Siggie Freundlich continuing to protest against Dr. Holloway's appointment. Other patients concluded that Freundlich was suffering from obsessive compulsive disorder and started to call him "Dr. OCD". Freundlich responded by starting to boast of his allegedly important "discoveries" in the field of psychiatry. After this, his fellow patients started to call him "Dr. DOG" (from Delusions Of Grandeur).

Ever since the visitors from Xypon had landed, Mayor Marlowe preferred to go by the name "Lord Moo". He also decided to hold regular elections for his unsalaried post, always running unopposed. Although turnout at these elections was low, he could now claim to be an elected mayor. He continued to earn his upkeep from operating the Fancy Turtle Saloon. After a lot of pressure from the members of the political science department, Lord Moo eventually relented on his ban of water pistols and even organized regular water pistol "shoot-outs".

Pastor Grace became a Buddhist and emigrated to Tibet. Debbie Sue Stefanovich, who had previously left her husband, now resigned as assistant dean and assumed responsibility for preaching at the nondenominational church, while taking night classes at UWU in the department of religious studies, in order to earn her pastoral license. Some people claimed that she was not as nondenominational as Pastor Grace had been, before he became a Buddhist. But Pastor Stefanovich replied that she was so nondenominational that she had no definite opinions about religious matters and was open to all points of view.

Agamemnon Alcibiades got tired of the jokes about his name and changed it to John Doe. He was also curious about how the Holloway/Maverick brothers had managed to steal the famed Grecian urn and decided to try, after hours, to break into his own museum and steal the replacement urn, which Governor Romulus had purchased from the museum in Athens. However, the state-of-the-art alarm system, installed at the behest of Bart Maverick during the time he was Chief of the Office of Historical Heritage, caught John Doe in the act, and the tougher police presence in Omaha, mandated by Chief of Police Rossini, resulted in his being taken into custody the moment he came out the front door of the museum. There were no potheads around to witness his arrest, however. John Doe is currently serving a 15-year jail sentence.

Floorboard, who had taken up the post of president of A.E.I.O.U., shut down four departments at that university and counted this as his greatest achievement, since it promised to save the university large amounts of money. The Rectors of A.E.I.O.U. were less than impressed and fired Floorboard, who returned to his native California. There, Floorboard accepted a job offer to manage Anaheim's world famous Disneyland theme park. His only major innovation there was to convert the Sleeping Beauty Castle into his private residence, so that he could live on the premises. After hearing rumors that unrehabilitated communists were visiting Disneyland, Floorboard had concealed microphones installed in various attractions, including in the boats at Pirates of the Caribbean and in the carriages on the Matterhorn attraction.

Paolo "Smiley" Lastorino, Nebraska's first and only foreign minister, had found that the various people he had appointed as ambassadors to various countries were not being accredited in those countries. He resigned in frustration immediately after Romulus stepped down as Governor. Lastorino's subsequent whereabouts became the subject of speculation, although some people say that he is now the de facto ruler of Kerguelen, a small island in the south Indian Ocean. Others claim that he fell victim to the curse of the Aztec dummy.

Gabe Carver, the political science department's erstwhile "expert" on alcoholic beverages, continued as Inspector General of the state's Liquor Control Commission, introducing wine-tasting seminars at the various shops run by the commission. He continued to promote the idea of ending the discrimination against driving while intoxicated. He also founded a nonprofit organization to fight discrimination of all kinds – not merely the discrimination which dead people and drunks face on a daily basis, but also discrimination against the certifiably disordered. When Dr. Siggie Freundlich learned about Carver's organization, he joined, even while still committed in the Happy Trails Institute. Freundlich argued that, even if he might have been diagnosed as mentally disordered, that should not prevent him from being restored to the directorship of the Institute. As for Perry MacPerry, he landed a job at the IRS, where he has repeatedly tried to raise taxes.

Pestalozzi and Perkins continued to teach at UWU with both of them winning prizes for excellence in teaching. The two friends also opened a "haunted house" attraction on the outskirts of Uptown, where customers had the chance to see a "real live" (? – or perhaps "real dead") ghost. Between the haunted house, Romulus' redesign of his steakhouse along the lines of an ancient Roman temple, and Bart and Katie Maverick's hunt for Aztec treasure, Uptown had the beginnings of a theme park, and Mayor Marlowe and former Governor Romulus started to discuss collaboration on developing Uptown into a proper theme park. Among their ideas was to offer a ride in the Okra Hills in goat-drawn carriages and the establishment of a Museum of Colorado History (for which they planned to use information they had obtained from their visitors from the Colorado Galaxy).

The bands at Uptown's two steakhouses – Los Capitanes and the Uptown Mafia Bah Bah Band – acquired international reputations and started touring the world, performing concerts across the Western Hemiphere as well as in Europe, Asia, Africa, and Australia/New Zealand, as well as Kerguelen. They coordinated their schedules so that at least one of the bands would be performing in Uptown at any given time.

Nebraska's anarchists eventually split into three parties: the original Nebraskan Anarchist Anti-Government and Anti-Party Party, whose representatives continued to sit in the Legislature but to abstain from all votes; the Nebraskan Pure Anti-Government Party, which refused to stand for election and condemned all cooperation with the government in any form; and the Nebraskan Subversive Anarchist Trojan Horse Party, whose elected representative took an active part in the Legislature and cast her vote on every measure being considered, always voting against the proposition in question. When asked to explain why she was always so "negative", she replied that one had to be negative in order to be positive.

At UWU, the physics department experimented with an antigravity device with great success and, one day, the entire physics department, together with all of its professors, simply floated into space, leaving behind only the newly acquired particle accelerator. As for the particle accelerator, it was therefore placed in UWU's Museum of Strange Objects, together with the museum's collection of toe-nail clippings from U.S. presidents and a collection of keys to locks that had been either destroyed or lost.

After the entire physics building had floated into space, there was a lot of controversy on campus about whether or not to hire a new team of physicists. Some faculty members in other departments felt that the physics professors had been "lording it" over them and suggested that having a physics department was a waste of space. Some people thought that the vacant lot where the old physics department had stood could be used to construct an observatory. Others championed other ideas, ranging from a law school to a department of lost sciences (no one was prepared to admit out loud that this meant astrology and alchemy) to a department of liturgical science, though the advocates of that last idea were not very clear about what they had in mind. Finally, it was decided that, since UWU had a tradition of cutting-edge research in physics, the university should look to hire the world's top physicists, whether dead or alive. It took some persuading, but eventually Sir Isaac Newton and Albert Einstein agreed to set aside their intellectual differences and come on board as co-chairs of the department. In fact, the department would come to consist entirely of dead physicists, including such luminaries as Benjamin Franklin, Amadeo Avogadro (who discovered Avogadro's number), Max Planck, Pierre and Marie Curie, and Enrico Fermi. Due to an error in paperwork, the brilliant American writer Gertrude Stein, who had died in 1946, was also invited to join the department of physics. She accepted but pointed out that, while she would show up for classes and faculty meetings, most of the rest of her time she would continue to haunt the Latin quarter in Paris.

One should not forget Uptown's popular weekly newspaper, which was shut down for a month, when its journalist finally took a much-needed vacation. When she returned to work, the newspaper revived an earlier name, and would appear, thereafter, as *The Uptown News Daily & Every Advertiser's Dream (The UNDEAD)*.

At this point, the paper expanded from six pages weekly to eight pages weekly.

As for Toby, it became ever more certain of its wisdom and even something close to omniscience and eventually opened up a counseling service. People paid good money to come in for counseling and have their clothes washed at the same time. They typically arrived confused about life and, after listening to their clothes spin around in Toby for more than an hour, they were told by Romulus that they were cured. They were usually, but not always, even more confused now than before but, after this experience, most of these clients decided that their problems probably did not matter and some of them came to believe that the wise washing and spinning by Toby had, in fact, cured them. Or maybe they were just too ashamed to admit that they had sat for more than an hour in front of a washing machine, expecting it to give them good advice. The satisfied clients were then very loud in promoting Toby's fame, while those who did not feel cured kept their feelings to themselves. The result is that more and more people came to sit in front of Toby, the washing machine, for counseling on life's difficult problems. Nor was that all on Toby's agenda, as it continued to advise Romulus on various matters and dictated its memoirs to the ex-Governor, for him to write down. The book, if published, will be called *Memoirs of an Unusual Washing Machine.* Ex-Governor Romulus hopes to see the book published not only in English, but also in Latin.